MW00943744

the Jagged Gate

Twelve Tangled Tales

the Jagged Gate

TWELVE TANGLED TALES

James Maxey

All stories copyright James Maxey 2017

"Joe's Spider Farm" originally published in *Soon*: *Four Chilling Tales* 2013

"Absolutely Brilliant in Chrome" originally published in *Absolutely Brilliant in Chrome* 2004

"Little Guilt Thing Goin' On" originally published in *Abyss and Apex* 2003

"Fall of Babylon" originally published in *Kaiju Rising: Age of Monsters* 2014

"Tendrils" originally published under the pen name Nigella Bryne on KDP 2012

"Sorry Honey" originally published in *the Raleigh Hatchett* 2005

"Eater" original to this collection 2017

"Greatshadow: Origins" originally published in *Blood and Devotion* 2006

"Tornado of Sparks" originally published in *Solaris Book of New Fantasy* 2008

"Girls' Night Out" originally published in *Nobody Gets the Girl Tenth Anniversary* Edition 2013

"Cherry Red Rocket Ship" originally published in *Intergalactic Medicine Show* 2017

"The Jagged Gate" original to this collection 2017

The author may be contacted at
nobodynovelwriter@yahoo.com.

ISBN-13: 9798876957696

Table of Contents

Dedication

For anyone who's ever lingered before a door

they've been warned not to open.

It's not too late to turn back.

THERE'S A LITTLE SIGN up where the dirt road connects to the gravel road that says "Joe's Spider Farm." It's easy to miss. Joe keeps saying he'll put up a bigger sign to make us easier to find, but I know he won't. Anyone set to find us will find us, sign or no. Joe's Spider Farm isn't a place you happen to stumble across.

We've got a pretty little home up here. Fifty acres total, although our trailers sit on just two of them, smack up against the Virginia border. Joe's great-granddaddy used to make moonshine up this way. Gives the place a seedy history to go with its seedy present.

Odds are good if you're the kind of person who knows about Joe's Spider Farm, you're into freaks. Used to be, we'd come up here in the winters to hunker down and wait it out until the weather was good enough to start the carnival circuit again. Of course, the world's changed a great deal even in my lifetime and now most of the trailers here stay parked all year round. Not a bunch of gigs for freaks these days. If you're a freak who can't find work anymore, Joe doesn't charge anything for you to set up your trailer and hook into his septic tank and well. Joe likes the company. He gets along with pretty much anybody as long as you don't mess with his spiders.

If you've got a thing about spiders, Joe's ain't the place to be. One reason the little sign at the end of the road is so hard to spot is because of the white cloud of webs hanging off it. During the summer when you're driving up, you'd think we were overrun with caterpillars from all the webs weighing down the branches; but no, they're spiders gone all feral. Joe's shipped them in from Argentina, from Australia, from Vietnam. He's got spiders round here that eat birds. You don't wake up to a lot of chirping on Joe's Spider Farm.

But there's nothing sinister about the place, if you're cool with spiders. We're actually a gentle people, a kind little family. We happen to make money by receiving visitors who'll pay twenty bucks a head to stare at us. Not that all we do is sit around and get stared at. We're showmen, professionals. We're always working on something new.

The latest addition to our show? Well, I have to say, there's a story behind it. It began on New Year 's Day. Round here, winter is an iffy thing. You're as likely to be walking around in shorts and sandals as you are to be needing your long johns and boots. New Year's this year was the warm kind, so Tibby was getting ready to show off his latest gimmick.

Tibby is actually one of the more famous members of our little family. You might have seen him on the cover of a newspaper in a supermarket checkout. They call him "Lizard Boy" although his real name is Tiberius Jackson. His friends call him Tibby. "Boy" is a bit insulting, since Tibby's a black man, and about seventy. He's a little guy though, skinny, and his scaly skin is more green than black. He's a good sport about being called "boy." He even tried to market himself as Dinosaur Boy when those dinosaur movies were big, but it never caught on.

Tibby got this little remote controlled boat for Christmas and, being a born showman, within a week he figured out a new act. On New Year's, we're all of us standing round waiting for the big debut. "All of us" on New Year's isn't that many. Even freaks have families to visit during the holidays. Only a handful of us stick around. There's Joe of course. He used to travel around as the "Amazing Spiderman" until a lawsuit put an end to that. Joe is a squat fellow, his torso is about as close to a ball as a human body is likely to get, even though his arms and legs are twiggy as a little girl's. That day he was hanging out without his shirt on, showing off the intricate web of tattoos that cover him. He kept grinning, displaying his teeth filed down to points, as Tibby squatted in the wading pool with the boat.

Joe wasn't the only one having a good time. Wolfman was there also, clearly stoned. His bloodshot eyes stood out like Christmas lights amid the silver fur that covered his face. He was swaying rhythmically, humming softly, looking for all the world like he might break into song and dance at any moment.

Of course Camilla, my sister, was there. She was clapping her hands with anticipation. Camilla's encephalitic, what in less politically correct times would have been called a "pinhead." She's almost forty, with the mind of a two-year-old. She's the happiest person I've ever met, getting all excited over the littlest things. She used to love going on tour, where she was known as the Chicken Lady, due to the way she bobbed her head as she walked, plus when she laughed she sounded like a chicken. She loved to laugh at the people who came to see her; she could find almost anyone funny. It's been almost twenty years since even the Mexican carnivals touched an act like hers. Our trailer's been parked in these woods a long time.

And me? I'm Pete Pyro, the Fire King. I'm the oddball of the group, which is to say I'm not odd at all. You wouldn't look at me twice if I were sitting next to you at the movies. Unlike a lot of the people who live here, there's still work for a man of my talents. I can spit flame almost six yards, and I don't just walk on beds of hot coal, I lay on them, and let the audience scoop glowing cinders over me. John Flower runs a show that tours with rock concerts and he used to beg me to travel with him. Finally, he got the hint that as long as Camilla was alive, my first and only duty was to stay with her.

Anyway, I was telling you about the new act.

Tibby was squatting in the water, launching his boat. Behind it were two balsa floats, joined together with toothpicks. Tibby reached into his overalls and pulled out Jasper, his pet squirrel. Camilla started laughing when she saw Jasper, clapping harder than ever. She loved that little squirrel.

Tibby sat Jasper down onto the balsa wood floats and handed him a little rope with a toothpick handle. Jasper held the handle and sat calm and steady as Tibby nudged the throttle forward on the remote. The boat puttered off, pulling Jasper behind. Camilla stamped her feet, she was so happy. Wolfman went ahead and burst into song, although that song was "Happy Birthday to You," which didn't have much to do with anything.

And Joe, Joe might have been the most choked up of all of us. He stood up straight, took off his ball cap, and gazed up at the clear blue sky.

"Praise the Lord," he said reverently. "We have a water-skiing squirrel."

I wasn't quite as moved. I guess because Camilla was always so excited, I tend to be rather stone-faced. So when Tibby wanted an opinion, it was me he asked. "What do you think?"

"There are worse things to look at," I said.

Looking back, it's the only time I've ever displayed a propensity toward prophecy. Tibby shifted his eyes from my face to something behind me. I swear I felt a chill run up my spine about the instant the shadow would have touched me. I looked over my shoulders.

Behind me stood a slouching, middle-aged man, his hair greasy and stringy, his flannel shirt glued to his body by weeks of sweat and filth. His eyes were fixed on me and he had the faintest hint of a smile as he sucked a drag off a cigarette. When he opened his mouth to speak, he revealed snaggled yellow teeth. A wave of stench watered my eyes from several yards away.

"Well if it ain't Pete Pyro." He chuckled as if this were somehow amusing. He flicked the butt of the cigarette toward my feet.

"Do I know you?" I asked.

Wolfman had stopped singing. Everyone was watching the stranger, except Tibby, who was stuffing his squirrel back into his overalls. Camilla had stopped laughing. She silently moved behind me.

"We worked together in Tijuana. I was the blow-off for the ten-in-one."

Instantly I remembered him, though his name escaped me. He was a geek … a pit geek. The ten-in-one was a standard layout for a freak-show. You put ten freaks under one tent and one ticket got you in to see all of them. There'd been me and Camilla of course, usually a midget, a fat lady, your standard fare. After the rubes had paid to get into the tent, the barker would pull aside the more jaded of the lot—you learned to spot them easy enough—and let them know that for an additional fee, there was one more freak to see, one so terrible and disturbing they dare not advertise him to the general public. It was only the strong-stomached, brave-hearted seeker of the strange that could stand what lay beyond the back tent flap.

The act behind the tent flap was known as the blow-off.

The people who paid to see the blow-off were the ones with dark needs that couldn't be satisfied by staring at Siamese twins or men with three legs. They were too dead inside to feel anything looking at a freak. To get their money's worth, they needed to see a monster.

They'd come to see the geek.

Geeks were the lowest act in the freak business. Literally, since their standard arena was a pit dug in the ground. The rubes would line up at the sides of the pit and watch the geek snarl and curse, his hair matted with mud and filth, his eyes mean and wild. The barker would toss in a live chicken and the geek would bite its head off and eat it whole, spitting out feathers, smearing the blood over his body. He'd throw the bloody entrails at the audience members. If he vomited, which he often did, he'd catch as much of it in his hands as he could muster and shove it back into his mouth.

Geeks and freaks tended not to associate with each other. Yet, here one was, grinning at us, staring with those spooky, unblinking eyes.

"I heard y'all got yourself a little freak village," the geek said. "Things been kind of slow for me of late. Figured I'd drop in and see if you had room for one more."

To my horror, Joe replied instantly, "Friend, there's always room for one more."

I cut Joe a glance that should have knocked him backward. He gazed back at me, slightly bewildered.

"We're always open to anyone willing to pitch in around here," he said, to me and the geek.

"Joe," I said, "Can I talk to you a minute? In private?"

"If it's about me," said the geek, "come on out and say it. I got a tough hide."

"Okay," I said. "The Spider Farm is a peaceful place. People sometimes bring their kids up here. I don't know that it fits in to have a guy whose only talent is to bite the heads off chickens."

"Only talent?" said the geek. "Pete, you wound me. There's plenty else I eat. I chew light bulbs, swallow razor blades, gulp mice whole and vomit them back up still kicking."

"Wholesome family entertainment," I said.

"Better than a damn squirrel on skis," the geek said. "Who are you to judge me? Ain't you the guy who spits gasoline?"

Joe put his hand on my back. "Pete, don't be hasty. I'm sure we can work out something."

I wasn't interested in working something out. I'd seen this geek in the pit twenty years ago and for long years after, I'd seen him in my nightmares. The way he'd vomited back up the head of that chicken and held it up into the beam of the barker's flashlight. The beak was still moving, the eyes still darting about. And the audience had loved it. They'd laughed and cheered this horrible thing.

I knew what I had to do.

"Sure," I said. "Hey, it's been a while. I have to admit I forgot your name."

"Don't matter. I forgot it too. Nobody used it in thirty years. Folks just call me Geek."

“Right,” I said. “Okay, Geek. If you join us, I don’t want any blood acts. No biting the heads off chickens.”

“You in charge here, Pete?” asked Geek.

“Joe?” I asked.

“No,” Joe said, sounding annoyed. Joe was a gentle man who hated getting dragged into arguments. “No, this is my land, and you're all my guests. Pete, you stop giving this fellow grief. But Geek, Pete’s right. No chickens in your act. I’m looking forward to seeing you eat other stuff though. Light bulbs you say?”

“Nothing to 'em,” said Geek. “Chew 'em long enough and it’s easy as swallowing sand. No challenge at all.”

When he said this, I thought of a way to get rid of him. It was mean, but I had to do it.

“You want a challenge?” I asked. “You ever drink gasoline?”

“Brush my teeth with it,” he said. “While smoking.”

“How about poison?”

“A rattler bit my tongue once as I was biting him. My mouth swelled up and turned black but I’m still here. Poison don’t bother me now.”

“Good,” I said. “Cause there’s a lot of poisonous spiders round here.”

“Spiders? Hell. I eat spiders too. I'll take a big bowl of black widders and pour some milk and sugar over ‘em and eat ‘em with a spoon. Then I eat the bowl and the spoon to boot.”

Joe breathed out a high, whistling sound, like steam coming out of a teakettle. He bounced forward like a basketball, leaping into the air as high as his spindly little legs could carry him, tackling Geek right in the center of his chest. They went down hard, with Geek shrieking obscenities as Joe sank a mouthful of pointy teeth into his shoulder. Wolfman sobered up and ran forward as Geek tore himself free from Joe and pushed him away. Wolfman grabbed Geek as he scrambled to his feet. I grabbed Joe, holding him back.

“Get out of here,” Joe spat. “You damn dirty thing!”

“Who are you to call me a damn dirty thing?” Geek shouted. “I’m a regular man. You're nothing but filthy freaks. You should beg me to come live with you!”

“Get the hell off my land,” said Joe. “You ever come around here, I got a .38 pistol in my trailer I won’t hesitate to use.”

Geek pulled himself free of Wolfman and rubbed his shoulder. “Well. Well,” he said. “Well, I think I can manage that. You not seeing me again. Freak.”

Geek turned, and staggered back toward the road, still cursing.

"You okay, Joe?" I asked.

"I'm fine," Joe said, though he was trembling. He wiped his mouth and stared at the blood on his arm. "Kind of lost my temper, huh?"

"Who can blame you?" I asked.

"You were right about him, Pete. Jesus. He'd eat a spider? Jesus. What a monster. Should of listened to you from the start."

Camilla was still behind me, her eyes clamped shut. I turned and hugged her, rubbing her back. "It's all right now," I said.

I was grinning, but not so anyone would notice. The whole incident had gone off a thousand times better than I'd planned. I mean, I knew Joe'd get angry, but not biting mad. Hooyaw!

That night, the adrenaline died down and I felt ashamed. Joe had shown me and my sister nothing but kindness. I'd manipulated him into a fight and he thanked me for it, all over some guy whose name I couldn't even remember. Geek had struck a nerve. Both of us built our acts on what we put into and took out of our mouths. But I breathed fire while he vomited blood, I danced on coals while he wallowed in filth. We were nothing alike. What could happen to turn a man into a geek? What could make a person dig that pit and wallow in it, more animal than man? I was glad I didn't know. Joe's Spider Farm was no place for such horrors.

THE NEXT MORNING, at dawn, Tibby's wail woke us all. We rushed from our trailers to his. He was sitting in the door, half-naked even though the night had brought a frost. He cradled something small and furry to his chest, weeping uncontrollably.

"What is it?" Joe shouted as he ran up.

By now I was close enough to see. It was Jasper. Or what was left of him. His head was gone.

"The geek," said Wolfman.

"Probably," I said, feeling very cold and small.

"Oh, God," said Joe as he realized what had happened. "Oh God, that S.O.B.'s done murdered Jasper."

I followed Joe back to his trailer, the only one with a phone.

"Sheriff, you'd better get out here," I heard him say as I waited outside. "There's been a killing."

I still wonder if things might have worked out different if he'd added the words, "Of a squirrel."

I walked back to my trailer, wondering if this wasn't all my fault. Camilla was cowering under her covers. I didn't talk to her. I didn't know what to say. I put on my clothes and boots then went back out.

Joe was waiting for me, carrying his pistol.

"He might still be around," said Joe.

We searched the trailers of those who'd left for the holidays, but found nothing.

Then Wolfman shouted from down the road.

We ran out to meet him. He was standing in the dirt road, looking down. We reached him and could clearly see boot prints in the dust. About this time we could also hear the wail of sirens.

"I remember Geek had boots on yesterday," said Wolfman. "These could be evidence."

Just then, the sheriff's car popped over the hill and began shooting toward us, bouncing wildly on the washboard road. We scattered as fast as we could as he came to a halt in a cloud of dust right where we'd been standing.

Sheriff Parker jumped from his car, his eyes fixed on Joe.

"Who was murdered?" he called out.

"Jasper the squirrel," Joe said solemnly.

The Sheriff pushed back his hat.

"What?" he asked.

"Oh God. Someone killed Jasper last night," said Joe, his lower lip trembling. "Bit his head off like a chocolate Easter bunny."

"Jasper was a … squirrel boy?" asked the Sheriff.

"No, a real squirrel," said Joe, who began to sob.

"That water-skied," Wolfman added.

"You think this is funny?" asked the Sheriff.

"No, Sir," I said. "There's a dangerous man around here. His name is, um, Geek. He's about six feet tall, white, maybe fifty, very dirty. He killed Tibby's squirrel last night and we think he's capable of worse."

If the Sheriff was listening to me he gave no indication of it. He walked up to Joe and grabbed him by the shirt.

"Look at me," he said.

Joe continued to blubber.

"Look at me!"

Joe wiped his tears and looked into the sheriff's face. He hiccupped.

"I put up with your little freak farm because I'm a Christian man who figures you have to live somewhere. But I'm not here to protect your squirrels. I'm not here to protect your spiders. I'm here to protect people, you understand?"

Joe stared at him.

"Understand?"

"But," said Joe.

"No buts," said the Sheriff. He looked around at the rest of us. "I protect people, of which I see maybe one standing in this yard. Don't waste my time again or I'll put a deputy up by your sign and tell him to arrest every one of those degenerates who come into my county just to see you. You'll never make another penny out here, understand?"

"But," said Joe.

The sheriff let go of him and stalked back to his car. He sat in it for a moment, talking on his radio, then turned the car around and headed back up the road, shaking his head.

"I can't believe it," said Joe. "I can't believe he won't help us."

"I can," said Wolfman. "But I admire that you can't. You're a good guy, Joe. You've built a kind, safe little world up here. It's easy to forget the rest of the world hates us."

"I pay taxes," said Joe. "It's his job …"

"Forget it," I said. "The geek's high-tailed it out of here by now, anyway. Let's go see what we can do for Tibby."

We headed off to Tibby's trailer, but I was looking up at the surrounding forests. Even in the light of morning, this was a place filled with shadows. I couldn't help but wonder if he was out there, laughing at us.

That night, it was decided that Wolfman and I would keep watch over the trailers. He would watch from 10pm until 3am, when I would take over and watch until dawn. I probably should have volunteered for the whole night. I didn't sleep anyway. I dragged myself out of bed, already dressed when the alarm went off. Camilla was sound asleep as I left the trailer and stepped into the cold night air.

The sky was frozen into little diamonds. The quarter moon was high overhead and the sky was clear enough to cast shadows. I made my way to Wolfman's trailer. It was up on the hill, higher than the rest, and from his front window you could see all the other trailers. His trailer was dark. I studied the window, unable to make out any hint of his face. I flicked on my flashlight. The light glared on the window. Empty. I went up the aluminum steps and tried the door. Unlocked. I pushed it open.

"Wolfman?" I said.

"Whuh?" he answered groggily.

I swung the beam around his living room. He raised his arms to cover his eyes from where he lay on his recliner.

"Dammit, Wolfman, I can't believe you fell asleep."

"Just resting," he said.

"What if something had happened?"

"Did something happen?"

"How should I know? You're the one watching."

He grunted as he rose, then shuffled to the door. He poked his head out and looked around.

"All clear," he said.

"This isn't a joke," I said. "That geek is obviously crazy."

"And probably gone," said Wolfman. "He made his point with the squirrel."

He flipped on the lights.

Then I heard something.

I put a finger to my lips and motioned for Wolfman to be quiet.

Behind the trailer, someone was clucking. It sounded nothing like a real chicken, only like someone imitating one.

"Stay here," I whispered.

I stepped outside, slowly and silently. The noise seemed to be directly behind the trailer now. Very clearly a man, saying, "Buck-buck-bucka."

Cigarette smoke wafted through the air.

I wished I'd borrowed Joe's gun.

On the other hand, geeks weren't noted for their bravery, and I had a pretty solid plan for scaring this one off. I pulled my lighter from my right pocket, and a can of lighter fluid from the left. Squirting in a mouthful, I crept around the edge of the trailer.

I didn't see anyone. Wolfman's trailer was right up against the woods. The moonlight wasn't much help back in there.

But he didn't stop bucking. He was still doing it, maybe ten yards away. Leaves crunched in the darkness. I moved carefully toward the noise.

"Buck-buck-bucka," the invisible voice said, now further away.

I stepped into the woods. Winter had reduced the trees to skeletons, through which the moonlight slipped. I paused to let my eyes adjust.

"Buck-buck-bucka," he said again, further away still. The sound of crunching became more rapid. He was running away. Geeks are cowards. I wanted him to stay scared. I moved forward as fast as I dared, following the sound, watching out for the fallen branches and weathered rocks that threatened to trip me.

Suddenly there was a crash from ahead, and a loud curse.

He'd fallen, maybe twenty feet from me, though I still couldn't make out anything amid all the shadows. Eager for the chance to catch him, I moved forward, no longer watching my feet.

The ground disappeared.

I fell into pitch-blackness, landing on my shoulder in muddy soil, spitting out the lighter fluid on impact. My lighter was knocked from my hand. Shaking my head, I rolled to my back. Above me was a little square of stars. I'd fallen into a pit.

A slouched, dark shadow appeared at the edge.

"Buck-buck-bucka," he said.

"Very damn funny," I said. "When I get out of here I'm gonna kick your ass."

"Very damn funny," he said, turning away.

"Come back here!" I shouted.

Muffled, growing faint, he answered, "Buck-buck-bucka."

I groped my way blindly around the pit. The rim was a good three feet over my head. I grasped at the muddy walls, trying to gain traction on twisted roots, but everything was too slippery to hold my weight when I tried to lift myself.

"Dammit!" I said, frustrated. I dropped to my knees. My lighter was in here somewhere. I needed to see what I was doing. Every second I was in the pit, the others were in danger.

"Help!" I cried out, as I ran my fingers through the stony mud surrounding me. "Help!"

"Pete?" came the answer, far away.

"Wolfman?" I stood up. "Wolfman!"

"I hear you Pete! Where are you?"

"Wolfman? Dammit, what are you doing out here? You need to be watching out for the others."

"You was the one calling for help," he said, his voice now very close. The beam of his flashlight flickered over the branches above me.

"Watch out!" I yelled, too late. His foot slipped and with a loud yelp he fell, feet first, his filthy boots crashing into my jaw.

I crumpled beneath his old skinny frame. He knocked the wind out of me, although not out of himself, judging by the string of obsccnities he spit out.

"You okay?" he asked, once his curses were exhausted.

I groaned. "Been better. You?"

"Feels like I busted my damn arm," he said.

The flashlight uselessly lit a tiny circle against the wall. I retrieved it and studied our surroundings. The pit was only about five feet from end to end, no more than ten feet deep.

"We gotta get out of here," I said, struggling to rise. I helped Wolfman to his feet. "How's your other arm?"

"Okay, I reckon," he said.

I laced my fingers together and braced my back against the wall. "I'm gonna boost you out of here. Then you find a big branch or something to lower down to me."

"I ain't strong enough to pull you out," he said.

"We'll think of something. You can do more out of this pit than in it, right?"

He nodded, then placed his good arm on my shoulder to steady himself while he put his boot into my fingers. With a grunt he stood, wobbling.

"Get ready to grab," I said. Then I lifted with all my strength, launching him upwards. Rocks and twigs rained down on me as his torso fell over the edge and he started kicking at the wall for traction. Apparently, he found something solid to grab onto, because he unleashed another string of expletives as he yanked himself further over the edge, until he was free.

"Oh God," he moaned from up above. "Holy God."

"What is it?" I said.

"Might be havin' a heart attack," he said. "Jesus."

"Don't you die on me!" I said. "You're bad enough alive. I don't want to put up with your damn ghost!"

I could hear him grunting, twitching around in the leaves, but he didn't say anything. I found the flashlight and beamed it up at the lip.

"Wolfman? I said don't you die! I mean it, man."

He stopped grunting.

"Wolfman?"

His face appeared in the beam. He stuck his arm into the pit. He had his belt wrapped around his fist, dangling the end down to me.

"You climb on out of there so I can whip you for being so mean," he said. "Come on. I got my leg jammed up under a root. I'm steady."

I grabbed the belt. The look on his face as my feet left the floor and my full weight was on him was horrible to behold. But I didn't dare let go. I scrambled up for all I was worth, grabbing his shirt, half pulling it off, but he was good to his word, and steady. My shoulders reached the edge of the pit and I grabbed the waist of his pants and pulled myself up until my torso was clear and only my legs were left dangling. I kicked until I was all the way out, all tangled up with Wolfman, who was gasping for air.

I was gulping down air myself. How long had I been in that pit? Five minutes? Ten? Too long was all I knew.

"We gotta get down there," I said.

"Let me catch my breath," he said.

As punctuation to his sentence, a crack rang throughout the hills, echoing back and forth.

"Jesus H. Christ," I said, taking off through the woods once more, stumbling over root and rock, until I was free of the woods. I half ran, half fell down the mountain toward Joe's trailer. His door was open. There was something dark and wet on the steps gleaming in the moonlight. I burst into the tiny room and found myself staring down the business end of Joe's .38.

Only Joe wasn't holding it.

"Slow down, Pete," said Geek, smiling pretty as you'd please. "Where's the fire?"

He was sitting at Joe's kitchen table, the gun in one hand, the lid of one of Joe's spider cages in the other. His chin was wet with blood and his shirt was soaked red.

Joe groaned next to me. He was propped up on his shoulder beside the door, blood pouring from his leg. He'd been shot, but was still conscious.

Geek pulled the spider from its cage. It was one of Joe's tarantulas, the one that was good with kids, Fuzzy.

Geek popped Fuzzy into his mouth. He bit down with a crunching sound, like a mouth full of potato chips. Black legs jutted from the corners of his mouth like whiskers.

"Kinda glad to see you out of that pit," Geek said, spraying the table with hairy-black goo as he spoke. "I realized something a minute ago. Guess I've known it all along. This job's no fun unless somebody's watchin'."

He washed the tarantula down with a swig from a bottle of Mad Dog he pulled from his hip pocket. The gun in one hand, the bottle in the other, he rose and looked through the other spider cages. Joe had dozens of them.

"Oooh," said Geek, setting the bottle down and grabbing one of the larger cages. It was filled with black widows.

"No," whined Joe. "Not my babies."

"Funny thing about widder spiders," said Geek. "They ain't poison if you bite them first."

He stuck his hand into the cage and pulled one out. He popped it into his mouth and crunched it, causing Joe to whimper.

"What're you trying to prove?" I said. "What did we ever do to you?"

"Besides knocking me down and biting me? Besides calling me names and chasing me off?"

"Yeah, besides that," I said. "We have a nice decent home here. You wouldn't have been happy."

"I got calluses in my mouth," Geek said, chomping down on another spider. "Callused fingers. Spiders try to bite, I don't even feel it. But there's still some things that sting."

"Maybe," I said, "Maybe I was wrong about you. Maybe you could stay around."

"After what I done? You're just babbling. Think, boy."

"What do you want?" I said.

"I told you. You're gonna watch me eat spiders. Then I guess I'll shoot you. Finish off the rest of the freaks as they come back home. Maybe build a little pyramid out of your skulls. This will be my own little peaceful kingdom, I figure."

He crunched into another black widow.

I was still in the doorway. Even with him watching me, I could jump back and sideways and get out of his sight. Of course, then he might put another bullet into Joe. For that matter, if he shot in the direction I jumped, these trailer walls weren't likely to stop a bullet. So maybe I could make a jump at him. Get my hands on the gun, keep it pointed up. I might get lucky.

But if I wasn't lucky, a lot of people might wind up dead.

I felt something tug my pants cuff. I casually looked down. It was Wolfman. It was his turn to hold his finger to his lips and motion for silence.

I looked back at Geek, worried I'd been staring.

Geek took a swig from his bottle.

He sat down at the table and leaned back in the chair. He pulled out a pack of cigarettes from his shirt pocket.

He took out a book of matches and looked up at me, grinning evilly. "Mind if I smoke?" he asked. Keeping his finger on the trigger, he clumsily struck the match against its cover. It sparked, but didn't ignite.

In the half second it took him to strike again, I jammed my hand into my pocket. He saw my sudden motion, and dropped the match just as it flared to life. The gun swung toward me. Time slowed to a molasses crawl. I squeezed the lighter fluid can with all my strength as he pulled the trigger. My aim was better.

His bullet kicked a hole in the wall beside me.

The lighter fluid drenched his shirt right where the match fell.

He jumped backward, shooting again, putting a hole in the floor as he smacked at the flames. He wasn't paying much attention to me at this point. I jumped across the table and grabbed his gun arm, smacking it back against Joe's kitchen cabinets. The gun went flying. I was right on top of him now, wrestling him, his shirt fire singeing my arms.

Fire never much bothered me, to tell the truth. I squeezed the lighter tin again, soaking his face and mouth good. He squealed as the flames licked over him, the baby. It was the fluid burning, not him. He'd survive, damn him. I pushed his head into the cabinets as strong as I could, trying to stun him. We knocked spiders everywhere as we danced around Joe's kitchen. I noticed some knives in the kitchen sink. I pushed Geek away and reached for them. I grabbed the first one I found and turned back to him. Only, Wolfman had reached him first.

Wolfman stood right next to Geek, holding Joe's pistol right up to Geek's shoulder, the one Joe had bit. He squeezed the trigger. Blood splashed my face.

The Geek fell to his knees. His arm was dangling by a pulsing rope of meat.

"Goddamn," he said, then collapsed, face forward, extinguishing the last of the flames.

"Goddamn," I said.

"Amen," said Wolfman.

"Call an ambulance," I said to Wolfman. "I gotta go check on the others."

"No ambulance," said Joe.

"We ain't gonna let you die," I said.

"Just put me in the back of the truck and drive me," he said. "Don't want no outsiders coming to the farm, you understand?"

I wasn't in the mood to argue. I stepped back outside. Tibby was in the door of his trailer now. "What's happening? Was that a gun?"

"Yeah," I said. "We gotta take Joe to the hospital. Can you watch Camilla for me?"

"Sure," said Tibby.

I headed back toward my trailer.

I couldn't help but notice how dark and wet the grass was between Joe's trailer and mine. I ran to my door. The lock was broken. I pushed my way inside.

I don't much like to talk about what I found. In the kitchen. And in the bedroom. And in the toilet.

I understood completely why Joe didn't want that ambulance.

CAMILLA'S BURIED up on the mountain now. There's a big old tree up there she used to like and she's near it, which is fine.

Joe and Wolfman patched up pretty good. Joe told the doctors he'd shot himself hunting, and Wolfman broke his arm trying to help him down off the mountain.

The finances of the farm have taken a little tick up of late. Word can get out fast among a certain segment of the market. We've had people fly in all the way from Japan to see what we keep out back of my trailer.

There we got a pit, twenty feet straight down. The bottom's nothing but mud and water. The customers pay us a hundred bucks to have us tie them to a rope that's attached to the hitch of my trailer and take them over to the pit. The rope's to keep them from slipping in, which would be bad.

You can hear him grunting and growling, almost sounding human, though I think it's been a month since he last used actual words. We throw our garbage down, kitchen scraps, the occasional bit of road kill. He ain't gonna starve. Still, as cold as the weather's been lately, he's stayed alive a lot longer than I would have guessed.

Not all the customers are happy at first. The pit is damn dark at the bottom. If you aren't there a little after high noon, you can't see much of him, all caked up with mud. For those who complain they can't see, I've a way of shedding a little light on what's down below.

I walk to the edge. I spit a mouthful of gasoline into the gloom. Then I open my hand to reveal a glowing coal, which drops in a red arc, trailing sparks. For a minute or so, there's light, and you can see him dancing around, shrieking, smacking the flames with the hand he has left.

The rubes who pay to watch this didn't come looking for freaks. They came looking for monsters. When they see the flames flickering in my eyes, hear the low chuckle of satisfaction that rises out of me as the screams rise from the pit, they know, at last, they've found one.

CURT ZANDER ONCE MORE, to his shame, found himself thinking about Skin. He sat in the third pew from the back, seated next to Andy, his five-year-old son, and Roxy, his wife. Reverend Perkins had just kicked into high gear, his voice rising with enthusiasm for Jesus. And Curt had something of his own rising. Shifting as subtly as he could manage on the hard bench, Curt hoped no one watched him, because Skin was on his mind once more, Skin and the message he'd received this morning.

"Live Your Fantasy," the e-mail had read. "New SkinEscort Service Now Open in Old Town."

He'd known of the existence of businesses that specialized in his particular interest. But they were found in the big cities, places like Atlanta or New York or LA. He never imagined one opening just a few hours away.

Curt went to the Old Town area almost every month. He was district manager for a check cashing chain and ran three branches in Old Town. Sometimes he'd spend a day in the area, then make a trip to the Northside branch the following day. More than once he'd stayed in a hotel rather than fighting the congested highways two days in a row. He shifted in the pew once more.

Every time he closed his eyes, he could see Skin like pearl, like emerald, like chrome. He didn't even imagine the women beneath the Skin any more. The days when he would fantasize about the dancers or the models in the magazine seemed almost innocent and quaint. Now it was as if Skin lined his eyelids, and this smooth, featureless surface was all it took to set his fantasies in motion.

Roxy glanced at him. She looked bored. Despite Reverend Perkins' enthusiastic style, his sermons followed a predictable pattern. It was 11:50, time for the Reverend to pound his fist on the podium then pause while his words sank in. *Thump, thump*. But maybe Roxy was bored by more than the sermon. Eight years of marriage, it would be natural for her to feel a little too settled in, wouldn't it? Curt could understand if Roxy found her thoughts wandering toward other men. If it were just her thoughts. If it were only fantasy.

She'd been his fantasy once. She was still beautiful, with blonde hair, blue eyes and a nice figure, more shapely now than eight years ago. Their lovemaking remained wonderful. True, it was hard to find time, with him working sixty-hour weeks and her working round the clock to raise a hyperactive five-year-old. But when they did make love, it was as good as it had been eight years ago. Except, it was only as good as it had been eight years ago. Did she ever think about anything more?

One thing for certain, Roxy didn't think about Skin. The word to her probably still had its old-fashioned meaning. When she heard the word skin, she thought of flesh, of the stuff you were born with. Curt hadn't thought like that for years. Skin, to him, was slang for Skintex, a registered trademark of the Dermantic Corporation.

A decade ago, Skintex was just another medical miracle. Developed to treat burn victims, Skintex was something temporary to place over a wound until the victim's real skin could be cloned and grown in sufficient quantities to transplant. Only, once they learned how to weave nerves and sweat glands into it, Skintex had a lot of advantages over plain old skin. It was woven from protein strands a dozen times stronger than spider silk, practically bulletproof. Skintex had no vulnerability to disease or cancer, and could survive open flame or a plunge into liquid nitrogen. So some doctors didn't see the need to replace Skintex with cloned skin, even on victims with burns over 90% of their body. And Skintex had one last advantage over the old stuff—it would never sag or wrinkle.

Eight years ago, a cosmetic surgeon in New York had been the first doctor to completely replace a healthy woman's skin with Skintex. This set off a wave of outrage on radio talk shows. This meddling with God's handiwork appalled people. Some people even wanted to outlaw replacing healthy skin with the artificial stuff. Reverend Perkins had advised his congregation to write their senators supporting the ban.

Curt hadn't been so closed-minded. True, at the time he found the idea repulsive, changing one's skin purely for vanity's sake. But he'd seen a fireman on a television show, talking about how Skintex had saved his life, and how he now wore his fake skin as a badge of honor. Dermantic had tried to slow the purely cosmetic applications of Skintex by no longer manufacturing it in flesh tones. Outlawing Skin just seemed too extreme.

Plus, even years ago, Curt had to admit that people with Skintex had an exotic glow to them, a sort of beauty that was, without question, only skin deep, but nice nonetheless.

Four years ago, during a weeklong visit to the home office in Atlanta, he'd seen his first Skin show. Jack Sanderson, a company bigwig, had taken him to dinner, and later invited him to a Skin joint. Curt hadn't been interested, not even curious, really, but Jack was easy to get along with, and what harm could it do?

Skintex is hairless. Sometimes, Skinners wear wigs, but not the girls at the club. Curt had sat in the smoky bar until his eyes were red and dry. He couldn't stop staring. Like silk, like satin, like chrome, their unblemished bodies slithered before him, all curves and shadows, the flesh made perfect. Their mouths. Curt had been especially focused on their mouths. Where did it change, he wondered. Their lips were Skin. Were their gums? Were their tongues? What would it be like to kiss such a mouth? To have those smooth, nail-less fingers caressing his cheek?

On his next trip, he went to an adult bookstore and paid twenty dollars for a magazine that told him what it would feel like and showed him what it would look like in extreme close up. He'd thrown the magazine away before returning home, but not before memorizing its web address. He resisted visiting it for many weeks. Had it actually been possible once not to think about Skin for as much as a week? As much as a day?

AFTER CHURCH, they went to the mall. He took Andy to the food court as Roxy went looking for a birthday present for a friend. It was an effort to get Andy to eat any food at all these days; the boy seemed determined to live on air and sunlight. The toy robot in the kid's meal didn't help. Fries and chicken nuggets were forgotten as the toy robot accepted the challenge of the evil salt and pepper shakers.

"Take that!" the toy robot shouted as he smacked Salt.

"Arg!" Salt cried as he toppled backwards onto Curt's chicken sandwich.

"Help!" Curt said, picking up his sandwich, lifting and closing the top bun so it looked like a mouth. "I've been assaulted!"

Andy found this hilarious, and fell back in his seat laughing.

Curt took a bite from his sandwich. He stopped in mid-chew. Across the food court, outside the women's bathroom, leaning against the wall, looking impatient, stood a man with Skin. He wore blue jeans and an athletic shirt that showed off his muscles. His Skin was metallic gold. Curt had seen men with Skin only in photos, never in person. Staring at the gleam of the man's shoulders, uncomfortable feelings stirred within him. What would Skin feel like stretched over hard muscle? Massaging shoulders like that–how could it not feel magnificent? He wanted to look away, but couldn't.

Then a woman came out of the bathroom, wearing a black hat and a skimpy black dress that showed off her opalescent Skin. She took the gold man's arm and they began to walk right toward Curt. He was at last able to tear his gaze from the man and fix it upon the woman's neck, and the delicate lines of her collarbones over shimmering cleavage. Somehow this felt safer.

But this wasn't safe. This was wrong. Dangerous. Not his obsession, or his staring, but Skin's presence here, in a mall food court for God's sake. Skin had a context, it was to be seen on web sites, or in magazines, or in smoky bars, or in his dreams every night. He'd made a little box in his head that Skin stayed in, unable to escape into the rest of his life. Now Skin was here, in his normal life, walking right toward him on graceful legs as if it recognized no barrier between the forbidden and the mundane.

Andy had stopped laughing. Curt kept staring. The couple walked by. As they passed, her eyes caught his. She smiled, ever so slightly.

"Daddy!" Andy shouted, pointing after them. "A robot! A big robot!"

Curt swallowed. He'd nearly squeezed his sandwich in two.

"Daddy!"

"It's OK, Andy," he said. "That … that wasn't a robot. It's just a man in … just a costume. Like Halloween."

"Oh," said Andy.

Curt felt that being a parent in this day and age was harder than ever. He remembered his own father trying to explain to him at Andy's age how it was that some girl at school had two daddies. But how do you explain people who want to peel off their own God-given skin and … it wasn't like they even tried to make it look like flesh anymore. They didn't want to look human. They were setting themselves apart as something different, something better, and Curt knew that wasn't right, that it was an affront to God and family and country, and … and Lord help him, she'd passed close enough to touch, if he'd dared. He knew, just knew, that despite the gemlike appearance, her Skin would be the softest, warmest, smoothest thing he could ever touch.

A hand fell on his shoulder. "Having fun, guys?" Roxy asked.

"Oh," Curt said. "Yeah."

"Mommy, I got a robot!" said Andy.

"You look a little pale," Roxy said, placing her hand on Curt's chin and tilting his face toward her.

"I'm fine," he said. "Find what you're looking for?"

"Close enough," Roxy said. "Here, watch my bag while I run to the restroom."

Curt watched her walk in her Sunday dress. Her legs were quite shapely; her hips had a nice swing to them. She was all of the woman he'd ever need. He wouldn't let this weird interest he'd developed affect his feelings toward her. Still as she vanished into the ladies room, he could see her, quite clearly in his mind's eye, with her skin smooth and polished and gleaming like pearl, with the fine shape of her neck and head unconcealed by hair. He imagined her looking back over her flawless shoulder to smile at him. He smiled dreamily back as he finished Andy's fries.

"DID YOU SEE THAT COUPLE at the mall?" he asked that night as he climbed into bed. "The ones with the, um, fake skin?"

"Sure," Roxy said. "That stuff's all the rage in California, I hear. The latest thing for people with too much money and not enough sense."

"I almost worked up the courage to speak to them," Curt said. Which wasn't entirely a lie, the way he was rewriting the encounter in memory.

"Really? Why?"

"Well, I was thinking about inviting them to church." Which also wasn't a lie, but nowhere near the truth. As he'd played the scene over in his mind the rest of the day, he'd decided that it was a relief that he'd felt attracted to the gold man. He knew beyond question he wasn't gay. So maybe this meant that his interest in Skin wasn't really sexual. Maybe it was just simple fascination with what could be done with a human body, no more dangerous than admiring a tattoo, no more aberrant in the grand scheme of things than a tongue ring. He could see himself talking with the gold man about sports, or business, and realized how natural and easy and satisfying it would be to shake his hand. But he couldn't tell Roxy this. So he said, "I thought it would be, uh, funny to have them sitting next to us on the pew. Can you imagine the look on Reverend Perkin's face?"

"Oh, you," said Roxy.

"So what do you think about it?"

"Inviting them to church?"

"No, just Skintex in general."

"Curt!" Roxy said in mock shock. "Don't tell me you think she was pretty!"

"What? When did I say that?"

"You're beating around the bush, my friend," said Roxy.

"But I didn't find her pretty. Really. I just wonder what makes people do things like that."

"Who knows?" Roxy shrugged. "They say that Skintex never wrinkles. Some people are afraid of growing old."

"Yeah," said Curt. "You know, when I was a teenager, I thought forty was old. Now I'm almost there and I still feel like a kid sometimes. Old's a long way away."

"I look forward to growing old," Roxy said. "I don't want to speed it up or anything, but I think there's something nice about the thought of you and me sitting in rocking chairs on the porch while our grandkids play in the yard."

"Grandkids? Andy's five!"

"But, you know, it's nice to think that he makes it. It's such a big scary world out there. I just find it comforting to think about twenty, thirty years from now, he's made it to adulthood safely, our job's done and I can … I can relax."

Curt nodded, then turned out the lamp by the bed. He slid down under the covers. But he had one more thing to say.

"Speaking of scary, I need to go to Old Town this week. The manager of the State Street branch needs a little fear put into him. He's dragging down figures for the whole region."

"Oh, Honey. I hate when you go up there. You're always back so late."

"Yeah. I know. Maybe I'll make an overnighter of it. Drive up to Northside once I'm done, spend the night, visit that branch first thing then head back here and spend the rest of the day with you and Andy. Beats two late nights, don't you think?"

"Sure, Honey. What day?"

"Actually," he said, "I'm thinking tomorrow."

"Tomorrow? This is short notice."

"Well, if I plan for later in the week, word inevitably leaks and they try to straighten things up before I get there. I'd like to catch them by surprise, just wander in unannounced like a customer, try to see things in a fresh light."

"Sounds like a plan," Roxy said. "Good luck with it."

"I'd better get some sleep then," said Curt.

He kissed his wife goodnight and placed his head upon his pillow. He would drive up to Northside tomorrow evening. Maybe he'd stop at a bookstore and buy a magazine, but that would be it. Nothing more.

THE NEXT MORNING, he stopped for breakfast and read the morning mail on his phone. Once again, the ad for the New Skin Escort Service was in his mailbox. He wondered how they'd found his address. He had a second e-dentity set up, with a second credit card under a different name to allow him to cruise Skin sites anonymously. But this one was coming to his work address, and he'd been very careful never to visit a Skin site from anywhere he could be traced. He hoped it was coincidence. Business travelers were routinely spammed with escort ads.

He jotted down the web address on a napkin and switched over to his other e-dentity. He tapped in the address and made the arrangements. He would call Roxy at 5:00, talk for a while, then tell her he planned to go see a movie. Then he'd go to the hotel bar, have a few drinks, and his date would meet him at 7:00.

He felt good about his decision. This obsession had hung over his head for too long, was costing him money, was making him deceive his wife, and after tonight, it was over. Tonight, he'd satisfy his curiosity, get it over with, put it behind him. He could predict the ending now. He'd touch his escort, find out that Skin was cold, or hard, or even warm and soft, but still only a covering, no more erotic than upholstery. He was looking forward to being disappointed. Tomorrow, he'd be free of this perverse longing.

HER NAME WAS SAFFRON and her skin was white and smooth as a glass of milk. She wore a clingy red dress and a wig of orange hair, with long curls draped about her bare shoulders. Her lips were painted to match her dress, as were the tips of her fingers where nails should have been. Her eyes were emerald green. She and Curt sat in a booth near the back. He worked on his fourth beer as she toyed with her Bloody Mary.

"You're not a cop," she said.

"No," he admitted.

"When you've done this a while, you can tell," she said, taking the lime from her drink and sucking on it.

Saffron certainly didn't look like she'd been doing this, whatever this was, for too long. Maybe she was 25, he guessed. But how could you tell, with Skin? She could be 65, or maybe 15. Had she been a pimply-faced kid just months ago? Was she someone's grandmother? He'd read stories about women from all walks of life getting Skin from dealers south of the border with the understanding that they'd pay for it by prostituting themselves. It was a cold, commercial trade, sexual service in exchange for a forever-youthful appearance. The business aspect of this night appealed to him. Once everything was stripped down to money, he felt comfortable.

"So look," he said. "I'm probably going to be a little different than most of your, uh, dates."

"Do tell."

"Well, I … I just want to talk. At first. I want to—"

"Find out why I did this?" Saffron interrupted. "Oh, Baby, that's nothing new. This is your first time, right?"

"With a Skinner," he said. "Oh. Wait. Does that word bother you? I've heard that—"

"No," she said. "I think the ones who don't like that word are mainly the involuntary ones. Burn victims and such. But I'm honest with myself. You didn't pay the agency a grand for my sparkling personality. You want to touch Skin."

Curt took a sip from his beer.

"More than anything," he said.

"Baby, I find it's best to just cut to the chase. Anything you want tonight, you just say it. You got a room here?"

"Yes."

"Then let's go to it. Just dive right in."

"I did say it," said Curt. "What I want. I'd like to talk a little first."

"I got the Skin because I really wanted to," Saffron said, rolling her eyes. "That's as complex as my story gets. The first time I saw it, I knew it was right for me."

"And you still feel everything normally?" he asked.

"Baby, what's normal? I don't remember what the old stuff felt like. But, yeah, I still feel things. I don't feel pain, really, but I notice heat, cold, pressure, all that. In a way, I'm more aware of them now than before. I pay attention." She reached out and touched his hand. Her fingers were cold and hard, moist with condensation from her drink. It was a relief, his best-case scenario for disappointment come true. Defenses lowered, he continued to explore. He took her hand in his, turning up her palm, smooth as a porcelain doll's. He touched it. It felt soft as a pillow, and warmer than her fingertips. He traced his fingers across her palm, over her wrist, up the long sleek curve of her forearm. It was unlike anything he'd ever imagined. If there were bodies in Heaven and not just spirits, this would be how they would feel. He bent down to the table and kissed her hand. She watched with emerald eyes.

LATER, HE USED HER. Every position he knew, everything he'd read about, he tried it. He explored her with his fingers, searching for the boundary between outside and inside, between the unbreakable china doll and the living woman within. He couldn't find it. He growled like a hungry animal as he bit her. She gave small, fake sounding gasps in response, but shed no tears. He realized that the woman inside the Skin watched him, bored, unconcerned. The Skin was a barrier between him and this woman, just as it was becoming a barrier between him and his wife, between him and his life, and suddenly all he could feel was anger. With rage he sank his teeth into her neck, he chewed her lips, he tore at her breasts and thighs, gnawing with all his strength until his jaws ached. His nails raked the length of her back, but never scratched her. He grabbed her wrists in viselike grips, dragging her from the bed, tossing her to the floor, and throwing himself upon her. By the end of the night, there wasn't a single surface in the room he hadn't pinned her against. Her skin was unmarked by his passion—almost. In the corner of her mouth, was a thin red splotch of blood. He reached out and wiped it clean. There was no visible wound. He touched his lip. He was the one bleeding. His anger vanished, the last glowing ember of his rage suddenly ashing over. Her cool, gentle eyes gazed out of the doll-mask face with a look that told him she understood what he felt; she'd seen it all before. She knew him. She didn't hate him. Tenderly now, he held her to him, all her warmth and mercy filling him, all her softness yielding, till he forgot himself, could no longer feel the boundary where he ended and she began, and found himself helplessly in love.

He said her name ten thousand times.

At dawn, when she left him, he cried himself to sleep.

CURT ZANDER ONCE MORE found himself staring at Roxy as she slept, watching her still eyelashes and the wrinkles surrounding them, studying the folds and pores and the few stray hairs that grew between her eyebrows, contemplating the ugly brown mole that sat upon her left brow like some tiny yet malevolent gargoyle snickering as it glowered over her face. Half a million dollars would replace all of her flaws with perfection. If he sold the house and cars and cashed in his stock, he'd have enough.

Of course, he would never approach her with the idea.

He knew that if he ever suggested it, no matter how gently, how jokingly, the deviant desires within him would be exposed, and their marriage would be over. Some people might be willing to surrender everything for Skin, but he wasn't one of them. He was happy with Roxy. He loved her when they met. He loved her now. Roxy's face would age and sag and wrinkle and he would cherish every fold. His fondness for Skin would stay in that box in his head now; he had other outlets to satisfy himself. He and Roxy could now peacefully grow old together.

But if it ever did happen—on some outside chance, some long shot chain of events, some terrible accident or disease, perhaps, or something as common and simple as a house fire or a car wreck—if it ever did happen that Roxy should lose her skin and slip into something new… Curt couldn't help but think she'd look absolutely brilliant in chrome.

Little Guilt Thing Goin' On

HALO SLUMBERED, her peaceful face visible through the empty tequila bottle. Rob rolled over, careful not to disturb her. He sat up, wobbly and nauseous. Sunlight slipped through gaps between the blinds. Rob blinked, gaining his bearings amidst the clutter. Halo lived on the fifth floor of a brick building that had once been a department store. Her collection of antiquities and oddities filled the huge space. In a near corner stood a razor-edged sword, its polished steel gleaming beneath dust. The far wall held old, beautiful paintings that could have been at home in any museum, with dozens of additional paintings propped up against support columns. And books. All around were books in great heaps, books written in every tongue, from coverless paperbacks to leather-bound tomes, the pages yellow and crumbling. Looking down, he found his feet rested on a medical encyclopedia, opened to a tangled map of blue and red blood vessels, its heavy pages propped open with a gilded monkey's skull.

"Sweet merciful Jesus," Rob whispered, his lower lip thick and swollen. "Not again."

His face hurt. No part of him felt good, but his face hurt with special intensity. It helped balance out the throbbing base of his skull. The pain reminded him of the time he'd been hit from behind with a hammer. He touched his face and winced. He looked back at the bed. Blood spotted the pillows.

"Ah, Jesus," he said. "How could this happen?"

Of course he knew. From time to time he would walk out of the studio of his ministry in Richmond, Virginia, get into his car, and drive down to the corner store to buy milk. Some of those times, not every week, but a few times a year, he'd drive past the corner store and get onto the highway, achieving speeds upwards of one-hundred thirty miles an hour down I-85 toward Atlanta. Toward Halo.

Yesterday, he'd forgotten the milk again.

Trembling, he tiptoed across the scattered clothing concealing the floor. A full-length mirror leaned against a support column. He brushed back the tangles of his red, shoulder-length hair to reveal his face. It had changed somewhat. Rings pierced his face, almost a dozen of them. Slender, shiny hoops, in neon shades of blue and pink and green, along the ridge where his left eyebrow had been just yesterday, balanced by three black ones in his lower lip, from which hung tiny bells. When had this seemed like a good idea?

Thin dark trickles had dried on his face. He looked into his red-rimmed eyes. For not the first time he felt like a helpless prisoner in his body, like the real him was some tiny doll man trapped inside his head, strapped into the driver's seat of a body without brakes.

Halo stretched, arching that long sinuous back, showing off those little dimples in her shoulders that drove him wild. She rose and tossed her dark hair back, and the streaming light accented the curves of her breasts and belly. She strode toward him on perfect legs, still wearing her black stilettos. She draped a slender-fingered hand across his shoulder and pulled his hair back, kissing his neck, before looking into the mirror with her deep green eyes.

"Hmm," she said, the hint of a grin on her succulent lips. "You look like you fell face first into the tackle box."

"How did this happen?" he whispered.

"You showed up like this, Sugar. You ever think tequila might not be your drink?"

"Dear God, I tried," he said. "I tried so hard."

His lower lip trembled, causing the tiny bells to chime.

"I've failed," said Rob. "How can I change the world when I can't change myself?"

"Oh Sugar," Halo said, hugging him. "It'll be all right."

Her warm lips pressed once more against the nape of his neck.

"Y'know," she said, "you're kinda cute when you got your little guilt thing goin' on."

His eyes caught hers in the mirror.

In a twinkling, Rob glimpsed the force that made him drive past the store. Halo loved him, more than anyone ever had. She never said it. That wasn't important. He'd heard the words before, spoken by more women than he could count. Words meant nothing. Halo was different. She carried her love in her eyes, in the gentleness of her fingers, in the sway of her hips. And he loved her. He could admit that, on these dark painful mornings, in this brief clear window between wanton abandon and shame-filled denial. He loved everything about her, her wit, her laugh, her gentle teasing and her rough touches, her soul and her body. Except … he wasn't sure about her penis. As perfect and beautiful as the rest of her, somehow feminine even when it was fully aroused, Halo's penis was a sticking point for him. No pun intended.

"ALL I WANT," said Rob, sitting half-dressed on the edge of the bed, "is to be taken seriously. OW!"

Halo stood over him with a pair of needle-nose pliers. She'd taken off her shoes and put on some panties and was wearing his shirt, unbuttoned. She slipped the skinny point of the pliers into another ring and pulled.

"Ow!" Rob said again.

"You ever think, Hon, that maybe you take yourself too seriously?"

"I don't think that's-OW-possible. People listen to me."

"Um-hmm," she said.

"I'm screwing everything up."

"Baby, I can't argue. You know about screwing."

"OW!" he cried as Halo gave a particularly vigorous tug.

She dropped the ring into the ashtray along with the others.

"That's the last of it," she said.

He went to the mirror, to examine his bloody, swollen face. He looked like he'd been a brawl.

"Anyone ever tell you you're a scary lookin' man?" asked Halo.

He nodded. Deep inside, he worried that he liked it.

Someone knocked on the door.

"Who's that?" asked Rob. "Jesus, if a reporter saw me…."

"Sugar, it's only Bubba."

"Your photographer?"

"We're shooting today."

"I don't want anyone to see me," said Rob.

"Bubba won't talk, Baby."

"I'd better go," said Rob, reaching for his boots.

"It's okay if you stay. I'd like it if you watched me work."

"I don't want to be around you and a camera at the same time," said Rob.

Halo looked miffed.

"You could phone ahead," she said, opening the door.

"Halo! Baby!" Bubba's ever-jubilant voice made Rob's head throb even worse. Bubba sashayed into the room. He was a tiny man, with a bleach-blond Mohawk and facial features that mixed the best of his Asian and African ancestry. He wore a pantsuit made of a shimmering purple fabric that creative and energetic vandals might use to reupholster a stranger's couch. "Oh," said Bubba, spying Rob. "You. Forget the milk again?"

"Morning, Bubba," said Rob.

"It's four in the afternoon," said Bubba.

Rob looked at his naked wrist. He had the faintest flash of giving his Rolex to some tattooed woman with a shaved head.

A grunt from the doorway announced the arrival of a young woman, in torn jeans and a black tee shirt, straining under the load of five bags of camera equipment. The hair on the back of Rob's neck rose. He didn't recognize this woman.

"Quite a climb," the woman said, gasping.

"Who's this?" asked Halo, eyeing the woman cautiously.

"Brandy quit," said Bubba, shrugging. "This is Lucy."

"I see," said Halo.

Lucy looked around the museum attic clutter of Halo's home and whistled. "Cool decor," she said.

"Just some things I've picked up over the centuries," said Halo.

Great, thought Rob. He didn't have to be around Halo long to be reminded that her penis wasn't the only thing waiting to scandalize his parishioners.

Lucy grinned, ready to take the bait. "Did you say centuries?"

"Didn't I mention?" said Bubba. "Halo's a demoness."

"Demoness?" said Halo, rolling her eyes. "Darlin', we prefer the term 'eternity challenged.'"

"Look at the time," said Rob, looking around the room for his leather jacket. "I'd best be on my way."

He spotted his jacket hanging on the corner of a bookshelf and snatched it. In doing so, he dislodged a stack of dusty magazines and sent them fluttering to the floor. Amidst the flurry of paper, a hard, marble-like object bounced, coming to rest at Halo's feet.

"Ah-ha!" she said, kneeling to pick up a smooth black pebble the size of a small egg. It was wrapped in fine braided hair which she held between her fingernails gingerly. "That's where I left it!"

She held it up into a bright dust beam, where it glimmered with the polish of ages.

"Know what this is?" she asked.

"A sex toy?" said Bubba.

"Please," said Halo. "This is the stone that killed Goliath. It's the oldest thing in this room. Not counting me."

"Cool," said Lucy.

"I'd stick around and help clean up, but, you know," said Rob, pulling on his jacket. "Long drive. Running late."

Lucy glanced at him as he spoke, turned away, then looked back, goggle-eyed.

"Oh. My. God!" she said.

Rob clenched his teeth.

"You're Rob MacDowell! From the Four Horsemen!"

Rob's teeth unclenched a little. For once he felt relieved that his other reputation preceded him. Lucy had that look on her face, that dreamy hungry look that Rob had seen countless times, a different life ago.

"I, uh, get that a lot," Rob said, heading for the door.

"Your song! YFM! It's, like, my favorite ever! You and Dirk Sinister are geniuses! Oh my God! Could I get your autograph? Could you get me Dirk's autograph?"

Rob felt a very strong desire to turn into water and seep between the cracks in the floor.

"Lucy," said Bubba, "you're going totally fanboy."

"Long drive," Rob mumbled, avoiding eye contact.

Halo intercepted him, planting a kiss on his cheek.

"You get that lip healed up," she said, tapping it gently with the stone that killed Goliath. "Come back soon, ya' hear?"

"I'll, uh, call," said Rob.

"That'll be the day," said Bubba.

"Sorry if I embarrassed you," said Lucy. "But you have no idea! Your song changed my life."

"Yeah," said Rob, shoulders sagging. "I get that a lot, too."

He slipped from Halo's arms into the hallway, and shut the door. He leaned back against the wall, his heart pounding. He could still hear their muffled voices.

"What?" said Bubba. "He ain't gonna call. You know that. What do you see in him anyhow?"

Halo sighed. "He's, you know, interesting. Always something new."

Rob nodded.

"He's a maniac," said Bubba.

Rob nodded again.

"I like his style," said Halo. "Rob goes through life the way some folks go through windshields. Faster than he ever dreamed and with the most precious look on his face."

"Leaving behind a bloody mess," said Bubba.

Once more Rob nodded, then pulled himself away. Time to take his bloody face back home.

I-85 FROM ATLANTA to Richmond is one long haul when you're stone sober and leaving behind the love of your life. Lucy had rattled him. He hadn't said good-bye. And this time… this time he wasn't coming back.

"Coward!" he cursed, then punched himself in the forehead. Insufficiently chastised, he struck again. "Idiot," he said.

Driving through the dark nothingness of the rural south, there was little to distract him from his shame and weakness. He was a minister of the Lord. If his relationship with Halo were discovered, his whole world would crumble around him. But, wasn't he a fool to fear what the world thought? It was the Lord's opinion that mattered, right? Of course, the Lord hadn't given his stamp of approval. Still, honesty was the best policy, right? Perhaps it was time to tell the world the whole story.

"Not going to happen," said the little doll man in his head.

"I know," said Rob.

He'd met Halo five years ago in Los Angeles after the release of the second Horsemen album. He'd slipped away, unnoticed once Dirk Sinister had entered the room. As always, he was practically invisible in Dirk's presence.

He'd walked to the top floor of the hotel parking deck and climbed onto the wall that surrounded it.

Thirty-seven stories to the pavement. He'd spread his arms and closed his eyes. The warm wind rushing through his fingers gave him the illusion of falling.

"You feeling okay, Sugar?" were Halo's first words to him.

He looked at her out of the corner of his eye. She was breathtaking. He assumed she was a prostitute Dirk had hired.

"Go away," he growled. "You got nothing I want."

Halo laughed. "I was worried you might kill yourself. Now I'm kinda lookin' forward to it."

"You think it's funny?"

"Oh, Baby, everything's funny."

"Not this. You can't know."

Halo brushed back her hair as the wind danced around her. She said, "You feel guilty about making the second album, right? *Die, God, Die.* Honey, you do have a way with words."

"Everything's happened so fast," he said, watching the cars streaming below him. "I'm tired. Folks back home… they think I'm some kind of monster."

Halo leaned against the wall. "Dirk's having a good time."

"Dirk *is* a monster. Nothing makes him happier than looking out his window and finding the villagers have brought out the pitchforks."

"Are you scared of him?"

"Why am I talking to you?" he asked, looking down at her.

"You looked like you could use someone to talk to."

"You aren't a reporter, are you?"

"Do I look like a reporter, Baby?"

"So who are you?"

"Would you believe that I used to be an angel?"

"Nope," said Rob.

"Wasn't real good at it," she said. "Got fired after this big dispute with management."

"Ah. Casual blasphemy," said Rob. "We have something in common."

"Sugar, you'd be surprised at how much we have in common."

"It's been a while since I felt surprised," said Rob. "Been a while since I've felt much of anything."

"Want to talk about it?"

"I don't spill my guts to strangers," said Rob, studying her. Her eyes had a fiery opalescence that caught his attention. "So. What's your name?"

"If I told you my real name your eardrums would explode. But my friends call me Halo." She raised a hand toward him. "Come on down from there before you do something ironic."

He had. They'd talked all night. She'd listened, mostly, and made a few jokes, as Rob had told her of the terrible weight in his life, how far he'd strayed from his childhood dreams. He'd grown up in West Virginia, singing in the choir, learning the bagpipes from his grandfather. He'd gone to college with the dream of becoming a gospel singer, not a rock star. As he talked to Halo, the path out of his terrible guilt suddenly came into focus. The following morning, he informed a very hung over Dirk Sinister that he was quitting the band and devoting his life to the Lord. That had been the morning he'd found out what it was like to be hit in the back of the head with a hammer.

WEARY FROM HIS DRIVE from Atlanta, Rob dragged himself into bed as dawn was breaking. He woke in the heat of the day, feeling lighter. This time, it really was over. He got dressed. His face was looking less swollen. A dab of make-up and he'd be fine on camera. In retrospect, the whole encounter with Lucy encouraged him. People listened to him. He was a role model. He just needed to sharpen the message. Focus in like a laser beam.

"A love laser," Rob said to himself in the mirror. "Jesus is a love laser."

He began to hum a tune to fit the words. He might be onto something. His thrash bagpipe gospel had never moved Horsemen level sales, but this one had potential.

Whistling the tune, his head full of lightning enthusiasm, he wheeled across town to the studio.

In his office, there was a postcard from Dirk.

"Love, love, love, love, love," it read.

On the front was a picture of a tiny dog humping a woman's leg and thinking, "Oh, Baby!"

Rob suddenly realized why his tune for "Jesus the Love Laser" was popping into his head so fully formed. It had the same baseline as "Burn in Hell, You Cocksucker," the Horsemen's first big hit after Rob left the band.

ROB WAS IN FINE FORM. His bagpipe sang like a living thing. He'd started into "Jesus the Love Laser." The whole studio clapped and sang. He'd found his groove, tapped into the underlying angelic chorus that vibrated through his world. He felt alive and free.

He brought "JTLL" to its climax, then basked in the spotlight, waving to the bright faces in the audience.

"What's it about?" he yelled.

"Love!" screamed the audience.

Rob handed his pipes to Mickey, his stagehand and took a microphone up into the seats.

"People," he said. "People, when I'm making music, when I'm making music, it's like I don't exist. I just disappear, and all that's left is energy. That energy is love, people. It's like nothing else. No drug can take you there, nothing you can smoke, drink, or stick in your veins is gonna get you there. It's God's love, moving through me, and I'm here to share it. God is ready to move through all of you. I need a witness. Can I get a witness?"

Hands went up all around.

He thrust his mic into the face of a blonde, blue-eyed girl wearing a tartan skirt and a lovely smile.

"I, like, feel God's love, Rob. I feel it when I'm cheerleading. When I start jumping around and shouting, I know that my energy is coming from someplace higher. I'm cheerleading for the Lord!"

The audience clapped and whooped raucously. Rob moved up the stairs. A college-age guy with a crew cut and leather jacket jumped from his seat to intercept him.

"Preacher," Crew-cut shouted. "Preacher, I've felt it! I've felt the glory, Preacher!"

"Testify!" Rob said, holding out his mic.

"I've felt the fire inside me, Rob," the young man said, taking the mic. "The fire that comes from doing the right thing, from living God's word."

"Tell it," Rob said, as the audience began to chant, "Tell it! Tell it!"

"Like, last week, there was this faggot, you know?" said Crew-cut. "He was all looking at me, and telling me that I had pretty eyes and shit, and I told him, I told him God hates faggots."

Rob grabbed for the mic, but the young man spun away, continuing to testify. "He was all, like, 'God doesn't care. God doesn't care who I put my thing into.' So I smote him, people. I smote that faggot good! I left him tied to a fence with blood coming out his ears and—"

Rob shoved the boy hard, snatching the mic away. The little doll man inside Rob's head gripped the wheel tightly, anticipating the worst.

"You fuckin' moron," Rob shouted, as the young man stumbled backward, tripping on the steps, falling down. "What's wrong with you? You think this is some kind of joke?"

The crowd hushed.

"It's in the Bible," Crew-cut said, stammering. "God hates faggots. He wants them dead."

"It is not in the Bible," Rob said. "God is not hate. God is not about hating. God is—"

"Sodom and Gomorrah," said Crew-cut. "God killed whole cities because they were faggots!"

Rob grabbed Crew-cut by his jacket and yanked him to his feet. In his cockpit, the little doll man struggled with the wheel as all around him dials rose into red zones.

Rob stared into the young man's mean little eyes and growled. "God. Is. Love."

"It's an act of love to kill a faggot," Crew-cut said. "What are you, some kind of faggot lover? Huh? Whose side are you on?"

Crew-cut punctuated his argument by raising his knee hard into Rob's groin.

The little doll man crashed into the top of Rob's skull.

Then, because occasionally these things happen, Rob pulled the young man closer, placed his mouth upon Crew-cut's eyebrow, and bit that poor bastard 'til he squealed.

ROB TROD SULLENLY toward his office, wiping blood from his mouth. Mickey had sent him away to cool off before the police arrived. He had a terrible ache in the pit of his belly that was only partially due to the nut-shot. The little doll man was awake again, and delivering a very scathing critique of Rob's handling of the situation. Rob could only nod, and sigh.

He opened the door to his office. The pain in his belly magnified exponentially. There, sitting at his desk beneath the yard long stainless steel crucifix that hung on the wall, was Dirk Sinister, all seven feet of him, dressed in a white silk suit, his skin bleached to a matching shade, his dark eye-slits twinkling with amusement despite his permanent frown.

The little doll man sighed, and clutched the wheel once more. Then he noticed Mikimbe in the corner, reading a year-old issue of Gospel Music Today. Mikimbe was Dirk's bodyguard, a 300 pound former linebacker with a fine aim to accompany the .44 magnum visible in his shoulder holster. The little doll man relaxed. Even Rob wasn't stupid enough to lose his temper around Mikimbe.

"My dear Mr. MacDowell," said Dirk. "Have you ever considered that live television might not be your friend?"

"You planted him," said Rob. "Of course. Brilliant. And I fell for it. You must be very happy."

"Happy. Wealthy. Every time you throw another tantrum, the Horsemen albums rise up the charts. But I had nothing to do with the boy."

"Sure," said Rob. "Why are you wasting my time, then?"

"I'm concerned about your reputation, old friend." Dirk folded his fingers into a prayer-like wedge as he spoke.

"Noted," said Rob. "I'll send a thank-you card."

"'That angry guy,'" said Dirk. "You get called that a lot, don't you?"

Rob shrugged.

"'That bagpipe guy.' Harmless enough. 'That crazy guy' galls you, I imagine."

"Dirk, can you speed this up? What do you want?"

"I want to help you not be known as 'that preacher who sleeps with she-male porn stars,'" said Dirk.

Rob tried to remain poker-faced.

"What are you talking about?" he asked in his calmest, most bemused voice.

Dirk pulled Rob's laptop from the top desk drawer and opened it. It was already on, lighting his pale face with an electric glow. He spun the monitor around.

It was Halo's web page.

"Impressive," said Dirk. "You're sharing the bed of a fallen angel who was around to watch the planet cool. I'm a teense envious."

"Huh," said Rob, with a disinterested glance at the computer. "Yeah, I know her. Didn't know she was a he. Certainly never slept with her. She's a soul in need, and I am a minister."

"This is why you've been an abysmal failure as a man of the cloth," said Dirk. "You're a pathetic liar."

"So you're planning to spread the rumor that Halo is my 'girlfriend,'" said Rob. "Who'll take you seriously? You're an aging rock-hack who earns most of his money off a song I wrote. I might be known as 'the angry guy,' but you're known as a past-his-prime burnout who desperately clings to his reputation for hedonism and the occult in order to keep his name in the tabloids."

"How pithy," said Dirk. "Did I mention I have photographs?"

Rob laughed. "You can whip up any picture you want in Photoshop. You really think Halo has black leather wings?"

"Yes," said Dirk. "Halo has black leather wings."

Rob shook his head, feeling pity for his insane former partner.

"Halo also has the stone that killed Goliath," said Dirk. "I want it."

"Dirk," said Rob, in a soothing voice. "I may not know Halo in the Biblical sense, but I know her, okay? She's not a demon. She doesn't have wings. She's someone who found a niche market for she-male demon porn and filled it. She makes up stuff. The stone that killed Goliath is probably a pebble she found in a parking lot."

"Believe what you wish," said Dirk. "Three millennia ago that rock was touched by divine wrath and turned into a weapon. The power of God's violence resonates within it. The stone is priceless. I want it; you'll get it for me. If not, the pictures hit the internet a week from today."

Mickey opened the office door. "Hey Boss, the cops are here," he said.

Rob turned from Dirk and Mikimbe and told Mickey he'd be right there. But, Mickey wasn't through. "There's good news, kind of. The guy's confession was real. He's wanted in West Virginia on attempted murder charges. You'll look like a hero for this."

"No," said Rob. "I'm glad the guy got caught, but we're not gonna spin this into me doing the right thing. I'm going to apologize. That clear?"

"Fine," said Mickey. "Your call."

"If you'll excuse me, Gentlemen," Rob said, turning toward his desk. Dirk and Mikimbe were gone. "What the … ? Where'd they go?"

"Where'd who go?" asked Mickey.

"You didn't see … ?"

"See who?"

Rob scratched the back of his head and left the room. "Never mind," he said.

ROB HAD MET DIRK SINISTER at a party. Dirk was the center of attention, being that he was nude with a bleeding pentagram cut into his chest. Rob in his "What Would Jesus Do?" tee shirt had instantly become the target of Dirk's barbs. Dirk had spent the night ridiculing Rob, his accent, his mullet, and everything dear and true Rob believed in. Somehow, though, Rob felt like he was in on the joke, and by the end of the night the two were friends.

Not long after, "The Four Horsemen" were born. Dirk's morning Tarot reading had been favorable toward forming a band, and Rob was the closest person with musical talent, albeit bagpipe oriented. Dirk showed promise as a lyricist. So, of course, the first song that really took off for them was "You Fucking Morons," which had been recorded one drunken night with Dirk squeaking and honking on the bagpipes and Rob mumbling his way through lyrics made up on the spot. The lyrics were dark and evil, welling up from a place inside Rob he still didn't dare examine. Listening to the song the following morning was both shameful and liberating. They'd posted the song to their website and forgot about it.

The following year, in California, a teenage boy named Johnny Ray Wilson had walked into a church, splashed a cup of gasoline onto an old man, and flicked a lit cigarette into his lap. He did this humming the music he was listening to on his headphones:

rip pages from the phone book,
go on pick a name
visit where he lives and introduce some flame
burn the fucking moron and dance in the laughing fire
feel the spark inside you
know that nothing gets you higher

These were the words to that had fallen from Rob's drunken lips that long ago night. These were the words that drove Johnny Ray Wilson to murder. After news of the "murder song" leaked out, these were the words that made Dirk Sinister and Rob MacDowell unimaginably rich.

THREE DAYS LATER, he was in Atlanta, parked in front of Halo's building.

"This is stupid," he grumbled.

For once, the little doll man was making trouble. Because the little doll man was worried. Dirk was right. Rob didn't want his relationship with Halo becoming public. Someone had told Dirk; it was easy to guess who. Rob wasn't surprised that pictures existed. Hell, Halo had a web-cam in her shower. Who knew where else she might have them hidden?

"Two birds," said Rob, "with one stone."

It was time to finish this.

Halo opened the door before he knocked. She looked worried. Cool morning air flowed through open windows, and her collection of eclectica seemed cheap and junky in the sunlight, an assortment of flimsy props gathered from garage sales and Goodwill.

"Lip's looking better," Halo said. "Except for the frown."

"Lucy ratted us out," said Rob, striding past her without looking at her eyes. "It's over."

"What?"

Rob looked around, searching amid the maze of clutter. He began to wander around the room, full of nervous energy. Where was the rock?

"You heard me," he said. "Dirk found out about us sleeping together. He's threatening blackmail. Lucy has to be the one who told."

"That little whore," said Halo. "I'm sorry, Sugar."

"I know," said Rob, continuing his seemingly random pacing. "I know. But, this is it. It ends. I let this whole thing go on too long. Today is the last time we see each other."

He placed his hand atop her dresser, as if to steady himself. He took a deep breath. The words sounded good, now that they were out. He had what he'd really come for.

Halo wasn't saying anything. He said, "I thought you deserved to hear it in person."

He turned toward her, to look at her sad eyes from across the room.

Only her eyes weren't sad. They were angry little daggers.

"You know what your problem is, Honey?" she said. "You don't believe a damn thing you say. You go on TV and shout about 'love, love, love.' You've never felt love in your life. It's always shame with you. It's always fear. Dirk only has power over you because you give it to him. You can shout about love all you want. But you'll only preach what you practice."

The venom in her words stunned Rob. Halo had never raised her voice to him before. *Good*, thought the little doll man. This made it easier.

He stomped back through the junk shop labyrinth, his practiced good-bye speech forgotten.

"You don't have a clue, do you?" he asked. "I know you've probably had a rough life. Something bad happened to you that's made you craft this little fantasy you live in. That works for you, fine. But I've had a man die because of something I said. Life has consequences. I've done a bad thing. I can never undo it. All that keeps me sane is knowing a loving God watches over me, that he forgives me for being me."

"Oh, Sugar," said Halo, taking a deep breath. "Sugar, God's not gonna forgive you. Trust me on this. God assumed you were guilty before you were born. You're wasting time expecting his mercy."

Rob didn't know what to say to this. He'd known, obviously, that Halo wasn't a Christian. Despite all of the Biblical mythology she wrapped herself in, he'd always assumed she was deeply non-religious to make such a joke out of the things he held dear and deep. It never seemed important to him. It seemed clear why, studying her perfect pretty face.

"I never loved you," he said.

"Tell yourself whatever it takes to get down from that wall," she said.

ALL THE WAY BACK to Richmond, the little doll man kept telling Rob how good he should feel. His shameful secret life was finally over.

"You've done the right thing," said the little doll man. "Now we give Dirk the rock and move on. Simple."

Maybe it would be that simple. In a way, he was grateful to Dirk for bringing the whole thing into crisis. He could start a new life, the life he'd pretended to start all those years ago.

"No more hypocrisy," said the little doll man. "No more lies."

Instead of going home, he drove straight to the studio. He paged Dirk. No point in dragging things out, the little doll man reasoned.

While he waited for Dirk to call, he paced around the room. The walls were decorated with photographs of him and his followers, smiling faces whose lives he had touched. Some people got his message, didn't they?

He came to the stainless steel crucifix, gazing up at the tortured face of Jesus. No forgiveness, Halo had said. But look what God had given the world. His only son, brutally tormented and slain, to pay for our sins. That was a kind of forgiveness, wasn't it?

Rob noticed himself in the mirror-smooth metal just beneath Christ's feet. He looked old and tired. He imagined his little doll man must be gray-haired by now, withered and weary from the effort of trying to do the right thing. Then, he noticed a flicker of white in the corner of the reflection. He turned, and found Dirk and Mikimbe waiting.

"I thought you'd call," said Rob.

"We were on our way here before you dialed," said Dirk. "Those occult hobbies of mine have their uses."

"Whatever," said Rob. From his jacket he produced a small, dark pebble. "So, what can your occult hobbies do with this rock? You planning to rule the world?"

"This world is already mine," said Dirk. "The stone will help me move into other realms."

"Whatever gets you off the planet," said Rob, tossing the rock to Dirk.

Spasms wracked the corners of Dirk's mouth. His smile muscles had atrophied.

"At last," he said, rolling the stone in his palm. He looked to Rob. "There's one last item of business between us."

"Oh?"

"Mikimbe," said Dirk.

Mikimbe reached into his jacket. Rob tensed, but instead of the gun being drawn, a small manila envelope appeared. Mikimbe placed the envelope on the desk.

"You cooperated nicely, betraying your boyfriend when I hadn't even shown you the photos."

"She's not my boyfriend," said Rob. "What's in the envelope?"

"Look."

Rob cautiously emptied the envelope's contents onto his desk. It was a photo of him standing in front of a window in an old brick building, and Halo was kissing his cheek.

"This was taken today," said Rob.

Dirk nodded. "As I said, you responded so well to blackmail when I had nothing but imaginary photographs, I'm anxious to try again with the real thing."

"We had a deal," said Rob, feeling the veins in his forehead pulsing.

"We're making a new one," said Dirk. "This photograph was taken after the old deal."

"You—" Rob swallowed hard. What had he expected?

"You look distressed," said Dirk. "Perhaps a little tequila would calm your nerves."

"What do you want this time?" Rob asked.

"I want full ownership of the first two Horsemen albums. I want your rights signed over to me."

"Why? You're filthy rich. Why take it all?"

"To help your reputation. Isn't it terrible you still make money off of what you consider to be your greatest sin?"

Rob ran his hand through his hair, contemplating Dirk's demand.

"That money funds my ministry," said Rob. "I use it to fund the homeless shelter on King Avenue. Also the prison outreach program.

That money makes amends for my mistakes, as long as I control it. You'd spend it on drugs and prostitutes."

"Then keep the money," said Dirk with a shrug. "Use it to hire more PR people once this picture hits the tabloids."

"It's just …" Rob swallowed. "It's just a peck on the cheek. You can't expect me to—"

"There's also a tape, made with a directional mike from across the street. You plainly say, 'Dirk found out about us sleeping together.' Your voiceprint can't be explained away as Photoshop trickery."

Rob sagged. He'd played right into Dirk's hands. But Dirk was asking too much.

"No," Rob said. "I'll take my chances."

Dirk clucked his tongue and shook his head. "Rob, Rob, Rob. You continue to delight me. You gladly betray your lover, but you refuse to turn loose of the money. Perhaps you do have what it takes to be a successful televangelist."

"Fuck it," said the little doll man, letting go of the wheel.

Rob growled like an angry Doberman.

Mikimbe went for his gun.

Rob reached behind his head, ripping the steel crucifix from the wall, then hurled it across the room. The thorny face of Jesus kissed Mikimbe's lips as the linebacker pulled the trigger. The bullet whizzed by Rob's ear and kicked a hole in the plaster.

Rob leapt onto his desk as Mikimbe crumbled to the floor. As Rob went airborne, Dirk turned two shades paler. Rob slammed into his reedy nemesis, knocking him to the carpet. Rob straddled him and wrapped his hands around Dirk's throat. Dirk scratched desperately at Rob's wrists, to no avail.

Rob noticed the small object that had fallen to the carpet. He laughed as he snatched it up, and pressed it into Dirk's lips.

"You want the stone? You want the stone? I hope you choke on it!"

Dirk struggled, jerking his head, his teeth clenched. Rob pinched Dirk's lips and stretched them with all his might, until Dirk's teeth popped open and the pale man gasped with pain. Rob pushed in the stone and jammed his palm under Dirk's chin.

"Choke on it!" Rob yelled.

Dirk didn't choke. Still, the look on his face as the stone went down was worth the price of admission.

Mikimbe groaned. The .44 sat next to the linebacker's enormous hand. His eyes fluttered open. Rob abandoned Dirk and scrabbled toward Mikimbe. His hand fell on the steel cross. He rose to his feet, clutching it overhead like an axe as Mikimbe closed his fingers around the gun.

"Drop it," said Rob. "Or I pop your skull like an eggshell."

Mikimbe dropped the gun, and began to curse. "Cowardly backstabbing freak!"

"You don't have to like me," said Rob. "You just have to crawl out of here and take your boss with you."

"I'm not cussing you," said Mikimbe. "That bastard left without me."

Rob looked behind him. Sure enough, Dirk was gone.

"Man," said Rob. "He's really good at this Batman thing."

"Ow," said Mikimbe, touching his bleeding nose. "I got no body to guard at the moment, so I'm off the clock. You got any aspirin? A wet washcloth, maybe?"

"Sure," said Rob, resting the cross on his shoulder and heading for the door. "Check the bathroom down the hall."

"Where you going?" said Mikimbe. "You ain't gonna find Dirk. He's halfway around the world by now."

"Couldn't care less," said Rob. "I'm just stepping out to get some milk."

HALO OPENED HER DOOR and smiled bright as the morning sun. Rob entered her apartment, and dropped the crucifix onto her couch.

"Brought you a prop," he said.

"I can use it, Sugar," said Halo. "Business really picked up after CNN played that tape."

"Sorry about that," said Rob.

"Don't be, Baby," said Halo. "I haven't had this much in the bank since I was mistress to Louis the Fourteenth. So where you been the last month?"

"Was it only a month?" asked Rob.

"Forty days," she said.

"I decided to walk to the store."

"That explains the weight loss. You walked all the way from Richmond, didn't you?"

Rob looked down at his ragged clothes. His pants were cinched up with a piece of clothesline.

"I gave my belt to some guy at a shelter in Durham," said Rob. "He liked the buckle."

"Who'd you give your jacket to?"

"Some kid. I dunno."

"I hear you signed over your Horsemen copyrights to a waitress at a diner in Spartanburg," said Halo.

"Yeah," said Rob. "I hope she didn't get too much of a hassle when she showed the attorneys the contract on that napkin. She needs the money to get her son a spinal operation."

"Good thing I never loved you for your money," said Halo.

"I'm down off that wall," said Rob. "I've got something to tell you."

Before he could speak, they were interrupted by a voice from the doorway.

"Look at the lovebirds," said Dirk, stepping into the room. Three seedy-looking thugs with guns drawn followed him.

"Rob," said Dirk. "You'll beg for a bullet when I'm done with you. But these are for the hellion."

Halo moved in front of Rob as the thugs aimed their guns at her and fired. Her hands moved so quickly they cracked like whips when they halted.

Halo looked back at Rob and smiled. She was holding a silver bullet in her teeth. She turned her gaze upon the gunmen, who suddenly dropped their weapons as the barrels began to writhe like serpents. She spat out the bullet, then studied the small silver cylinders in her open palms.

"Oh, look, you've carved little crosses into them," she said to Dirk with a giggle. "How cute. Child, you done got me confused with werewolves and vampires."

Then, once more with unwatchable speed, she spun around and jammed the bullets into Rob's ears. He gasped. They were burning hot. Halo said something, but he couldn't make out what. He clawed the bullets out and heard the wails of the three gunmen, who tripped over themselves to get out the door, blood gushing from their ears.

"A predictable counter move," said Dirk, still looking confident. "Are you surprised to see me still standing?"

Halo shrugged. "The bullet flub didn't make you look like a master sorcerer, Sweetie. So you know a little magic. I'm not impressed."

"Then be impressed by this," said Dirk, holding up a small dark stone that Rob recognized. "With the divine anger that echoes within this object of power, you are mine to command! Now turn, and kill Rob!"

"Whatever," said Halo. "What's so special about that rock?"

"Don't play the fool," said Dirk. "This is the stone that killed Goliath."

Halo reached to the bookshelf and picked up something small and polished. Light played across its ancient surface.

"No, Baby, this is the stone that killed Goliath."

Dirk stared at the stone she held, then gazed at the rock in his fingers. "Then this…?"

Rob grinned. "That's a pebble I found in the parking lot."

"Son of a bitch," said Dirk.

"Now here's how that mind control thing works," said Halo. "You're gonna go throw yourself in the river for me, ain't you, Dirk-baby?"

"Sure thing," said Dirk, smiling as best he could manage. He turned and left without further comment.

Halo faced Rob, who hadn't blinked for about two minutes.

Rob rubbed his temples. "So much for my theory about you."

"I'm the genuine article, Baby. I never tried to hide it."

Rob placed his arms around her slender waist and pulled her close.

"I'm not going to hide who I am, either," said Rob. "This doesn't change how I feel. I've been thinking about Jesus, all busted up on the cross. Forgiveness can't be an easy thing for a God who'd do that to his own kin. Maybe God doesn't love me, or much of anyone, really."

"Ah, Sugar, he's just cranky."

"Maybe. But it also may be that the only love in this world I can count on is what I feel for you and what you feel for me. I've treated you wrong, Halo."

"It's okay, Honey. You're only human."

"I love you," said Rob. "I want the world to know. Halo, will you marry me?"

Halo blushed. "Aw, Baby. The laws of Georgia frown all over that kinda thing."

She pulled him tighter and tilted her head, as he lowered his lips to meet hers. He closed his eyes, basking in her fragrance, her salty skin upon his lips. In the lingering stillness that followed, he heard her gentle moan, and the soft, leathery rasp of wings unfurling.

And the woman was arrayed in purple and scarlet color,
decked with gold and precious stones and pearls,
having a golden cup in her hand full of abominations
and filthiness of her fornication.
Upon her forehead was a name written a mystery:
Babylon the Great,
the mother of harlots and abominations of the Earth.
~ Revelation 17:4-5 ~

IT'S RAINING BLOOD.

I'm on my belly atop the Statue of Liberty, jammed against one of the wedges of brass that radiate from the crown, hoping the wind doesn't blow me from my perch before I take my shot.

The Lamb is marching straight toward me, balanced on the heaving Atlantic like it's solid and calm. The Lamb would look at home in a medieval painting of Hell. He's part-sheep, part-human, a cloven-hoofed devil covered in thick wool. Of course, if this were a devil, you'd expect him to be red, or maybe black, not pure white, glowing bright as dawn through the blood rain. Seven ram horns curl atop his head like a crown, with lightning crackling between the tips. The Lamb's been gutted; I'm told he was sacrificed earlier in the day, but that doesn't seem to have slowed him. His purple entrails snake from his chest cavity like tentacles in a hentai movie.

Did I mention he's big? It's hard to pin down his size while he's out on the water, but I can already tell he's a hell of a lot taller than Lady Liberty.

Despite the howl of the wind, I hear Baby and that crazy preacher going at each other in the room below. I think, between the two of us, she's got the tougher job.

All I have to do is shoot a judgmental god in the face. My odds of hitting the Lamb between the eyes are improved by the fact the thing has seven of them. Halo didn't mention they'd be full of fire.

The thing's almost in range. I wipe blood from my eyes, taking slow, steady breaths as I rest my finger on the trigger of the crossbow.

What a fucked up day.

THE DAY STARTED BAD the second I crossed onto Long Island and got caught in snarled traffic. I made it to the rehab center three hours late, with the fuel gauge on my Olds Cutlass hovering on E.

People who know I'm related to Baby are surprised I drive such a wreck. My sister's worth millions. It seems like a little of that money might have flowed my way. Alas, Baby and I aren't close. It's been three years since we last saw each other. She was supposed to come to Christmas at our stepmother's place last year. She even texted me the day before confirming the plan but never showed up. It wasn't until New Years that she texted again, saying she'd come down with the flu. I knew it wasn't true. I follow her adventures in the tabloids like everyone else. Baby spent Christmas in custody for underage drinking and public nudity, her fifth arrest.

She wiggled out of jail by checking in to a rehab center in the Hamptons. I knew I'd found the right place from the crowd of paparazzi in front of the gates. They were snapping shots of a bearded man waving a placard. The front read, "For all the nations have drunk the maddening wine of her adulteries," which struck me as curiously poetic. Then he turned, and the other side said, "GOD HATES WHORES!"

Poor Baby. I can't imagine a nut like Jude Barnes stalking me 24/7.

The guard at the gate was skeptical of my identity at first, but I had the letter from Baby asking me to pick her up. Why she'd reached out to me was a mystery. Maybe rehab really had changed her.

The Coast Wellness Center looked more like a country club than a hospital. The valet looked mortified when I pulled up, but was saved from getting behind the wheel when Baby burst through the front door and bolted toward the station wagon.

She was dressed in jeans and a neon purple long-sleeved T-shirt, skin tight, but still conservative for her. Her hair was dark brown. I thought she'd let it go back to her natural color, but when she reached the car I realized it was a wig. Large sunglasses hid her eyes.

Her expression was unreadable as she leaned into my open window and said, "You're late, bro."

"Traffic was a bitch."

"You brought the bag I had shipped to you?"

"In the back seat," I said, getting out of the car and spreading my arms. "How 'bout a hug? It's been a long time."

She nudged against me, lightly touched my back with her palms, then stepped back away before my arms closed around her. "Let's go. I'll scream if I'm here another minute."

"It can't be that bad. This place looks pretty swank."

"It's still a prison. You can't even pee without people watching you." She slid into back seat of the station wagon. "I can't believe you're still driving this heap."

"I can't afford a new car."

"I could have helped out if you'd asked."

I started to say that, if she'd bothered to keep in touch, she might have known I was still driving our grandfather's old car. I held my tongue.

She zipped open her duffel bag. "At least there's room to change in this boat."

I got behind the wheel. "What's wrong with what you have on?"

"Are you kidding?" she asked. "Now that I'm not kissing up to my jailers, I can stop dressing like a nun. I've a reputation to maintain."

I couldn't think of a delicate way to tell her that her reputation wasn't exactly a positive one.

Perhaps to head off what I was about to say, she said, "Just drive."

So I drove. Out of the gate, right into the paparazzi. I was half-blinded by the flashing cameras.

"Awesome," she said. "I was worried the world had forgotten me."

I glanced into the rear view mirror and practically choked. Baby was stripped down to her bra and panties, taking a swig from a huge bottle of Kahlua.

"Where the hell did you get that?"

"From the bag, duh."

"I searched that bag!"

"And didn't find the false bottom, obviously."

"You'll get us both arrested!"

"Don't get your panties in a wad. Nobody gives a—"

Before she could finish her sentence, the rear driver's side window shattered. Baby shrieked as a brick landed in her lap. The Bible-thumper, Jude Barnes, thrust his head through the window and shouted, "Babylon! Mother of whores! Only the blood of the lamb can cleanse the filth of your fornication!"

He thrust a yellow Solo cup through the window. Baby's torso was suddenly coated in foul-smelling, brown-red goop.

"Son of a bitch!" she shouted.

I leapt from the car, not bothering to put it in park, and grabbed the lunatic by the collar. He punched me in the chest. I drove my fist into his nose and felt something pop, then pushed him away. I spun around to find the photographers scrambling out of the way of the driverless car, still rolling. I jumped into the driver's seat just as the rear passenger door opened and Baby jumped out, running down the sidewalk in nothing but her underwear, holding the Kahlua tucked against her like a football. The paparazzi gave chase. I blew the horn, threw the car into neutral, and stomped the accelerator. The growl of the engine caused the vultures to look back toward me. I threw the car into drive as they scattered.

As the car lurched forward, one of them jumped on the hood and pressed his business card up against the window.

"Andrew Carrick, Weekly World Magazine!" he shouted. "We'll pay top dollar for info on Baby. Top dollar!"

"Get off my car!" I shouted, cutting the wheel hard to the right, lurching us up over the curb onto the sidewalk. The sudden jolt knocked him free and he slid from my hood and disappeared from view on the passenger side. There was a sickening jolt a second later. I felt suddenly sick, worried I'd run him over.

Then, I had to jerk the wheel the other direction and get back onto the road since I was now about to run my sister over.

"Get in!" I shouted, as I pulled up next to her.

She dove inside.

"Fucking maniac!" she screamed, grabbing the purple shirt she'd discarded and wiping the blood off her breasts. I fixed my eyes on the road as she tore off her bloody bra. "Drive! Drive! Drive!"

I gunned the engine, tires squealing as we went around the corner at breakneck speed. A motorcycle with two riders pulled up beside us. One guy was driving, while the other a camera in hand, snapping photos of my topless sister.

"Fuck this," I growled, jerking the wheel to the left, cutting them off. The bike veered to avoid me and disappeared into a ditch on the other side of the road.

Baby threw her bloodied shirt out the window, then stretched out on the seat, face down, her body trembling. I thought she was crying, until I realized she was laughing.

"Why on earth is this funny?" I demanded, jerking the wheel to take another corner.

"Oh hell," she gasped. "Why isn't it?"

In the rearview, another motorcycle was now on our tail. I did a double take as I realized it was that Carrick dude, his face all bloodied. I was relieved I hadn't killed him, and slightly disappointed I hadn't disabled him. I pushed the station wagon to its top speed, a bone-rattling sixty miles an hour. Carrick was able to easily pull alongside and shout, "Top dollar!"

He suddenly slowed, skidding to a stop and craning his neck toward the sky.

I looked up. My jaw dropped. I pulled the car to the curb.

Baby stuck her head out the window, then took a long swig from the bottle.

"Shit," she said. "It's the Apocalypse."

I got out of the car. The whole sky was red and glistening, like someone had applied fresh red paint to a previously unseen ceiling above us.

"It's Judgment Day!" came a shout from behind.

I turned and saw Jude, the preacher, running toward us.

The maniac made a bee-line for Baby, screaming, "With violence shall Babylon be thrown down!"

I leapt into his path, putting everything I had into a roundhouse punch. I knocked him flat, cutting my knuckles on his teeth.

Jude writhed on his back, but sounded ecstatic as he babbled, "Fallen, fallen, is Babylon the Great!"

I stared at the sky, listening to sirens from every direction. Were they coming for Baby, or was something bigger going on? Another terrorist attack? Nuclear war? What causes a sky to look like blood? I glanced back at that reporter and was relieved to see he thought the sky was more interesting than my sister, at least for the moment.

"You're hurt," Baby said, looking at my hand from the busted open window of the backseat.

"Why the hell don't you hire a bodyguard?"

"A bodyguard would have found the booze in my bag before he brought it to me," she said. "The agencies are legally liable if they sit back and watch me drink or shoplift or whatever."

"What the hell happened to you?" I shook my head, no longer able to suppress my feelings. "I try not to believe half the stuff I read, but…"

"Are you ashamed of me? You used to be proud."

Which is true. We had a rough childhood. Our mother was killed in a wreck when we were young. Dad remarried, but when he passed away, we bounced back and forth between our step-mother and our grandfather. Back then, I was the wild child with a chip on my shoulder, always in trouble. Baby was the good girl, the straight-A student and musical prodigy, a bookish nerd whose quiet accomplishments were overshadowed by my dumb antics.

When I was 18 I joined the navy, just as Baby got her first taste of fame. Only 14, she'd recorded a video of her singing "Like a Virgin," doing her own choreography and editing six different music tracks on her PowerBook. The video got a couple of thousand hits on YouTube, until Warner Brothers threatened to sue her for copyright infringement. The story of the giant corporation unleashing its lawyers on a teenage girl made the Drudge Report. Within a week, twenty million people had watched Baby's performance.

Then Baby released her own song, "Not a Virgin Anymore." The lyrics were full of double entendrés about a young girl having her innocence stripped away. She'd performed the video with big puppet hands ripping off her clothes, leaving her naked by the end of the song, though with carefully placed props hiding enough of her to keep the clip from getting yanked from YouTube. A lot of pundits denounced the video, decrying the exploitation of a minor. Only, it was hard to say exactly who was exploiting her, since everything in the video was her creation.

While I was stocking vending machines aboard an aircraft carrier, she hired a lawyer and had herself emancipated, a legal adult at the age of 15. She had her own apartment in LA and a million-dollar record deal. Overnight, the quiet nerd became an out-of-control party girl. The more she misbehaved, the more songs she sold. I'd always hoped that her wild girl persona was an act. I figured Baby was cashing in on her fifteen minutes of fame. But… what if it wasn't an act?

"That's a long pause," she said. "Are you pissed at me?"

I crossed my arms. "It hurts that you only reached out because I'm more gullible than a professional bodyguard."

"That's one way of looking at it."

"Is there another way?"

"Probably not," she admitted. She got out of the car. She was now wearing a red halter-top and a short skirt she'd retrieved from her bag. Her wig was gone, revealing her bleached blonde curls. "I'd say I was sorry, but you wouldn't think I was sincere."

"Would you be sincere?"

"Dan, there's stuff you don't know about me. Stuff you can't know. There's a reason I act like I do. A greater purpose. If I could explain, I would, but…" her voice trailed off. "Let me see your hand."

I looked down at my bleeding knuckles. "Note to self: Don't aim at teeth."

"We should take care of that. Mouths are rife with bacteria."

I looked at the sky. "If there's been a terrorist attack, the emergency rooms are going to be too busy to look at my hand."

"I can disinfect it," she said, placing her bag on the hood and fishing out a steel flask. "Vodka should do the trick."

"You got a whole bar in there?"

"I wish," she said, taking out a small plastic box. "A Bloody Mary would be exactly the right drink for the apocalypse, but I didn't pack any tomato juice. Fortunately, I do have a first aid kit." She produced a roll of gauze. "I keep this stuff handy. I fall down a lot."

I offered her my hand. She dabbed my wounds with gauze doused in vodka. It stung like hell.

As she bandaged me, Jude tried to stand, but fell onto his hands and knees, his legs still rubbery.

"Stay down," I growled.

"It's the whore who will fall!" Jude cried, lisping through loose teeth. "Repent! The hour of judgment is at hand!"

"If he were stalking me, I'd drink too," I said.

"Don't give him credit for my being a lush," she said. "I started drinking before I even made that first video. I was just good at hiding it."

"What's his problem with you?"

She shook her head. "He blames me for his daughter's death."

"Murderer!" shouted Jude.

"Apparently, she got knocked up when she was thirteen, and there's not a lot of places to get a legal abortion in Texas. She'd heard the old wives tale that, if you throw yourself down stairs, you lose the baby. She broke her neck."

"Why's that your fault?"

"The girl was kind of a fan. When they found her body, *Mystery* was playing on her headphones."

Mystery was Baby's debut album.

As she finished my hand, she asked, "Want to know why I named the album *Mystery*?"

"Not that I don't want to talk about anything you'd like, but right now our priority should be to find someplace safe."

"Safe?" She shook her head. "It's Judgment Day. There's no safe."

"It can't be that bad," I said. "There has to be some rational explanation."

"Even for that?" She pointed over my shoulder.

I turned to find an army of knights on horseback galloping across the sky. Maybe horseback isn't the right word, since the steeds had the heads of lions and tails like scorpions. They raced among the clouds in eerie silence, their flaming hooves finding purchase on thin air. Black armor encased the knights, who carried long lances that crackled with internal lightning.

"Take me!" Jude shouted, rising to his feet, lifting his arms. "Take me!"

One of the riders heard Jude and peeled away from his fellow riders. He landed with a thunderous boom at the far end of the street, throwing up a pillar of smoke as he gouged a crater in the asphalt. The shock wave knocked me from my feet. I tried to get up, but the ground kept shaking as the monstrous steed thundered toward the preacher.

From nowhere, the reporter, Carrick, leapt into the path of the monster, camera in hand, snapping shots like crazy. He looked prepared to jump aside at the last second but the beast was faster than it looked. I blinked, and suddenly Carrick was impaled on the knight's lance. The lion beast paused for a second to shake the corpse free. The knight turned its gaze toward Jude.

The preacher's shouts trailed off as the knight lowered his lance, aiming it straight toward Jude's heart. His face went pale as the monster steed galloped forward once more. Jude might have been crazy, but even he could see the thing wasn't coming to save him, but to kill him.

"Run, you moron!" Baby shouted.

That sounded like excellent advice, so I pulled myself back into the car. I turned around to make sure Baby was in the back seat. She wasn't. She was running toward Jude.

"Snap out of it!" she screamed, grabbing the preacher by his arm. From where I sat, it looked like they'd both be trampled. The lion-thing was the size of a rhino.

Cursing my own stupidity, I threw the Cutlass into drive and stomped the accelerator, aiming for a collision course with the onrushing beast. Instead, the thing leapt onto the hood of my station wagon, killing my car. I slammed into the steering wheel.

The beast flew over the roof. Behind me, I heard Baby scream.

Then, I heard her cheer.

I twisted to see what was going on, wincing. The steering wheel hadn't done my ribs any favors. The rhino-sized steed was on its side, its severed head a good ten feet distant from its body. The black rider, at least ten feet tall, had drawn a sword and was hacking at what could only be described as a demon with a pitchfork.

I pushed open the car door and managed to drag myself out. The demon looked female, with long black hair and porn-star breasts, though her feminine traits were matched by an equally impressive length of male genitalia. She was no taller than Baby, but leathery bat wings at least thirty feet long jutted from between her shoulder blades. A black, scaly tail, thick as an anaconda, snaked from her lower back. With a laugh, she used her tail to jerk the knight from his feet, then buried her pitchfork in his torso. The thing disintegrated into a swarm of black flies.

Baby ran up to the demon, lifting her hand to give a high-five. "Way to kick ass!"

"199,999,999 to go," the demon said.

"Why?" Jude said with a sob, dropping to his knees. "Why wasn't I taken?"

"Idiot," the demon said. "You weren't good enough."

I limped forward, not fully convinced of my sanity. "What's going on?"

"Really?" the demon asked. "You don't know?"

"Vile succubus," Jude said, tears streaming down his cheeks. "You're a demon, come to drag our filthy souls to Hell."

"Demon? I'm not one of those saps."

"You're not a demon?" I asked.

She rolled her eyes. "I'm an independent angel. My real name is seventeen syllables long and would rupture your eardrums, but my friends call me Halo. You must be Dan."

I wasn't sure what was more disturbing, that I was face to face with a supernatural being, or that she knew my name. I couldn't do anything but stare at her.

"An angel?" asked Jude, who evidently had more of his wits at the moment than I did. "Then… I am going to heaven?"

"Yeah, no. I'm not that kind of angel."

"You're a fallen angel?" asked Jude.

"There was no falling involved. I walked out."

"Don't be so insulting, asshole," Baby said to Jude. "She just saved your hide. That thing—" she pointed at the swarming flies— "was an angel. One of two-hundred million spreading across the globe, charged with killing a third of mankind."

"What?" I asked.

"The seven seals have been broken," said Halo. "The Lamb has returned to Judah and now walks across the ocean for his final battle with Babylon."

"What?" I asked again.

Halo looked puzzled. "How can you not know what's been going on? God's like the Riddler. He spells out his crimes in advance. The world's had 2000 years to get ready. What the hell do they teach in school these days?"

"They pollute innocent minds with lies of evolution!" said Jude, clenching his fists.

"That's still at thing?" asked Halo.

I looked back at the bloody sky.

"So… that Bible stuff… it's real? Shouldn't we… I dunno, find someplace safe to—"

"The great day of his wrath is come; who shall be able to stand?" Jude said.

"What he said," said Halo. "We need to get someplace a whole lot more dangerous if we want to have a chance. Let's hope your sister's ready."

"I'm getting there," said Baby, tilting back the vodka. She belched and wiped her lips. "Can we loot a liquor store or something?"

"Ready for what?" I asked. "Why are you being so cryptic?"

"Reality is cryptic," said Halo.

"This isn't the first time Halo and I have met," said Baby. "She's been giving me career advice for a while now."

I'M NO BIBLE SCHOLAR, and Halo and Baby took all of two minutes to explain the entire Book of Revelation to me, so if some of this gets muddled, I'm sorry. The takeaway is that Judgment Day begins when a lamb with seven horns and seven eyes is sacrificed and found worthy of judging the world. The sacrificed Lamb then opens a book that's held shut by seven seals. With each seal that opens, he unleashes various horrors upon the earth. The Four Horsemen of the Apocalypse aren't just something heavy metal bands put on album covers. Instead, they're set loose to punish a wicked world, along with an army of two hundred million angels charged with killing a third of mankind.

"That's what's happening now," said Baby.

"You're telling me two billion people are being slaughtered while we're standing here?" I asked, incredulous.

"That's more or less accurate," said Halo.

"Why is there wiggle room?"

"You noticed the sky's changed to blood?"

"Kinda caught my attention, yeah."

"We're not in the material world any more. The Lamb has shifted the globe into the spiritual realm. Here, the physical laws are subservient to symbolism and faith. It's a world of waking dreams. People believe they're being killed, so they're dead, at least until they wake."

"This is just a dream?" I asked. "Then what's the problem?"

"As long as we're here, there's no waking. The Lamb will keep us here for all eternity if we let him."

"Let him? We have a say in the matter?"

"With this, yes," said Halo, holding out a small wooden chest, barely big enough to hold an egg. "Open it."

I took the box. It wasn't very heavy. The wood was fine grained, etched with stars and swirls, which were coated with dust. The clasp was simple, made of brass. I flipped it open and looked inside.

"A golf ball?" I asked, rolling the contents into my hand. It was a smooth black stone, maybe marble. It was warm to the touch. There was a single thin braid of white hair wound around it.

"That's the stone that killed Goliath," said Halo.

"Whoa," said Baby, leaning in for a closer look. "You've got the best toys."

"You know how the Old Testament God was a bully?" asked Halo. "A sadist who slaughtered the firstborn children of Egypt? Who blasted Sodom and Gomorrah to gravel because he disapproved of how the residents used of their genitals? The maniac who drowned the whole fucking world in a fit of spite?"

"A God of righteous vengeance," Jude murmured.

"Then, you notice that around the time David became king, God mellowed out? No more smite-fests?"

"I'll take your word for it."

"The mellowing out wasn't voluntary," said Halo. "When David fought Goliath, God placed the spirit of his wrath into this tiny stone. The pebble punched a nice, clean hole through Goliath, but some buddies and I were waiting on the other side. We grabbed the stone before it hit the ground and encircled the rock with a braid woven from the hair of a fetus, trapping this aspect of God inside."

"And that works why?"

"Because God can't hurt you if you're sinless, and original sin doesn't pass into a person until they're born. The hair holds him as securely as a chain. But, even if the wrath can't escape, this is still one bad-ass pebble. It might be the only thing in the world that can kill the Lamb."

"If God's wrath is trapped inside, why is the Lamb dangerous?"

"The Lamb is the manifestation of God's judgment, not his anger. It's a fine distinction, but the end result is still destruction."

"So… we're going to put the stone into a slingshot and throw it at the Lamb?"

"I'm thinking crossbow," said Halo. "I've got a modified bolt with a little cage to hold the stone."

"Wouldn't a rifle be better?"

"We debated using a musket, but worry that might destroy the hair. Fortunately, Baby assures me you're good with a crossbow."

"I am?"

"You're not?" asked Baby. "Didn't Pop-Pop used to take you hunting with one?"

I shook my head. "He used to hunt with one during bow season, but the only thing I ever shot was a straw target out behind the barn."

"How was your aim?" asked Halo.

"I mean, not terrible, but… look, why can't you take the shot?"

"Even with the hair around it, we free angels are sensitive to the power radiating from the stone. It's only safe for me to touch the gopherwood case. If I tried to use it as a weapon, I'd be dead before I had time to pull the trigger."

"So… you want me to kill…"

"The Lamb of God," said Baby.

"Is that… is that even… remotely ethical?"

"It's always ethical to protect yourself from a bully," said Halo.

"But… isn't this bully… God?"

"An aspect of God, yes."

"Don't let that intimidate you," said Baby.

"I'm intimidated as hell."

"If you don't help, he's going to kill me," said Baby. "And I don't mean as one of the faceless billions the angels are going to slaughter. I mean he's going to rip me limb from limb and personally toss me into the fiery pits of Hell."

"Why?"

"Because I'm the current manifestation of Babylon."

Seeing the confusion in my face, Halo jumped in. "The Lamb's judgment ends in a final battle with a woman known as Babylon the Great. She's the last embodiment of the goddess Ashera, once worshiped throughout the Middle East. She was a goddess of female sexuality, of life and fertility, the embodiment of sexual freedom. Then a band of zealots with a commitment to patriarchy and strong opinions about who should sleep with whom came out of the desert carrying an ark filled with an angry God and wiped out all the tribes that worshipped Ashera."

"But," said Baby, "as long as men worship female sexuality, the worship of Ashera continues, even if almost no one knows her name."

"A lot of men lust after your sister," said Halo. "Basically, anytime a man downloads nude pictures of Baby, he's worshipping her, imbuing her with spiritual energy, making a rival god of her."

"And God is jealous," said Baby.

"That's why the Lamb's heading for New York," said Halo.

"To find Baby?"

"Because New York harbor is where the most famous idol of Ashera is located."

"It can't be that famous. I've never heard of it," I said.

"To the Romans, Ashera was worshipped as Libertas," said Halo.

I was still confused, so Baby spelled things out: "The Statue of Liberty. He's coming to tear down the Statue of Liberty. And when he gets there, I'm going to be inside." She tilted back the flask, frowning to find it empty. "And, I'd like to be a lot drunker."

WHICH BRINGS ME back to my perch atop the Statue of Liberty. Did I mention it's raining blood? And that I'm having to listen to my sister engaging in loud sex in the room below, losing her virginity to a creep like Jude Barnes? News that Baby was a still a virgin took me by surprise. Apparently, by maintaining her virginity, she's been able to protect all the accumulated sexual energy of the mobs who pay tribute to her. It seems that Halo explained all this stuff to her when Baby was still fourteen, when Halo discovered my sister the same way the rest of the world did, via YouTube. Record producers saw a future superstar. Halo saw a goddess waiting to blossom. As to why Jude is her partner, I'm a little fuzzy. Maybe the preacher was the nearest warm male body she wasn't related to. As to why Jude agreed, I suspect he's been lusting after Baby all along. Once he learned he hadn't been raptured, he didn't have any reason not to give in to his baser instincts.

The Lamb strides closer and keeps getting bigger. I thought I'd be shooting more or less on the level of his eyes, but I'll be shooting almost straight up. I'm holding out to the last second. I've only got one shot.

He's close enough I can smell those prehensile entrails he's waving. I pull the trigger.

The bolt is instantly caught by the wind. It's not only going to miss the eyes, it's not going to hit at all. Suddenly, Halo's dark wings unfold from below and she launches herself at the falling bolt. The second her fingers wrap around the shaft she screams. Flames wreath her as she falls from the sky, the bolt clasped against her breasts. The Lamb kicks out with one of his cloven hooves, catching Lady Liberty dead center of her chest. There's a rending sound as the statue twists on its pedestal. I'm flying through the air, buffeted by the storm, dropping toward the raging waves.

Then Liberty drops the tablet she carries and stretches her arm toward me. Giant green fingers gingerly pluck me from the air as the statue lands feet first in water that, for her, is only knee deep. The statue's features shift from a stoic stare to a sly grin.

The torch in her other hand flickers, then flares into a blinding light. She rises from her crouch, thrusting the white blaze into the Lamb's dangling entrails. There's a horrible sizzling sound and the smell of burnt meat as she stands on tiptoe to twist the torch in the Lamb's guts. The big guy roars. He grabs her by the crown and lifts her as easily as I could lift a toddler. As she rises, the hand that holds me passes near the now vacant base of the statue and she drops me. I land without breaking my legs, but the whole base is slick with the oily blood. I lose my footing and slide toward the edge before my fingernails find purchase.

Above me, the Lamb holds Liberty over his head with both hands. He roars again and throws her toward the city. She spins head over heels for half a mile before crashing into a skyscraper. Every window in the building shatters as she slides down the face, landing with her limbs limp, the torch guttering in her lap. Her face twists. At first, I think it's a look of pain, but then she raises her fist and shouts, with a voice like a thousand megaphones, "That all you got?"

The Lamb stomps across the waves in pursuit. She aims her torch and blasts him with a beam of light. By the time he reaches her, his wooly coat has caught fire, but it doesn't slow him. He grabs her by the throat and slams her into a nearby building. When she keeps fighting, he slams her again, and the whole skyscraper twists and topples.

The Lamb tilts back his head and unleashes a bleat that sounds like sadistic laughter, as if he's pleased by the falling building. They're stomping through the financial district; maybe the Lamb hates Wall Street as much as the next guy. As evidence of that theory, he uses Liberty's flailing form like a club to batter another building into rubble.

I can't just stand here and watch this. I don't know where Halo fell, but I have to try to find her. There's a big shaft ahead of me, what's left of the staircase that used to go up into Liberty's body. I slip and slide across the bloody rubble, then make a jump for the nearest intact step, a good six feet down. I land less than gracefully, but pull myself up and start racing down the steps three at a time.

I find Halo near the bottom, midway to the first landing, crawling. Carrying the bolt hasn't been good for her health. The voluptuous succubus I met earlier is now little more than a skeleton. Her skin, once creamy and translucent, is now charred and crispy, falling off in big flakes, revealing a good chunk of her skull.

"You… missed…" she gasps, as she lifts the bolt.

I grab the missile. "Won't happen again. For one thing, I've lost the crossbow."

"Great," she says.

"It's not important," I say as I get my shoulder under her arm and help her limp out of the building so we can get a view of what's going on. "With this wind, I'd never make the shot. We need a helicopter or something, some way for me to get above this thing. I'll jump down and stab him."

"How… heroic," she pants.

"Just desperate. Baby's getting her ass kicked."

Halo nods. "Prophecy's hard… to shake. At least we know… she won't be fighting alone."

"For all the help we've been, she might as well be alone."

"No." Halo shakes her head. "There I saw a woman… sitting on a scarlet beast that was covered with blasphemous names… and had seven heads and ten horns."

"Um," I say.

"Revelation 17:3."

There's a howl from the other side of the statue's base. I turn the corner to see the Lamb staggering backward. He's on fire again. Jets of what look like lava splash against his torso. I strain to find Baby amid the destruction. Their battle has left half of Manhattan flattened. I wonder where Baby is.

Finally, I spot her. She's in the sky, riding a dragon with a wingspan so wide the tips disappear among the clouds of smoke. The scaly thing has seven long necks, like a hydra, with its dragon mouths spitting geysers of molten brimstone at the Lamb.

"Is that—"

"The great dragon," says Halo. "He has the most to lose if the Lamb wins. If he loses this battle, he'll be cast in to the pits of Hell for all eternity."

"I don't think he's going to lose," I say. As big as the Lamb is, the dragon is bigger. The creature lands amid the ruins of Manhattan, bracing himself on legs the size of sequoias as he sinks his teeth into the Lamb's charred flesh. Baby is blasting the Lamb with dazzling beams of light, blinding him. In his agony, the Lamb stumbles, howling. The dragon presses his attack, destroying buildings with each sweep of his massive tail.

The Lamb drops to one knee. He raises both fists, then pounds them against the earth. The ground cracks open, revealing a massive pit of smoke and flame that grows beneath the dragon's feet. The dragon flaps his wings to fly away, but the Lamb grabs the nearest neck and breaks it, then uses it as a line to reel the beast in, snapping its necks one by one.

Baby's still on the dragon's back, holding on for dear life. When this thing goes down, she's going with it.

"We have to save her," I shout. "Can you fly us—"

"I can barely stand," says Halo. "Though… there's a way to regain some strength."

"How?"

"Jude wasn't completely wrong when he called me a succubus."

"What does—"

"I'm a bit like a vampire," she explains. "Only instead of sucking your blood, I drink your soul."

I furrow my brow.

"I won't drink it all. There's no time to fully drain you anyway. But a kiss will restore some small portion of what I've lost."

"Take what you need," I say, closing my eyes.

Her dry, thin lips crackle as they press against mine. She smells like a steak that's been burnt to a crisp. Her nails dig into my back.

Without warning, her tongue snakes between my teeth, forcing itself down my throat. I gag, but she doesn't let go. I can't breathe. The world spins. It feels like she's licking my heart.

She lets go and I drop to my knees. The backs of my hands are wrinkled, aged. My arms look thinner than they did a moment ago.

I look up. She's not as voluptuous as she was when I first saw her, but she looks filled out, full of life. My life.

"Don't drop that bolt!" she says, grabbing me by the collar. "Definitely don't let it touch me!" Her long wings flap and we lift into the air.

Five of the dragon's heads hang limp.

We lurch across the sky, tossed about by the tempest. My heart rises in my throat as we plummet in a downdraft, but Halo laughs and folds her wings, diving even faster, until she spreads them wide and we zoom upward.

"I've been flying since the dawn of creation," she boasts, clutching me tighter as we rise above the struggling monsters. "Nothing can touch me in the—"

Her voice cuts short as her arms go limp. As I tumble, I see one of the mounted angels looming above us, his lance jutting from her left breast, wet with gore. I spin and see I'm falling right toward the Lamb. There's still a tuft of wool relatively intact amid his crown of horns. It's like landing on a mattress, jarring, but nothing is broken. Was it luck I fell here, or did Halo aim me?

It doesn't matter. I scramble on my belly until I'm between the closest eyes. I gaze out at the destruction, the city blocks flattened, the flames stretching for miles. Any doubt I had about whether fighting this thing was right or wrong vanishes. I rise to my knees, lifting the bolt overhead with both hands, then plunge it with all my strength into the Lamb's brow.

The bolt bounces off. I don't even scratch him. I nearly lose my balance from the recoil. Why didn't this work? If this thing is some all powerful weapon…?

I eye the braided hair that wraps the tip. Removing it will free the wrath of God. It might make our situation infinitely worse. Or maybe…

The dragon only has one head left. Baby's still hanging on, unable to do a thing while the Lamb is thrashing the dragon so badly. I've no choice. I tear the hair away with my teeth and strike again.

This time, the bolt plunges into the skin and through the bone as if they were mashed potatoes. I keep pushing until my arm is shoulder deep in the Lamb's boiling gray matter. The Lamb howls, jerking his head, throwing me into the open air. As I fall, I see the Lamb's grip on the dragon's last head weaken. The beast latches on to the Lamb's throat with a thunderous growl. Lava splashes through his teeth as he blasts brimstone directly into the Lamb's jugular. But I can't focus on whether or not this attack is working, since I'm plummeting directly toward Hell.

Liberty's hand juts out and snatches me from the air. She places me atop her crown, then takes her torch in both hands. The Lamb is writhing in agony, his skin bubbling and boiling. There's a huge smoking crater in his brow, right at the point I pierced him with the bolt. Liberty leaps from the dragon's back and plunges her torch into the crater.

Light explodes from every orifice of the Lamb. He stops howling in agony. He stops everything and simply falls. His ropy entrails entangle the dragon and they both tumble toward the hellfire. Liberty makes a jump for the edge of the pit and hooks a single arm across the lip. The ground shakes violently as the Hell pit starts to close.

"Run!" she gasps, the word tearing from her giant brass lips with the sound of groaning metal.

I run, sliding down her face to land on her shoulder, scrambling toward freedom. I make a leap for a steel beam near the edge of the pit and stick the landing. I turn, shouting, "Get out of there!"

But she loses her grip and vanishes into the ever-narrowing gap. Before I can even call out her name, the crack closes, and Baby's gone.

I throw myself onto the broken earth, vainly, foolishly clawing at the rubble, as if I might somehow free her. My tears blot away my vision. I rub my fingers raw for a while, then wipe my eyes. I study the ground, searching for any sign of an opening.

It's then I discover that the sidewalk I'm sitting on is completely intact.

I look up and find myself surrounded by towering skyscrapers. Through the haze of light cast by the city, I see a single star in the night sky, Venus I think. I rise, and see a dozen people on the street staring at me. I look at my ruined hands … and suddenly it all makes sense.

Halo was right! It was only a nightmare, and now we're awake! I race down the sidewalk, heading for the waterfront, laughing like a maniac. I feel like Scrooge on Christmas morning. All a dream! A dream!

Then I reach the harbor and my laughter dies. I stare across the waters, toward a distant island, where a hundred floodlights illuminate the base of a vanished statue.

Not everyone woke, it seems.

Fallen, fallen, is Babylon the Great.

But she went down fighting.

And she didn't go down alone.

ANGEL "SKY-DEVIL" SILVERMAN floated from the warp with the RV balanced over her head. She'd cancelled the vehicle's gravity so weight wasn't a problem, but the change in air pressure between Primordia and Earth left her dizzy. The RV tilted, the oily driveshaft slipped from her fingers, and ordinary physics took over. She darted aside before the vehicle crashed sideways on the beach.

"Sorry," she said, tugging off her helmet. She squinted in the midmorning sun; the dazzling white beach and crisp blue sky were an assault on her eyes after the endless haze of Primordia.

The driver's door creaked open and Adam "Apex" Grausam climbed out, with Dr. Pumpkin emerging a second later. Neither looked injured. Of course, Adam was almost indestructible, and the doctor was a ten-foot-tall sentient, ambulatory plant. She wasn't sure what might constitute a wound on him.

"I don't know why you wanted to bring the RV back," Angel said, frowning as she surveyed the wreck. "The motor's completely shot."

"We wouldn't leave empty cans in a forest," said Adam.

She found his tone condescending, but held her tongue. The RV had been transported to Primordia via the same warp technology the thinkweed used to kidnap them. The vehicle had been worthless for transportation but had provided reasonable shelter on a world with no concept of hotels. The air conditioning had been especially welcome, until the mildly acidic atmosphere chewed up the engine.

The aliens had returned them within fifty yards of Angel's beach house. Her private island off the coast of Florida was the sane hub of her crazy life. The gamma rays released when the warp arced had fused a ten-foot circle of black glass on the beach, and the dried palm fronds along the shore had caught fire. Dr. Pumpkin recoiled at the flames. Adam hopped from the RV and snuffed the fire with his boots.

Angel drifted toward the house. "I wonder how long we've been gone?"

Adam shrugged. Dr. Pumpkin curled into a ball and bounced after her. Angel surveyed the patio as she floated over the pool. The place looked unchanged, like she'd only been gone a few hours. They'd been fighting the alien war for what felt like years, warping between worlds with completely different time systems. Her internal clock was so out of whack she couldn't even guess what month it was. She'd had two periods since leaving earth, but felt sure they'd been off schedule. The last seemed so distant that she must have missed some due to stress.

The biometric scanners recognized Angel. The glass door slid open as the house said, "Welcome back. You have 3,427 new messages."

Angel sighed. "Probably all from Mother."

Adam walked in behind her. "Date?"

The house informed them it was October 3, but she took some comfort that at least it was the same year they'd left.

Neither of them said anything. Almost four months. July 31st was long gone. Angel wondered if it wasn't for the best.

"Our guest looks wilted," said Adam, heading for the kitchen. He filled the stainless steel sink and Dr. Pumpkin unfurled before it, rising into his walking configuration, a shape resembling the unholy union of orange-hued aloe vera stalks, a sunflower, and a praying mantis. Tendrils snaked out of the yellow disk of petals that Angel thought of as the head and slurped the fresh water.

Angel felt grudging admiration that Adam had thought of the alien's needs. He was so clear on priorities. On the other hand, the cells of Adam's body were genetically perfected to adapt instantly to any environment, so acid fog never gave him a rash. He was also lucky enough to have a highly evolved gut and had avoided the four months of diarrhea and cramps that plagued her. The gooey, stinky pollen that hung in clouds throughout Primordia had caked every crevice of Angel's flight suit, but Adam's navy blue uniform was built of self-repairing nanobots and looked as pristine as the day they'd gotten kidnapped.

Angel's Sky-Devil outfit was in tatters. Her skin was covered with red blotches, and her hair felt like it had melted to her neck. Now that they were home, she knew her first priority should have been to call her mother and let her know she was alive. Instead, all she could think of was a shower. She floated toward the bedroom, peeling off clothes. There was a time when this would have driven Adam crazy with lust, though perhaps he could be forgiven his lack of desire given her shabby state. It wasn't fair. The beard he'd grown off-world made him more ruggedly handsome; her unshaved legs and pits left her looking like a yeti.

"That can't wait until you're in the bedroom?" he asked, glancing at her as she pulled off what was left of her once-white tee shirt.

"Not everyone has hyper-adaptive skin. I'm itchy."

"But we have… company." He flicked his gaze toward the alien in the kitchen.

"He's seen it all before. He's a doctor."

Adam shook his head and picked up the remote and flicked on the TV. Angel sighed and kept floating toward the bedroom, leaving a trail of boots, pants, and bra. She was down to panties and socks when she heard someone on television say, "Still no information on the whereabouts of Apex?"

"Typical." She rolled her eyes. "They don't even miss me."

Adam frowned, possibly at the TV rather than her. She felt angry at him for not responding; he'd clammed up during their alien adventure. Objectively, she knew she'd been bitchy, complaining about the harsh conditions. He'd only gone deeper into his strong and silent mode. At first, she'd been grateful for his silence, glad he was maintaining his composure while she was falling apart. But, as the weeks wore on, she sensed that his quiet calm had shifted to unspoken scorn. She'd grown to hate every word that did not pass from his lips.

A woman's voice from the television: "When Apex and Sky-Devil didn't show up for their wedding, rumors spread that they'd been killed. For Apex not to respond to such a well-publicized disaster lends credence to these rumors. Still, while several super-villains have claimed responsibility for the couple's demise, none has produced evidence."

Angel drifted to see the television. Why were they the subject of conversation at this exact moment?

On the screen was a picture of dark clouds beneath the sea and the words, "Disaster in the Gulf." Adam reached out and touched the screen, switching it to computer mode. Images flashed by quicker than Angel could follow as Adam's hand dashed back and forth across the screen. Articles and photos blinked for the tenth of a second it took Adam to read them. Thirty seconds later, the screen changed back to normal.

Adam said, wearily, “Six days ago, an oil well ruptured a mile beneath the ocean. Everything they’ve thrown at it has failed. They’ve been calling for us since day one. Let’s fly.”

“Now?”

“It’s an environmental disaster of unprecedented magnitude. Every second counts.”

She rubbed her eyes. Deep down, she loved Adam for the very quality that was now on the verge of exasperating her. He lived as if every moment not spent saving the world was a moment wasted. He was selfless to a fault. Right now, she needed a tiny bit of selfishness. “If the well’s been gushing for almost a week, how much worse can it get if we wait a day? I don’t have the energy to deal with this.”

“You won’t have to deal with it,” he said. “I just need a ride. You can fly faster than I can swim.”

“Seriously, this can wait,” Angel said, crossing her arms.

Adam shook his head, looking disappointed as he headed toward the patio.

“So, what?” Angel yelled after him. “You’re really going to swim?”

“Looks like it,” he said.

Angel knew what was going on. She flew after him. “You’re running away so we don’t have to talk.”

“I asked you to come,” he said.

Angel clenched her jaw. She landed in front of him and placed a hand on his chest. “I know you feel as if the weight of the world is on your shoulders. But, for at least a few minutes, can you forget about saving the Earth and pay some attention to us?”

He pressed his lips tightly together. He wasn’t looking directly into her eyes.

She ran her hands along his chest. “I just… we need some time together. We need to focus on making things right between us again.”

“Nothing’s wrong between us,” he said. He wrapped his arms around her in an awkward hug. “But something’s wrong with the world right now. I can’t ignore my responsibilities. When I return, I promise to devote my full attention to you.”

She ran a finger down his spine. “Is there nothing I can do to get your full attention now?”

“Angel, I…”

His voice trailed off as she pressed her hand against his fly.

"There's no time," he whispered.

She unzipped his pants. If he wanted to, he could simply push her aside and leave. The fact that he simply stood still as a statue she took as a sign of encouragement.

Adam had a different emotional toolkit from most people. His grandfather, Heinrich Grausam, had been a Nazi surgeon during WWII who had gathered mountains of data about the adaptability of the human body from his subjects in the camps. In the closing days of the war, Heinrich had fled with his pregnant wife to a secret underground base at Ultima Thule. For seven decades, Dr. Grausam and his offspring had remained hidden from the world as they labored to create the ultimate Aryan superman. Adam was that perfected human, physically unmatched, but with somewhat limited social skills.

Angel had long ago gotten used to Adam's lack of warmth. She knew he loved her because he'd been created as a conqueror, but in order to make her happy he'd changed himself into a champion. She still recalled the shocked look in his eyes after they first made love when she'd revealed she was Jewish. She'd witnessed a lifetime of brainwashing crashing down inside him. Dr. Grausam had designed Adam's mind to be as advanced as his body, and in the end, Adam had been too smart to believe in the warped ideology that had created him.

She felt cheap slipping her fingers into Adam's pants without so much as a kiss. But, until she had a shower, she was too grungy to bring her face near his. She wanted to encourage him to stay, not drive him away. She slid slowly down his legs until she was kneeling. She looked up into his eyes, giving him her best look of lustful hunger. He looked down at her, his face a mask of conflicted emotions. She knew that the unfolding disaster was a powerful tug he had difficulty resisting. She needed to prove that she was even more irresistible.

"Angel," he whispered as she unfastened his belt and folded back the high-tech material of his uniform. The self-repairing nanobots were fueled by sweat and dead skin, meaning that, unlike her, he was as clean as if he'd just stepped from a bathtub. A bit too clean, perhaps, as she pressed her nose into his pubic hair and inhaled. She preferred it when he'd been out of his costume a while and had time to build up a scent.

She didn't know what was going on in his head, but the superhuman shaft before her showed its full appreciation of her efforts. His flesh was hot as a furnace as she brushed her fingertips across it. He took a deep breath and held it as she opened her mouth and leaned forward.

The submissiveness of the pose struck her. With her anti-gravity powers, they often made love weightless in the air. Now she was grounded, hot sand burning her knees. She was nearly naked, emaciated from her alien diet, her dirty hair a mess. He loomed over her with his pants bunched at mid-thigh, but otherwise fully clothed, every hair in place. With his dark uniform and shiny boots, he could have been a military guard, and she a helpless prisoner, forced to service her captor. Before they left for Primoria, this mental image might have aroused her. Now, her body felt numb to pleasure. Was it only because of the physical stress she'd been under, or was something wrong on a deeper level?

No matter what she felt, Adam wrapped his fingers in her hair and held her immobile as he began to thrust his hips. She sensed he was trying to be gentle, but with his inhuman strength even his most careful movements made her fear for her teeth.

It was over much faster than she'd expected, perhaps because it had been months since they'd been intimate. Adam's semen often took on the taste of any strongly flavored food he'd eaten recently. The worst of the alien diet of Primordia suddenly flooded back across her tongue, a fishy, fermented flavor, with undertones of licorice and kerosene. Reflexively, she pulled away, spitting. She wiped her lips and said, "Blech. That was fairly awful."

She winced as she realized what she'd said. She glanced up and found him frowning, looking hurt.

"It's not your fault," she said, apologetically. "The diet of Primordia has messed up our chemistry."

He turned his gaze from her face as he nodded. He softly answered, "I was thinking the same thing."

Before she could ask what he meant by that, he pulled his pants up. As he zipped, he said, "Perhaps… we would benefit from a… quarantine. To give any alien chemistry within us a chance to work through our systems."

"So you're staying?" she said, feeling happy he was seeing things her way.

"I meant," he said, "a quarantine from each other. Until we've had time to readjust to normal life."

She floated into the air until she was even with his eyes. "We're fucking superheroes, Adam. You grew up in an underground bunker with a robot for a best friend and I was flying before I learned to walk. What the hell is normal? We don't do normal."

"You're right," he said. "And one reason I'm not normal is that I can hold my breath for three hours and walk on the sea-floor without being crushed. I'm the only one who has a chance at capping that oil-well. I can't waste any more time."

He crouched, then shot into the air with one of those jumps that showed up on seismographs. He flew a mile out over the water, then vanished beneath the waves with a splash. When he came back to the surface, he left a plume like a jet-ski as he tore across the water. Grausam had perfected Adam's neurotransmitters to render his grandchild exponentially faster than an ordinary man. Angel could leave him in the dust when she flew, but on foot or in the water, Adam was unbeatable.

Angel was in turmoil as she watched him go. She was furious about his charge that she'd wasted his time. Adam was increasingly acting as if time spent with alone with her had no value. This gave Angel pause, not just because it boded ill for their relationship. It also was a potentially bad development for the world.

Adam was a decent man deep in his soul but his upbringing had left him with more than a few fascist tendencies. Fortunately, his love for her let her sway him away from his darker instincts. But what if that love was fading? She wasn't blind to the fact that their romance had been sparked by sheer animal lust, and she sometimes wondered if they'd even be friends if not for the intensity of their sexual passions. Not that Adam couldn't have found sex elsewhere—women were constantly throwing themselves at him—but, with the help of her superpowers, she was doing all she could to ruin sex with an ordinary woman. They'd literally made love upon a bed of clouds, which was another reason she regretted she'd knelt and serviced him like a common whore.

She brushed the sand from her knees. Quarantine. What did he mean? Or was she making a mistake in trying to read too much into his words? He wasn't emotionally sophisticated enough to toy with her. If he was done with her, he'd say so, wouldn't he? Maybe he was more right than she cared to admit. Maybe they did need time apart to get their chemistry back in order.

Angel drifted back into the house. The phone rang five seconds after the door closed.

"Hi, Mom," she said as she activated the speaker phone on the television. She left the video mode toggled off.

"Angel! You're alive!" her mother screamed over the line. "Where have you been?"

"How'd you know I was back?"

"Pierre reported a seismic spike from your island consistent with Adam making a jump."

"Right."

"I've been worried sick. What happened?"

"The standard craziness. Kidnapped by aliens."

"What?"

"They needed us to fight their war. We weren't happy about it, but then we learned it was kind of our fault. Remember that Star-Thief guy? The one who tried stealing that warp engine from NASA?"

"The one Adam literally punched out of our universe?"

"That's him. Apparently, he wound up on a technologically advanced world in the Andromeda galaxy. He conquered the planet with a pistol because the aliens had never developed the concept of war. Once he finished with the main planet, he tried conquering that world's moon, a place inhabited by telepathic plant-creatures called thinkweed. They mentally stole the warp technology and Star-Thief's knowledge of us, then kidnapped us to save them."

Her mother didn't say anything. Angel didn't know what response she was expecting. She knew that, even by the standards of her unusual life, her explanation of why they'd been missing was flat-out crazy.

At last, her mother said, "I take it you kicked Star-Thief's ass again?"

"Yeah." She sighed. "But we only managed to do so by teaching the aliens all about fighting and battles. Some of the aliens seemed really impressed by how effective violence was at resolving differences. I suspect that, if we go back ten years from now, we might find we did more harm than good. The whole trip was one big clusterfuck."

"I'm just glad you're home," her mother said, which was the only sensible thing to say. Then she said the thing that Angel didn't want said. "When you disappeared so close to your wedding, we thought perhaps you and Adam had eloped to escape the media circus."

"We wouldn't have done that to you." In truth, she'd thought about it. "Anyway, sorry. I know that you'd spent a fortune getting things just right for the big day. I hate that our, um, careers got in the way."

"You've nothing to be sorry for. Have you and Adam discussed a new date? Or… or did you get married by some alien priest? That would be romantic!"

"No. No alien wedding. And now, maybe no wedding at all."

"Oh."

"It was a rough trip. We … we learned stuff we didn't want to learn about… about how we behave under pressure."

"Honey, your whole life is spent under pressure."

"Yeah, but here, I call you when I need to clear my head. There it was just me and Adam. I was complaining constantly, and he shut down emotionally as the days dragged by. We kind of ran out of stuff to say to one another."

"Any couple can have a rough patch. Now that you're back on earth, maybe things will still work out?"

"Maybe."

"Do you want them to work out?"

Angel nodded. "Yeah."

"Then you should tell him that."

"I should. But I don't think it will matter. He just ran off to handle that leaking oil well in the gulf even though I practically begged him to stay."

"Begged?" her mother sounded skeptical. "Begging's not really your style."

"I literally was on my knees."

Her mother was silent for a long moment. At last she said, "You sound exhausted."

"Nothing a shower and a night's sleep won't fix," Angel said, trying to sound upbeat, though she knew it wouldn't be that easy. "Ironically, the thing that'll really clear my head is the thing I told Adam not to do. I need to get back into action. I'll fly over to the gulf tomorrow to see how I can help. Of course, by the time I get there, Adam will probably have the whole thing under control."

"Ever the hero, isn't he? Back from another galaxy and off to save the world." Her mother sounded almost dreamy as she spoke of Adam, which bugged Angel.

"If only he cared about our relationship half as much as he cares about the damn planet," Angel said as irritation welled within her. She rubbed her eyes. She knew she sounded bitchy. "I should go. There's a bottle of Tylenol calling my name."

She downed four tablets as she shed her panties and flitted into the shower.

"Max heat." The water jets hit her at a temperature slightly shy of scalding. Her skin was as raw as if she'd been rolling in poison ivy, but the pain was worth it if the water cut the stink. She stuck out her tongue and let the water rinse it. She spun slowly, buffeted by the spray. The water bounced from her body in every direction as the droplets entangled with her anti-gravity aura. As a child she'd been unable to wash without drenching the bathroom. Her custom built shower was fully enclosed and had drains in the ceiling.

As she emptied two bottles of shampoo and another of conditioner, she kept thinking of Adam. The longer she spent in her costume, the funkier she became. Adam always emerged from his nanosuit cleaner than when he went in. She wondered if, by keeping him so clean, the suit might be somehow messing up his pheromones. He hadn't removed his uniform in months. Maybe it really was chemistry that was interfering with their connection to one another.

But, what if they'd never been as connected as she believed? He claimed he didn't feel pain when bullets bounced off his chest. If bullets couldn't hurt him, how much did he feel the caress of her fingertips? Sure, he got off when they made love, but one thing she'd learned early about men was that her skills and talents in bed were somewhat superfluous. Men could enjoy sex with just about anyone or anything. That long ago realization had only made her even more sexually aggressive and driven. She was determined to prove that her sexual talents were as superhuman as her defiance of gravity. Only amazing sex could keep men interested once they learned she was a mutant. Her most satisfying long-term relationship before Adam had come in the years when she'd maintained a secret identity. But, she'd always known it wasn't true love if she hid her true self. Adam was, in some ways, the last man on earth. He was the only man who could hope to love her as an equal. But, was he even capable of love?

The time when she could have asked these questions and expected an honest answer was gone. Adam had been charmingly, sometimes hilariously, blunt when they first met. But, as they'd become a couple, he'd grown more adept at hiding thoughts and feelings that she wouldn't approve of.

The irony, of course, was that they were supposed to be the superheroes without any secrets. Several years ago, following a super-powered battle that wiped out a city, masked vigilantes had become public enemies. Angel and Adam had tried to restore the good name of superheroes by making their true identities public and agreeing only to take action in coordination with lawful authorities. They held regular press conferences and made a show of hiding nothing. While most superhumans still skulked in the shadows, she and Adam were celebrities, as hunted by paparazzi as any movie star. She winced as she contemplated the possibility that someone with a telephoto lens might have seen them on the beach.

She was pulled from her train of thought as the hot water ran out. She did a quick spin to fling off as much liquid as possible before wrapping herself in a towel. She floated to the mirror, and barely recognized the woman staring back. It wasn't just the blotched skin; she'd shed twenty pounds on Primordia. Her eyes looked sunken, her cheeks skeletal. She was ten years older than Adam, her features etched with lines. Her roots were showing and strands of gray were everywhere. No wonder Adam had run away.

She sighed. Where had this streak of self-pity come from? Adam wasn't going to judge her for gray hairs and bad skin. No, if he was going to judge her, it was because she didn't approach the superhero life with level of zealotry he did. She needed sleep and he didn't, and even before the kidnapping he'd stopped spending full nights with her.

It was impossible to describe the loneliness of waking in bed alone and having to discover where Adam was by turning on the TV each morning. Adam was mostly fireproof, so it made sense that he went to Arizona to fight wild-fires. His lungs could neutralize any poison, so slogging through shafts filled with poisonous gas to save those miners in Chile had been a no-brainer. And who else could carry a Russian submarine to safety across two hundred miles of arctic sea-floor?

She'd developed the world's most twisted case of jealousy. Adam wasn't cheating with another woman. Apex was giving his heart to a world that needed him more acutely than she did.

BACK IN THE BEDROOM she drifted horizontal, lazily twirling to face the ceiling fan as she hovered over the bed. In her exhaustion, she had difficulty finding the switch in her brain that made her body feel gravity. When at last she found it, she dropped six inches onto the soft center of the king-size mattress, flat on her back, staring up at the slowly spinning fan, the bronze blades shaped like giant leaves.

She felt like she was forgetting something. She closed her eyes with some hesitation; she hadn't had a good dream in weeks. But there are times when exhaustion wins out over even the most troubled mind. She was asleep in seconds.

ANGEL'S EYES JERKED OPEN. It was dark; it had been mid-morning when they got back. How long had she been asleep?

She looked toward the clock and saw the LED blocked by a shadowy form. As her vision adjusted, she realized Dr. Pumpkin was standing by the bed. The thinkweed were all clones; their telepathic minds linked to form a communal intelligence. Angel was able to communicate with Dr. Pumpkin via this telepathy, but it was a frustrating exercise. Lacking ears, thinkweed had no concept of sound. The words in her head were meaningless static to them. Fortunately, the thinkweed could see in a similar spectrum. To communicate, Angel had to perform mental charades, visualizing pictures in her head. She could enhance these with smells, since the thinkweed had amazing chemoreceptors. Some sensory data of the skin, like texture and temperature, translated reasonably well. Even with this overlap, their minds were so different the simplest "conversations" could wear her out.

Dr. Pumpkin had been sent back to Earth against her wishes. To repay the Earth for borrowing its champions, his brethren had decided that earthlings should be given a gift. Dr. Pumpkin was that gift. Angel had tried to discourage him from coming back. She'd tried to convey that there was no way they could hide him from the authorities. He would be taken into custody and studied, most likely under military supervision. It would be like prison. The thinkweed indicated they understood her, but seemed undisturbed by the idea. With a single mind distributed among ten-million independent bodies, the fate of any individual was of little concern.

"Sorry I forgot about you," she said, leaning up on one elbow. She was in the habit of speaking to him despite the fact he couldn't hear her. The towel she'd wrapped herself in had come off as she slept but she didn't feel self-conscious. This was a plant after all. Curled into a ball, he really did resemble a pumpkin. The "Doctor" title attached to this one had come after it had bandaged her wounds with leaves. He'd also been instrumental in guiding her to the safest foods. Without Dr. Pumpkin helping mitigate the hazards of Primordia, Angel might not have survived.

Dr. Pumpkin was constructed from dozens of orange stalks, like thick, jointed spikes of aloe. He stood with four limbs on the ground and two limbs folded in front of him, like a praying mantis. Atop this structure was the large yellow flower Angel thought of as his head, though apparently his brain was in his torso, and his "head" was more akin to a crotch, housing waste excretion organs and reproductive apparatus. Long green tendrils swept back from the flower and draped down his back like curly hair.

Dr. Pumpkin reached out with one of his smooth forelimbs and lightly touched Angel's left nipple. She raised her eyebrows, but didn't shy away. He had to make contact to establish telepathic rapport. She was sure he'd simply selected a random portion of her exposed skin.

She waited for a stream of images to flood her mind, preparing for the jigsaw challenge of arranging them into a coherent idea. But, instead of images, a pleasant warmth flushed through her body. A little too pleasant.

She pulled back, breaking the contact. Her left nipple was hard as a pebble. The heat spreading through her body was indistinguishable from sexual excitement. She was certain that wasn't what Dr. Pumpkin had intended. She reached out and placed her fingers on the large paddle she thought of as his torso. Dr. Pumpkin was warm; he'd probably been standing in the sun all day. His skin was waxy and slightly dimpled, like a grapefruit. At this proximity, he smelled like overly ripe cantaloupe.

She paused to think of what images would indicate she hadn't understood his initial signal. But, before she could visualize her question, new images began to flash into her mind, pictures of the scaly patches on her skin. She saw Dr. Pumpkin caressing these patches with the tangle of tendrils that hung from his blossom. In her mind, the patches healed beneath his touch.

"Oh," she said. Was he saying he could help her? She had no reason not to trust him. "Okay." Even though the word meant nothing, she hoped he would understand her consent.

Dr. Pumpkin climbed onto the king-size bed, looming as he straddled her. He lowered the tendrils to brush her shoulder. A pale yellow oil seeped from the vines and slicked across her itching flesh. Instantly, she felt relief. Dr. Pumpkin brought the claw-like appendages of his fore-limbs to the oil and began to gently rub. His flower "face" moved even closer. The central disk within the petals dilated, revealing feathery fringes like the heart of an artichoke. This organ latched onto her shoulder with a raspy suction. It felt like being on the receiving end of a hickey. When Dr. Pumpkin pulled back, the feathery fringes had scrubbed away the dead cells, leaving unblemished skin behind. She touched her shoulder, amazed.

Dr. Pumpkin again placed a forelimb on her nipple, despite the fact that this area of her body was relatively free from damage. Warmth surged through her. She tried to pull away, but he was persistent. Scents flooded her mind, strawberry and lemon and mint. Her saliva was suddenly as sweet as if she'd bitten into a fruit salad.

"I'm not sure what you're saying…," she mumbled, squirming, as he brought his forelimbs up to his oily tendrils and spread the healing balm over her ribs. He folded his legs to drop closer to her, his tendrils tickling her throat. Her breath caught as she tried to think of a way to communicate that what he was making her feel was highly inappropriate. She tried to force her knees together as he rubbed her inner thighs. Her trembling muscles proved no match to the smooth, well-lubricated pods that pried her legs open.

Then his flower face twisted in a way nothing with an internal skeleton could ever duplicate and he brought his feathery rasping disk between her legs. She let out a short, sharp cry. Images flooded her mind; bright sunlight, warm rain, the scent of rich soil baking in the heat of the day. Drowning in a flood of sensations, she could no longer form coherent thoughts.

As his slender tendrils snaked inside her and began a slow, steady exploration, she screamed, long and loud and wordless, shuddering as tears ran down her cheeks. She climaxed so violently she saw stars, and fell back to the bed gasping.

"You don't understand…," she whispered when she finally caught her breath enough to try again to push him away. "There are parts of my body you shouldn't touch."

Dr. Pumpkin ignored her struggles as his flower face drew close to hers. His feathery orifice pressed against her lips, which she clamped tightly shut. She tried to squirm away but his tendrils wrapped around her wrists, clamping them together. Other tendrils encircled her ankles and drew them apart.

Panic rising, she screamed, but was instantly silenced as something thick as a cucumber slipped between her lips. She choked, and in desperation bit down. The organ that filled her mouth had a tough and fibrous core that she couldn't bite through, but the outer surface was no tougher than a banana peel. When she cut through it with her teeth sap exploded into her mouth with a strong citrus palette with a hint of saltiness. Dr. Pumpkin shifted in response to her assault but didn't pull out. She could suddenly breathe through her nose. She inhaled deeply trying to calm herself, to make sense of what was happening. The thinkweed had no concept of war, or at least they hadn't until they'd learned by telepathically absorbing all that Adam knew of it. Could they… could they also have absorbed the concept of rape?

As if in answer, something hard pressed against her labia. She squirmed, but succeeded only in spreading her nether-lips open wider beneath the probing intruder. Her muscles spasmed as a smooth, mushroom-shaped head far larger than Adam's penis stretched her wider than she'd ever been opened before. She dug her nails deep into the vines that wrapped her hands, arching her back as the unseen organ slid deeper, deeper, until it pushed against her womb. She was dizzy, bewildered, helpless, and violated. She knew she could cancel their gravity and throw them up into the ceiling fan. Perhaps this would shake the alien off.

But she didn't. Because there was no longer any mistaking what Dr. Pumpkin was intending. The mental images that flooded her weren't images of violence, but images of warmth and comfort and healing. Any fundamental outrage over what was happening was drowned beneath a flood of pleasure. Dr. Pumpkin had shown an instinct for healing in the past. He must have sensed her mental and physical distress after her encounter with Adam. The alien was no doubt mistakenly attempting to make her feel better both mentally and physically by sexually stimulating her.

Or was it a mistake? She clenched her thighs tightly around his trunk as she came again, the most powerful orgasm of her life, wave after wave of energy washing out from deep in her belly. As her vagina locked tightly on the alien pod inside her, the organ suddenly burst like a water balloon filled with honey. She felt sticky sap gush out of her, coating her thighs, seeping down her ass. It tingled like eucalyptus oil and smelled lightly of roses.

The tendrils redoubled their efforts to fill her every orifice and she came again, then again, until there were black spots dancing before her, and she passed out.

SHE WOKE AFTER DAWN, sitting up in the bed, covered in sweat. She was alone in the room. For a flicker of a second, she felt relief that the whole encounter had been only a dream.

Then she saw the lime green puddle of alien that soaked the sheets and her heart skipped a beat. It wasn't a dream.

And she felt absolutely amazing. The juices the thinkweed had smeared across her skin had left her without the faintest hint of rash or scratches. Her various knots and bruises had also melted away beneath Dr. Pumpkin's ministrations. More importantly, she felt like her insides had been completely scrubbed clean of all the unpleasant alien toxins that had stressed her system for months, and that somehow the earthly nutrients and vitamins she'd been missing had all been restored. She rose from the bed, her feet not touching the ground, feeling light as a feather. In truth, she was even lighter.

All the tension and fear she'd carried inside her were gone. Her relaxed, euphoric mental state reminded her of the high of top quality weed, but without the fogginess and forgetfulness. She felt lucid, completely aware of her body, fully in possession of her memories. Even the most horrible of her experiences now felt as if they'd been properly filed and organized in her mind. It was as if she'd gained perspective and wisdom overnight, and saw how her struggles and pain had been processed into the finer emotions of gratitude and compassion.

"Wow," she whispered. "That was one hell of a fuck."

She saw a trail of dried green droplets leading from the bed to the door of the room. She floated forward, following the trail down the hall into the living room. The front wall of the room was all windows, and Dr. Pumkin had come here to unfold before the rising sun. He didn't turn to face her as she hung in the air behind him.

He looked for all the world like an exotic houseplant. She again wondered how morally culpable Dr. Pumpkin was for what had happened. He was part of a species that reproduced asexually. In treating her wounds, he might not have been cognizant of the difference between touching her shoulder and licking her cunt. Maybe his actions had nothing to do with making her feel anything. What if he'd eaten her dead skin for sustenance, like those little Japanese fish they used for pedicures? The tendrils he'd sent inside her might have been seeking moisture and nutrients, absorbing the chemicals from his home world that she'd carried in her gut.

But what if he had understood what he was doing? Could the alien have pulled some sort of rape fantasy out of Adam's mind?

Or out of hers?

Her jaw went slack at the possibility.

She decided against touching him, turning back toward her bedroom. She pulled fresh panties from her dresser, then floated into the bathroom to wash up. She only used a warm washcloth at the sink instead of showering; the oils coating her skin felt like a soothing lotion she wasn't eager to get rid of.

She dipped a finger into herself, pondering whether she should douche. She decided against it. She pulled on the panties, soft cotton, pure white. In the mirror, they rendered her crotch virginal. Curious, she sniffed her finger. The rose-aroma was still there, mixed with her own briny scent. Underneath it all was the hint of freshly cut grass.

She felt herself growing aroused from the smell and decided it was time to get out of the house. She went to her closet. Her back-up Sky-Devil uniform was mostly black leather with Kevlar reinforcement. Bat-like wings jutted from the back. She could fly without the wings, but a human body was remarkably unsuited to perform the kinds of aerial acrobatics her superheroic persona was known for. The wings allowed her to catch and control the wind to perform banks and turns at high speed. She was fast enough to break the sound barrier, more than fast enough to kill herself if she didn't control her flight perfectly. Her costume was skin-tight and revealing not because she enjoyed running around in public looking like some biker-slut, but because any gap between her and her costume would fill with wind at high speed and shred her clothing.

She grabbed a modified motorcycle helmet to protect her face. At low speeds, she liked feeling wind through her hair, but she'd learned as a child that at anything much faster than the speed of a bicycle, seemingly empty air turned into an obstacle course filled with a thousand buzzing dangers. She'd almost lost an eye as a teen after smacking into a beetle at 90 miles an hour.

Moving into the media room, she flicked on the television while her helmet booted up and ran a systems check. The news was on and there was Adam, big as life, the giant white "A" in the center of his chest gleaming in the blackness of the deep ocean. He was holding a giant concrete dome over his head as he trudged through knee deep sludge.

The television anchor said, "Still no word on where Apex has been, or why he waited so long to intervene."

She touched the screen, switching to GPS mode and sent the oil-rig coordinates to her helmet. Flying there would take three hours. She'd check in with the authorities once she arrived. Presumably Adam had already made contact.

Dr. Pumpkin didn't look toward her as she floated out to the patio. Or, maybe he was looking at her; she didn't know what he used for eyes. Her ignorance of his anatomy made her stomach tighten. What if… what if the alien had impregnated her? She shook her head, knowing it was a stupid thought. Dr. Pumpkin didn't even have DNA. A banana was more likely to impregnate her than he was. And why was she thinking of him as "him"? The thinkweed was asexual. She hadn't had sex with "him," she'd had sex with "it." And the sex was probably an accident. A mind-blowing, body-restoring, soul-renewing accident that left her feeling as if every muscle fiber had been pulled apart, washed in cool water, dried in warm sunlight, then reassembled to perfection. It was an experience Adam's thick-fingered fumbling could never hope to achieve.

She knew she would probably think about the experience for the rest of her life. But, for the rest of the day, she needed to think about playing superhero. She rocketed straight up half a mile before spreading her wings and streaking westward.

"Standard signals," she said. The on-board computer quickly made contact with air traffic control in Tampa and downloaded flight plans. A light above her left eyebrow turned green as her helmet completed a handshake with NORAD, ruling her out as an enemy missile. In minutes she was over the mainland, sun glistening on the swamps below. Radar information played across her visor. She could spot a plane or a large bird on her own, but smacking into a robin at 700 miles an hour could prove deadly. Alas, even with the radar, she still couldn't spot the small bugs that smacked into her visor like bits of gravel.

By the time she left the gulf shore of Florida, there was enough goop on the faceplate to disgust her, so she veered into a fluffy bank of clouds. The suspended water droplets impacted like a high-speed car wash. On the other side, she was bug free. The wind dried her in seconds.

The ocean flashed beneath, blue and dazzling. She was several hundred miles from the accident, but having heard that the spill was bigger than the Exxon Valdez, she'd imagined that the whole gulf was one big slick. Hope stirred that things weren't so bad.

Then she could smell it. Mixed with the briny air was the faint essence of spent motor oil. Soon, rainbow films appeared like paisley splotches on the water beneath her. She zoomed toward the speck that her systems identified as the Coast Guard cutter Memphis, the command hub for the containment operations. Booms had sketched out an uneven circle of contamination several miles across, a sinister bruise upon the ocean.

The helmet responded to her eye movements to open a window streaming news headlines. Almost immediately she learned that Adam had been successful in fixing the containment dome. Apex was expected to make a statement to the press aboard the Memphis at any moment. She could see a crowd on the deck before a small podium.

Angel normally took the lead at media events. Adam answered most questions in monosyllables. He wasn't able to banter amiably with reporters the way Angel was. Not that Sky-Devil always had a pleasant relationship with the press. Before she met Adam, she'd gotten into a fight with a super-powered assassin known as the Silver Knife and had faked him out by shedding her costume and using it as a decoy while she snuck up behind him. To this day, though she'd done probably a thousand press conferences fully clothed, there seemed to be a law that no article written about her could run without the picture of her in her bra and panties standing over the unconscious villain.

She could only imagine the pictures that ran when they were no-shows at the wedding. Still, there weren't going to be any tabloid hacks out on the ship. Only reporters with genuine credentials would have been granted access. Hopefully, she and Adam could answer questions about where they'd been without it turning into a feeding frenzy.

On the deck of the ship, faces craned skyward as she decelerated. Between her flight plans and the ship's tracking radar, her arrival wasn't a surprise. She slipped down from the sky, drifting to a halt behind the podium. Hanging a few feet off the ground, she pulled off her helmet.

"Good morning," she said, brushing stray hairs from her face. "I know you're expecting Apex. He'll be along any moment, but I thought I might be able to answer your questions about where we've been these last few weeks."

There were about twenty reporters in the group, some familiar faces. Jackie Jones from ABC and Peter Hampton from the New York

Times were people she'd sat down with for one-on-one interviews. This wasn't going to be bad at all.

"We'll be issuing a more detailed press release after debriefing with officials, but the short answer is that we were summoned to deal with an off-world threat. We undertook this mission with little notice and, due to the distances involved, weren't able to communicate with Earth." She paused, pleased she'd avoided using the word "kidnapped." It sounded better if the mission was voluntary.

Before she could continue, Hampton shouted out a question: "Are you saying that the government approved your mission and allowed you to go off world?"

She shook her head. "We didn't inform anyone. There was no time."

"So you undertook this mission without consulting with the government? Isn't that contrary to your vow to always coordinate your activities with local authorities?"

She smirked. "I'm not sure who the 'local' authority would be. We were in the Andromeda galaxy. It's the exact opposite of 'local.'"

A reporter she didn't recognize butted in: "In light of the unfolding disaster, do you regret your decision to leave? Shouldn't your first priority have been to stay and protect the Earth?"

"Protecting the public remains our top priority," she said. "I personally regret that our mission lasted as long as it did. It made me miss my own wedding, after all." She offered the last bit with a half-smile, hoping for a little sympathy.

She instantly regretted mentioning the wedding when Jackie Jones raised her hand and asked, "Will the wedding be rescheduled?"

Angel's face froze. She wanted to smile and make a joke. Instead, she could only mumble, "We… uh, we're not ready to make a statement at this time."

Now she'd really done it. Every reporter erupted, shouting questions about her and Apex. She couldn't make sense of the cacophony. She felt like shooting back into the sky, when one by one, all the voices fell silent. The eyes of the crowd were no longer focused on her. She looked over her shoulder. Apex stood behind her, frowning. At her? At the reporters?

Apex brushed past her and gripped the podium with both hands. He leaned in close to the microphones and glared out at the reporters.

In a calm, deep voice, he asked, "What is wrong with you people?"

The reporters looked stunned.

"You're dead center of the worst environmental disaster of a generation and you waste even one second asking about our wedding?" Angel could tell he was upset because hints of his former German accent were slipping out.

Peter Hampton cleared his throat. "Apex, you're absolutely right. These are serious times, demanding serious questions. While you were missing, my colleagues at the Times looked into the information you've publicly released about your past, hoping to find clues to your whereabouts. What we discovered is that many of your publicly released documents appear to be forgeries."

Angel clenched her jaw. Almost everything about Adam's public identity was a forgery. Explaining to the world that he was a Nazi superman who owed his powers to data collected from death camp victims was too large of a PR challenge.

Hampton said, "Our research revealed that your birth certificate seems to be an altered version of a certificate issued for the birth of a child named Andrew Stanton, who died when he was only three weeks old. Do you have any explanation of why we discovered this?"

"Yes," said Apex, clenching his hands on the edge of the platform. "You discovered it because you devote more of your resources researching celebrities and gossip than you spend documenting the monumental crimes unfolding around you. For years, I've fought to defend this world from a variety of menaces and disasters, which are almost always self-inflicted. You can devote a team of reporters to look into my past, but spare no resources to examine the corporate and government decisions that allowed drilling in such a risky and fragile environment?"

Hampton shouted back, "We've reported on that non-stop since the spill—"

Apex cut him off. "But none of you so-called guardians of democracy could be bothered to look into this issue beforehand because the space your papers is reserved for running photos of my fiancé in her underwear. My grandfather told me that democracy was doomed to failure because mankind had become too mongrelized to have the intellectual capacity to manage itself. You're living proof, and a disgrace to—"

Angel placed a hand on Adam's shoulder. Slipping on her helmet with her free hand, she cancelled his gravity and they shot into the air before he could finish his statement.

Luckily, Adam didn't resist. Flying with Adam was a challenge due to the off-center aerodynamics, and he wouldn't have to work hard to break her grasp. Instead, he was still as she wrapped her arms around his chest and cranked up her speed. Adam was tough enough to withstand bug impacts. The wind whipping past made conversation impossible.

But what needed to be said? As they streaked across the heavens, she thought about old times. They'd seemed like such a good match. She was in command of the air, light and swift and agile. Adam's strength was on the ground, playing both unstoppable force and immovable object. She was the sarcastic quipster, born to wealth and comfort, while he was the tight-lipped stoic, born in a frozen wasteland, bred for constant struggle. They were yin and yang, opposites in balance, or at least they had been.

Yet, she couldn't ignore Adam's rigid tension as they flew over Florida. She hugged him closer but he never relaxed into her embrace. In the past when they flew together, he would often clasp his hands over hers. Now, his arms were stiff at his sides, as if he were standing at attention. Never had he seemed so distant.

She thought of something her mother had told her when they were planning the wedding. She'd said, "It's not the times when you're talking that determine if love will endure. It's whether or not the silences between you are comfortable." They'd been comfortable with each other's silence before departing for Primordia. She couldn't point to a single moment when she'd felt that comfort slip away, but it was gone all the same.

Hours later, they touched down on the sands of their island home. He broke free of her embrace and started walking toward the house.

"Are we going to talk about what happened back on the boat?" she asked.

"If you feel we must," he said, sounding weary.

"Don't let those jerks get to you," she said. "Anything they print, we can deny, deny, deny. The public will side with you. You're their hero."

He shook his head. "We shouldn't have to live in a world that requires heroes."

"What do you mean?"

He turned to face her. His mask of stoicism was gone, and genuine pain showed in his eyes. "When we decided to get married…." He voice trailed off. He took a deep breath and looked her directly in the eyes. "I only wanted… I decided to give you the best possible present. I wanted to give you a safe, healthy, peaceful world. I've worked non-stop. I've broke up terrorist cells, carted icebergs to countries gripped by drought, moved entire villages threatened by floods. All this, and I haven't changed a thing. It's like trying to empty the ocean with a bucket. I bail and bail, but the water never goes down."

"I had no idea you felt this," she said.

"I do," he said. "And I can't help but think that I've been approaching the problem the wrong way."

"What do you mean?"

"I mean that I dash off to emergencies like a fireman only to discover again and again that the people I've gone to save have set their own house on fire. So many of the world's problems could be avoided if men were capable of self-government. Instead, the governments of the world are a catalogue of human weakness. They're either corrupt, inept, or cowardly. The masses are too stupid and uneducated to save themselves from the failings of those in power."

Angel crossed her arms. "I don't like where this train of thought is heading."

He sighed. "I can see there's only one way to give you the world you deserve."

"What the fuck are you saying? That you're going to obey your grandfather after all? That you're going to go out and conquer the world and rule over it like some kind of goddamn Nazi overlord?"

"Only as a temporary measure, a stopgap for a few generations while I put in place systems that will improve mankind. I've no desire to rule anyone," he said. "But, I was created with a mind as advanced as my body. If I alone have the wisdom to save mankind from itself, is it not my duty to do so?"

"I swear to God, Adam, I will fucking stop you."

"I know… you'd try," he said, his voice choking. "Don't you understand the irony? Before I met you, I'd never felt love. I'd no desire to save anyone, no instinct for altruism. Now, because you taught me love, I want only to do good, even though I know that doing so will cost me your heart."

She threw her hands into the air. "You think taking over the world is doing good?"

"You saw the damage caused by that well. We live in a world where man has advanced technologically far enough to poison the planet in a thousand thoughtless ways. The best, most rational minds of mankind have managed to build arsenals of nuclear weapons that could reduce the world to a cinder in a single afternoon. What higher good can there be than to ensure that humanity survives this troubled era?"

She let out a slow breath. Here were the unsaid words that haunted his silences, spoken at last. She wasn't surprised. It was the destiny he'd been designed for. How had she been so foolish to think that her love could save him from the darkness bred into his soul?

She shook her head. "I know that this probably makes perfect sense to you. But, if you honestly love me, please stop and think. You've been operating under a superhuman amount of stress for a long time. Please, take some time before you decide to do anything. Promise that you'll do something to relax and get your mind clear."

"My mind is perfectly clear right now. This isn't some whim. I've traveled a long road to this point. I'm 99% certain of my decision."

She raised an eyebrow. "What's the 1% hesitation?"

"The possibility that I can persuade you to see things my way. There is a 99% chance I'll have to do this alone. A 1% chance you'll join me."

"Wow," she said. She bit her tongue before she told him how crazy he was. He'd admitted he still desired to be with her. Perhaps he could still be persuaded to abandon his plans.

"Okay," she said, taking a deep breath. "I agree to listen to you make your full case with as much of an open mind as I can muster. All I ask in return is the same respect, and that we at least sleep on it before we make any decisions. How long has it been since you had a night's sleep anyway?"

"Six months," he said. "I had a brief nap after we made love in Paris last April."

"Sleep will do you good. I slept like a log when I got back and felt a thousand times better afterward." She decided it was best not to mention Dr. Pumpkin's role in this.

"I've been designed to not require sleep."

"But you can sleep when you want to. You just admitted it. Let's go into the house right now and change into pajamas." She smiled as she said this, trying to hint that there might be more than just sleep in store if he went along with her.

Adam seemed to miss the cue. He shook his head. "I've got too many loose threads to wrap up. Dr. Pumpkin is still inside?"

"I suppose."

"The coast guard gave me instructions to deliver him to Cape Canaveral. They're putting together a team to study him."

"Gave you instructions?" she said. "What does that matter if you're planning on starting issuing the orders?"

"For now, it's best that those in power still believe I'm their servant. Besides, what else are we to do with our alien houseguest?"

"That's kind of cold, turning him over like that."

"That was always the plan. Plus, think of how you suffered in Primordia's atmosphere. Dr. Pumpkin might be feeling the same way in our air. The scientists can create a safe habitat for him."

"I know but…." She tried to think of a rational objection, but couldn't. "Fine. Want me to fly him?"

Adam shook his head. "It's only a short swim and a jog for me. I'll be back before sunset."

"Whatever," she said. In truth, she was a bit worried about what might happen if she touched Dr. Pumpkin again. The last thing she needed was to have the alien try to "heal" her in front of Adam.

Minutes later, Apex jumped back into the Atlantic. Dr. Pumpkin was curled into a ball that rested between Adam's shoulder blades, with several sturdy vines wrapped around Adam's torso. They left a wake as they shot toward the horizon.

Drifting into the living room, she turned on the television. It took all of two seconds to find footage of the press conference. The house announced an incoming call.

"Hi, Mother."

"I saw the video," her mother said. "You looked fantastic, dear. Your skin was practically glowing. Have you lost weight?"

"I've been an involuntary bulimic for a while. But, you're not calling to talk about how I look."

"I'm trying to put a positive spin on what must certainly be the worst press conference of your career."

"I take you already have people working to discredit the birth certificate story?"

"That will be simple. It won't be as simple explaining Adam's rather politically incorrect outburst. 'Mongrel?'"

"Bad PR is the least of our problems," said Angel. "Adam's gone all super-Nazi on me. He's seriously talking about setting himself up as supreme dictator of Earth."

Her mother was silent.

"You still there?" Angel asked.

"Do you… do you have a plan to stop him?" her mother asked. By coincidence, the silent video stream of the news coverage of Sky-Devil and Apex picked that exact moment to show the old picture of her in her underwear standing over Silver Knife.

Angel sighed. "I think the bigger question is whether or not he'll convince me to join him."

"Angel!"

"That's a joke, Mother. Look, I'll get back to you. I need some time to think."

Signing off, she drifted back to the window to gaze upon the spot where Apex had plunged into the ocean. The tide had risen and waves were lapping at the overturned RV she'd dropped on the beach. It was an ugly scar on her pristine, private paradise. The waves were probably washing alien microbes into the sea, which could lead to God knows what kind of ecological disaster. In all the comic books she'd read as a kid, the one thing they'd never bothered to put into the stories was how much of a superhero's life was spent cleaning up.

She carried the RV from the beach and dropped it into the swimming pool, figuring the chlorinated water would zap any alien bugs. Of course, now she had an RV in her pool. Sometimes, life seemed like an unending sequence of solving one problem by changing it into another problem.

Shaking her head, she floated back into the bedroom. She stared at the sheets, remembering the previous night. Then she stripped off her clothes and stayed in the shower long after all the hot water had run out, removing the last evidence of her alien sex romp from her pores. The euphoria she'd felt upon waking this morning was long gone. She was all that stood between the world and conquest by a super-Nazi. A super-Nazi that she still loved with all her heart.

After she'd dried herself, she plopped down in the center of the bed and watched the shadows on the walls, as the light streaming through the blinds grew ever redder.

She slept poorly, tossing and turning. She always slept so much easier when Adam was in bed beside her. What was wrong with her that she was so needy that she still longed for him despite what she now knew about his innermost thoughts?

It was still hours before dawn when she woke up and got out of bed to go pee. She walked back into the bedroom with the lights still out, her eyes bleary and unfocused. Then, in the dim light, she saw a large white "A" on the bed before her.

"Lights," she said. She blinked as the house turned on the lamps. Adam was sitting on the edge of the bed. He looked… relaxed. Loose. He smiled at her with an expression approaching serenity.

"How are you feeling?" she asked, surprised by his changed demeanor.

"Happy," he said. "I hope I didn't startle you. I've actually been here a few moments, watching you sleep."

She ran her fingers through her hair. "You were watching me sleep?"

"I'm sorry if that sounds… inappropriate. But… but I was thinking how good it would feel to lie down beside you. Of how good it would feel for us to share a bed again."

"Nothing in the world would make me happier," she said. "But, I want it to be this bed. Not a bed in some dictator's palace you build yourself when you take things over."

He shook his head. "Have I been a fool? I've tried so hard to give you the perfect world," he said. "Have I been blind to a simpler way of making you happy? Was it always as easy as sharing a bed with you?"

"Sharing a bed isn't all that easy," she said. "But, yeah. Yeah, it does make me happy. I was kind of a mess before I met you. I felt so alone. When I met you, that loneliness vanished."

"While I'd never known loneliness until I met you. The first time we parted company after we met, I felt such yearning for your return. It was like nothing I'd ever experienced," he said. "The thought of a world without you by my side fills me with emptiness."

"I want to be by your side," she said. "But as heroes, not as conquerors. You're right. The world is fucked up and run by fools. But if we think we can do better, aren't we bigger fools?"

"There's wisdom in your words. I want to follow the path that keeps you in my life." He moved from the bed to kneel on one knee before her, taking her hand. "Do you still want to get married?"

She smiled. "Oh God, yes."

"I meant, to me?"

Her jaw dropped. "Wow. You just made a joke."

"You didn't laugh," he said, in mock disappointment.

"It took me by surprise. You've never told a joke in your life."

"Let's keep being surprising. Let's elope. Have your mother call the president and arrange a midnight ceremony."

Angel looked down into his face. She could tell from his eyes he meant what he was saying. But she couldn't help but sound skeptical as she asked, "What's different?"

"It helps that we finally talked. My thoughts have weighed me down for some time. I thought I could bear the heaviness alone. I let myself forget that you make everything weightless."

She gently took his arm to pull him back to his feet. "This is quite a change of heart in, what? Five hours? Six?"

"More like seven," he said, with a shrug. "The mission to deliver Dr. Pumpkin had a detour."

"Oh, who cares how long it took?" she said, throwing her arms open. "I knew you'd come around."

He wrapped his powerful arms around her, pressing her against his sculpted chest. All his stiffness and awkwardness had vanished.

He looked into her eyes. "Will you get used to being called Mrs. Apex?"

"Shut up and kiss me, Mr. Sky-Devil."

She closed her eyes as he bent his head toward her. They lifted into the air, weightless, free of care. His lips met hers and his tongue slipped between her teeth for a long, lingering kiss that she never wanted to end. She sucked on his tongue like it was candy.

Her eyes snapped open. His saliva tasted exactly like the scent of roses, with an undertone of fresh cut grass.

AS JOSEPH WALKED into the living room, a hatchet in one hand, Becky's head in the other, he realized that the person he was really angry with was himself.

JANE LIVED IN THE SWAMP near the sound, down a seemingly endless gravel road lined on both sides by ditches of black water. The high beams of the cruiser painted the gnarled, vine draped trees in ghostly shades of white. Deputy Gray hated going out to see Jane. She was crazy, probably schizophrenic. It broke his heart to see how she lived. He wished the sheriff would let him bring Jane in, bring her before a judge, and get her sent to an institution. The sheriff said as long as she didn't hurt anyone, there wasn't much they could do.

Gray suspected the real reason the sheriff didn't do anything about Jane was that he'd bought into the bullshit. Like the steady stream of new-agers who made pilgrimages to this backwater, the sheriff believed Jane's prophecies—he thought Jane could see the future.

Gray stepped out of his cruiser into the August night; the woods buzzed and chirped and whirred. He swatted a cloud of mosquitoes away as he moved forward, the shadows from his headlights stretching before him.

The far reaches of the beam touched a half-dismantled RV. The hood of the RV yawned like an open mouth. The long dead motor was propped on the ground, the fan blades facing skyward, the perfect black circles of the camshafts turning the rusted block into abstract sculpture. Jane sat with her back against the engine. She wore a grungy trench coat that hung open revealing her otherwise naked body. A bottle of Everclear rested against her crotch, an offering, no doubt, from someone who came seeking knowledge. Bring her food, or water, or clothing, and Jane would return the gift with some vague fortune. Bring her booze to loosen her tongue, and she could talk about your tomorrows as if she was watching them on a movie screen.

No one knew how old Jane was—her face was leathery with sun-damage, but her body was pale and smooth as a virgin bride's. Her tangled hair was an oily black, without a hint of white. Jane watched with a half-focused stare as Gray approached. She lifted the bottle and took a deep gulp.

"You're not who I'm waiting for," she said, wiping her mouth on the trench-coat sleeve.

"Sheriff's busy," Gray said. "There's a big hoo-hah at the country club tonight and he's gone to slap flesh. Bill's wearing cowboy boots with his tux."

"Like to see it. I'm watching the Eater," Jane said, staring into the darkness, "else I'd gaze at him."

"Emma says you're goin' on about a murder," Gray said.

Jane nodded, focusing her eyes on something far beyond Gray. She mumbled as she said, "Two boys. Brothers? Nice clothes. Weird hands. Green. Swollen. He's going to eat them."

"Who's eating who now?" asked Gray.

"The Eater," said Jane. "He's nephilim."

"That's his name? Neville M.?"

"Genesis 6:4. Angels bred with the sons of men. Their offspring were the nephilim."

Gray rubbed his eyes. He didn't read the Bible any more, not since Linda died, but he didn't think that mattered. Jane was probably making this up.

"Jane," Gray said, "you been doing any drugs tonight?"

She shook her head. "Past and future already get tangled. Drugs make it worse." She lifted the Everclear and swigged another mouthful. Her whole body spasmed.

"He's coming," she said.

"Who?" Gray asked, before hearing the faint thrum of a motor behind him. He looked over his shoulder to see headlights. The twisted trees cut the lights into sweeping rays. He raised a hand to shield his eyes as a black van pulled up beside his cruiser.

The van looked like it belonged to some TV station, with a satellite dish on the roof, and a dozen antennas. The passenger door swung open and a man stepped out dressed like a Roman Catholic priest, wearing a long black coat despite the August heat. The small patch of white at his throat seemed almost luminous. He was thin, tall, and youthful. His hair was cropped short, black and thick as seal's fur.

"The local authority's already here," the priest said.

Gray wasn't sure who the guy was talking to. He noticed a Bluetooth headset in the man's ear.

"Keep scanning all bands. I'll check back," the priest said. Then he headed for Gray with his hand outstretched. "Father Daniel Spare," he said, in a firm voice.

Gray shook his hand. "Deputy Thomas Gray," he said. "Fancy van you got there."

"It's important to stay connected," Spare said. "What's she told you?"

"Who? Jane?"

Spare nodded.

"She's drunk," said Gray. "Said something about someone getting eaten, but I can't make heads nor tails of it."

"Mind if I talk to her?"

"It's a free country," said Gray.

Spare approached Jane and squatted before her. He reached out and grabbed the edges of her trench coat and pulled them to cover her breasts and genitalia.

"How are you tonight, Jane?" he asked.

"Busy," she muttered.

"Awfully hot out here. Can we take you into town? Get you an air-conditioned room?"

Jane shook her head.

"How about dinner? Are you getting enough food?"

"Ain't been hungry," she said. "But the Eater is."

"You've seen him? You know where he is?"

She shrugged. "Things don't stay focused."

"What have you been seeing?"

"He's rich," Jane said. "Big house. Swimming pool. People like him, or whoever he was. He hasn't started feeding yet, but tonight he'll eat those little boys."

"What little boys, Jane? What do you know about them?"

"Already told Gray. They got nice clothes. But their hands are funny. Big and green. Swelled up."

Spare looked back toward Gray with a puzzled expression. Gray shrugged.

Jane took a deep breath. "It might be what Gray said that put this in my mind," she said, tentatively, "but I think he's wearing a tuxedo."

Gray said, "I told her about the party at the country club tonight. Sheriff's in a tux. So are a hundred other guys."

"The club has a pool?" Spare asked.

"I suppose," said Gray.

"Jane," said Spare. "Try to look closer. I need a description. Hair color. Eye color. Some real detail."

"He's balding on top, salt and pepper on the sides," said Jane. "And… and he's looking at a pocket watch. It's got a monogram… GCH. It's just before he kills the boys. It's midnight. But, of course it's midnight."

"Of course," said Spare. "Thank you."

He stood up and pressed the headset. He walked away from Jane and said, "Amber, get me a list of local country clubs and their member directories. Look for someone with the initials GCH."

"GCH is George Clayton Hungerford," Gray said. "You don't need a fancy computer for that. He's the mayor."

"He's at the country club?"

"Should be," said Gray. "Look, what's going on?"

Spare looked Gray straight in the eyes and said, "Given that we have less than two hours, I don't have time to fully explain. I'm going to ask for a bit of faith on your part, deputy."

Gray shrugged. "Try me."

"I've been chasing a demon down the eastern seaboard for the better part of a year. The Eater is a jumper… it can move from body to body with only a touch. Tracking it through conventional means has been a challenge, to say the least. Now the Eater has popped up in a county that contains one of the most powerful seers in this hemisphere. If I don't stop him tonight, it might take months to get this close again."

"Father," said Gray, hoping that was the right way to address him, as there weren't many Catholics in this neck of the woods. "Folks believe Jane sees the future, but I don't. I think she's sick, and it makes me sick to see a man of the cloth taking her act seriously. She needs to be in a home, not out here in the swamp spouting off nonsense to strangers."

"I share your concern," said Spare. "Jane may, indeed, be insane. Bartlett's Guide to North American Psychics rates her as a class six seer; the Black Wiki ranks her as class eight. She's bombarded by random future events she'll never be present for. Living with so much sensory data pouring in from outside the boundaries of your skin can break anyone's mind."

Gray rolled his eyes. "You're as crazy as she is."

Spare shook his head. "Deputy, it's 10:15. In one hour and forty-five minutes, two little boys are going to be killed. I can GPS the country club, I can download photos of the mayor, and I can proceed on this mission without your help. On the other hand, you know the area and the people involved. If you help me, it might provide the crucial minutes needed to save innocent lives."

"Forget it," Gray said. "The sheriff would have my badge if I let you crash the party and harass the mayor."

Jane called out, "Bill always believes me. You go kill her, you hear?"

"Her?" Gray said. "Her who?"

"Him," said Jane. "The Eater."

The priest reached out and placed an arm on Gray's shoulder. "We're another minute closer to midnight. We need to go. I can tell you've got a good heart, Gray. Maybe we can do each other a favor."

"What kind of favor?" Gray asked.

"I'll call the diocese in Raleigh. Tomorrow, I'll have people here to help Jane. Does she have family?"

"No one knows anything about her," said Gray. "She tells lots of stories, but can't keep her facts straight."

"Whatever her history, we can put together a support team that can get her out of this swamp and into a more structured environment. I'll make the call whether or not you help—this isn't a quid pro quo arrangement—but, since I'm willing to assist Jane, which is something you want, would you give me a few hours of your night and help me find something I want?"

Gray sighed. "Fine. I'll take you to see the mayor. But if you do anything suspicious, I'll have you in cuffs before you can blink."

"You're the man with the gun," said Spare. "Speaking of which," he paused, digging into a pocket of his coat, "take these." He pulled out his hand and revealed three bullets. "Your pistol's a .38, right? These are blessed. Each tip contains a tiny sphere of holy water."

Gray took the bullets and looked at one, unable to see any difference between it and an ordinary bullet.

"I'm not going to use non-regulation ammo," he said.

"Just hold onto them, okay? What's the harm?"

Gray shrugged, and dropped them into his shirt pocket.

"Do you mind if I ride with you?" Spare asked. "There's stuff I should fill you in on."

"You'll have to ride in the back," Gray said. "Policy."

"No problem."

Gray let Spare into the cruiser. He went around and got into the driver's seat, wondering how this night had gotten so weird. He felt a little sentimental. Before Linda died, this was exactly the sort of night she liked hearing about. Crazy people made good gossip, and a priest with holy bullets was exactly the sort of quirky detail that Linda loved. With Linda, Gray had never gone a day without laughing. Even when she got sicker with her cancer, her humor had only gotten sharper. Now, Gray couldn't remember the last time he'd really laughed.

As he headed down the dirt road, he noticed the priest's van following. He hadn't seen anyone else with Spare.

"Who else you got with you?" he asked.

"Hinako's driving," Spare said.

"I didn't see him when I walked past."

"Her," said Spare. He started to say something else, then stopped.

"What," said Gray.

"You're already skeptical," said Spare.

"So?"

"So you probably won't believe me if I tell you that Hinako is a seven-hundred-year-old invisible ninja with a demon-slaying spirit blade."

Gray smirked. "Yeah, probably not. Anyway, a demon-killing ninja won't work. Jane said it was something else. A nevilsomething."

"A nephilim?" Spare said. "Really? That doesn't make sense."

"Well, at last we agree on something."

"Nephilim are the offspring of humans and angels," Spare said. Gray was a surprised to discover Jane hadn't just made the word up. "According to the Spirit Codex, there are two breeds; the greater nephilim were giants, but since they had human mothers they were mortal, and have long since died out. The lesser nephilim were birthed by angels with female aspects. They're the most cursed beings in all of creation, born into hell though innocent of original sin. Unlike the greater nephilim, they're immortal creatures of spirit. When they come to earth, they cause a lot of grief, but they aren't powerful enough to turn into something like the Eater. This thing has to be a fallen angel."

"Whatever you say," said Gray.

"Plus, a nephilim wouldn't be able to digest the sin. Jane's wrong about this."

"Should I turn the car around?"

"No. She's probably right about the boys at midnight. The Eater kills children because they have the purest sin."

Gray glanced into the rearview mirror, trying to judge from Spare's expression if this was some sort of joke.

"Until they're old enough to know right and wrong, children possess only original sin," Spare elaborated. "This is a pure strain that runs through the mother's blood back to Eve. Sin is like caffeine in the diet of fallen angels. The Eater consumes sin to feel more powerful."

Gray really, really missed Linda. He thought of skipping the country club and taking this priest—if he really was a priest—straight to jail. On the other hand, Emma had started all this by calling in with talk about children getting killed after she'd taken Jane some dinner. Emma was the town grandmother, the one old lady that nobody talked back to. "What would Emma do?" was the town motto. He'd let Emma deal with Bill if he got any grief.

"I'm sorry for the personal question," Spare said, "but have you ever shot anyone?"

"Nope." It was actually a question Gray was asked all the time. For some reason, people thought it made good small talk with cops. "Once took a shot at this guy who was threatening his wife. Missed, luckily. His gun turned out to be empty."

"You may need those bullets tonight, Deputy. Hinako's spirit blade doesn't work on the living. As long as the Eater is inside its host, she can't touch it."

"Uh huh," said Gray, who suddenly realized there was an important step to take before he let this guy get too far from the car.

The country club was all the way on the other side of the county. Gray listened as Spare called a church in Raleigh to explain Jane's situation. Whether the guy was crazy or not, at least he was keeping his promise. Gray had a lot of respect for churches. He and Linda had been Baptists. It had been an important part of his life, once. But, with Linda gone, he no longer had the patience to go sit in a pew and listen to talk of Heaven or Hell.

It wasn't so much that he didn't believe in God. Instead, he no longer believed in souls. He'd watched Linda slip away over the course of three long weeks. She'd been unconscious, and at first, he'd held her hand and talked to her, hoping she could hear him. But, all the time, the machines she was hooked to told a different story. Her heart beat the same whether or not he was standing there telling her he was praying, or sitting across the room trying to remember how to pray. He soon realized that there was no spirit lingering over her, listening to his words. As her body died, she died, and there was nothing left behind save memory.

It was after 11:00 when they drove through the country club gates. A stream of cars was heading the other way. The party was officially over. Gray knew the mayor would be the last to leave. He'd stick around to make sure every last hand got shook.

Gray parked a fair distance from the club, near the tennis courts. He got out and opened the back door as Spare's van pulled to the curb next to them. As Spare emerged, Gray grabbed him by the arm, then slammed him up against the cruiser.

"W-what are—aaah!" Spare protested, before Gray silenced him by twisting his arm halfway up his back.

"Be quiet," Gray said. "Don't fight and this will be over in a second."

He started to pat the priest down. Sure enough, beneath his coat, he found a holster strapped to the priest's belt. He pulled the coat aside and found the holster contained a large golden crucifix.

"If you're looking for my gun, it's strapped to my ankle," said Spare.

"Oh," said Gray, bending down to search. He found the pistol, a .38 similar to his own. "Thanks," he said, taking the gun. He checked the safety, then stuck it into the waistband of his pants to free up his hands. He did a more thorough pat down, from ankle to neck. The priest now seemed clean. Spare pulled the man's wallet from his back pocket.

"Kind of odd for a man of the cloth to be packing heat, isn't it?" Gray asked, flipping through the wallet.

"There's no time for this," said Spare. "The gun is legal."

Sure enough, there was a permit from the state of Texas for the concealed carry.

"I wouldn't have pegged you for a Texan," said Gray. "Anyway, you're not in Texas now. I'll hold on to this gun the rest of the evening if that's okay by you, cowboy."

He walked over to the van. He didn't see anybody in the driver's seat. He opened the door and looked around. The back of the van was a little office in which several laptops sat open, their monitors glowing softly.

"The crucifix is all I need to get the Eater out of its host," Spare said. "The gun was just for back up. Is that a swimming pool on the other side of the tennis courts?"

The change of subject caught Gray off guard. He looked up, beyond the courts. "Yeah," he said.

"Let's go look. Jane said there was a pool."

Gray didn't see any harm in it. They walked over. There was a pool attendant wandering around picking up toys, a blonde teenage girl in a red bathing suit. The lights were still on, but a sign said the pool was closed. As he got closer Gray realized he knew the girl, Becky Sue, Fred Cole's oldest daughter.

The cement around the pool was wet with children's footprints.

"Kind of a late night for you, ain't it, Becky Sue?" Gray asked, as they walked up to the fence.

The girl looked up, startled. She relaxed when she saw Gray but looked a little bewildered when she saw the priest.

She said, "Mr. Hungerford had his grandkids with him. He paid me extra to keep the pool open so they could play."

"He spoils them boys rotten, don't he?"

"I'll say. That Tommy's a real terror. He had his Hulk hands with him and spent the better part of an hour chasing Johnny around screaming 'Hulk smash!'"

"Hulk hands?" Spare asked.

"They're toys," said Becky Sue. "Big green gloves. They go BOOM! when you whack them against something."

A knot formed in Gray's gut. Green, swollen hands, like Jane had said. But… now that he'd heard the toys described, he realized he'd seen them in stores around Christmas. Maybe Jane had been into town at some point and seen kids playing with them.

"Where are the children now?" Spare asked.

Becky Sue looked at him suspiciously.

"Are they with the mayor?" Gray asked.

"Not yet," Becky Sue said. "I sent them to the locker room to change."

"We need to talk to them," said Spare.

"Ummm," said Becky Sue.

"It's okay," said Gray.

Becky Sue tilted her head toward the locker rooms on the far side of the pool. “All right, but I’m not going into the men’s side to get them.”

Spare was already moving toward the locker room. Gray quickly followed. Spare pushed the door open and said, “Johnny? Tommy?”

No one answered. They looked around, opening each stall in the bathroom. Gray’s hands grew sweaty as each stall turned out to be empty.

Gray went back outside. “Becky Sue, the boys aren’t here.”

“Hmm,” she said. “Well, I got a call on my cell phone right after I sent them in. Could be they finished and went up to the main club.”

“Thanks,” said Gray. “Let’s go,” he said to Spare.

“You seem to have a sense of urgency now,” said Spare.

“Two kids shouldn’t be wandering around alone, that’s all.”

As they approached the main clubhouse, Gray caught a familiar scent, the medicinal stink of mentholated cigarettes. “Bill must be around somewhere.”

“Gray?” a voice answered from behind a nearby bush. Gray poked his head around the bush and found the sheriff, still in his tux, peeing against the wall of the country club.

“Dammit, can’t a man take a piss in peace anymore?” Bill grumbled. The cigarette dangling in his lips dropped a line of bright embers, which vanished as they fell.

“Don’t they have bathrooms inside?” Gray asked.

“Not where you can smoke,” the sheriff said, zipping himself up. “Damn health Nazis.” He stepped around the bush and noticed Spare. He wrinkled his brow, then said, “Pardon my language, Reverend.”

“Father Daniel Spare,” Spare said, extending a hand.

The sheriff shook it, saying, “Bill Wilson, Sheriff.”

“Jane sent us,” said Spare.

“I see,” said Bill. “What’d she tell you?”

“Crazy stuff,” said Gray.

“We think the mayor’s grandchildren are in danger,” Spare said.

Gray said, “We don’t know—”

“I saw them with the mayor not five minutes ago,” Bill said. “What’s the problem?”

“The mayor may currently be possessed by a demonic entity known as the Eater. Did he recently travel to Philadelphia?”

“Last week. Some kind of conference.”

"That's where the Eater's trail went cold. He must have made the jump then."

"What's an eater?" Bill asked.

"It eats sin by consuming the hearts of children at midnight," said Spare.

The sheriff glanced at his watch. "Shit," he said. "How do we stop it?"

"I'll need to perform an exorcism," said Spare.

Gray closed his eyes and rubbed his temples. "Don't forget about the invisible ninja."

"I'll help however I can," said the sheriff. "Still, Jane can be a little… fuzzy."

Gray was grateful for at least this mild hint of skepticism. The sheriff believed in ghosts and witches and all that crap. Gray knew that the sheriff ran up bills of $300 a month calling some Caribbean psychic from late night TV and hid the charges in the department's budget.

The sheriff said, "George is right inside with the kids. Let's go talk to him."

Inside the ballroom, the mayor was nowhere to be found. There were only a few stragglers left at the party, plus some of the waiters. They made a circuit of the room, asking if anyone had seen the mayor. No one had noticed where he'd gone.

Spare wandered around the room talking to unseen people on his headseat. "Good work," he said, a moment later.

"What?" said Gray.

"Amber's been doing a multi-database search on Mr. Hungerford. He owns a Lincoln Town Car with On-Star. We've hacked their data stream and the car is still in the parking lot."

"Is that legal?" Gray asked.

Spare ignored him. "Sheriff," he said. "Can you get the rest of your men out here? We need to do a full search of the grounds."

Bill looked at his watch. "We've only got twenty minutes. They won't get here in time."

"Take these bullets," Spare said, handing some of the blessed .38 slugs to the sheriff. The sheriff nodded. "We need to split up. It's possible the Eater is fogging people's minds." He reached into his pocket and pulled out two small wooden crucifixes on leather cords. "Wear these and you should see him."

"This is crazy," said Gray.

"Wear it," said Bill, loading his pistol.

"I don't believe in this stuff," said Gray. He wasn't an atheist, exactly, but he wasn't a believer, either. To ask him to change his entire worldview in the next twenty minutes to accept demons and holy bullets and blessed necklaces was asking too much. Still, an order was an order. He put the necklace on.

He instantly felt completely the same.

"Sheriff, take the right wing. Deputy, go left. Hinako and I will search the grounds. Use your radios if you find anything. Amber's patching me into your system."

"That's definitely illegal," said Gray.

"Hinako doesn't have a driver's license either," Spare said, sounding annoyed, "in case you want to start a list."

Gray tried to put together a snappy comeback involving how an invisible ninja probably didn't photograph well, but Spare bolted toward the front door before he could work out the quip in his head.

The sheriff darted off as well. The few people left in the room stared at Gray, murmuring. Gray went down the left hall, opening doors to meeting rooms. He felt like he was hurrying, but every time he checked his watch another minute had flown past.

He eventually made his way to the kitchen. The lights were all on. There was a radio playing, and dirty dishes were stacked in the sink, yet, curiously, the room was empty. He stepped into the kitchen, feeling a little creeped out. The room looked as if everyone had been here only a minute before, then suddenly vanished. He crept into the kitchen, his hand on his pistol. He saw that the back door was open. In the shadows beyond, he heard hushed voices.

His skin felt clammy as he inched forward. An unnamable, irrational dread possessed him. He made it a few feet from the door when he heard a soft, high-pitched giggling.

He drew his gun and stepped outside.

The three dishwashers he found there stared at Gray with wide eyes. They were all young, dark-skinned men in their teens or early twenties. One of them was smoking weed, and a fragrant cloud of smoke hung around his head. He let the joint fall from his open mouth, then held up his hands in the universal posture of surrender. The other dishwashers also held up their hands, their eyes flickering between the gun and Gray's face.

Gray clenched his jaw, feeling stupid.

He holstered his gun and drew his shoulders back. He said, in an authoritative voice, "I'll let you off with a warning this time."

The dishwashers sagged with relief. The one who'd been smoking ground the joint out with his sneaker and said, "I'll never touch it again, sir."

"Have you seen the mayor?"

The dishwashers shrugged. "I don't know the mayor," the smoker said. "I'm new in town."

Gray nodded, then went back into the kitchen. He saw the clock on the wall. 11:55. The last hour had flown by. He started to leave the kitchen when he noticed a door at the far end of the room. On a hunch, he opened it. Stairs led down to the wine cellar. A dim light gleamed on the dark bottles.

He walked down the stairs. The tension that had hung over him a moment ago now dissipated. The wine cellar was fairly large, lined with brick. The place stank like fresh urine.

He saw the boys. They were staked to the ground in the far corner, unconscious or dead. They were naked, and wet pools glistened on the ground around them. Gray reached for his gun with one hand and his radio with the other.

A loud crash deafened him as shards of glass went flying out in front of his eyes. His hair was suddenly wet and everything smelled like wine. He staggered forward, dropping the radio, his head pounding with each step, bright flashbulbs popping before his eyes. He turned around to find the mayor standing behind him, a jagged, broken wine bottle in his hands. Gray straightened up, feeling wine trickling down his spine. He raised his hand to find the gash the bottle had left in his scalp.

The mayor smiled, and said, "You've got a thick skull. I'll ride you next."

The mayor lunged toward him.

With a movement that came as gracefully as dance, Gray aimed his .38 and put a bullet into the center of the mayor's left thigh, halting his charge. When the mayor didn't fall down, Gray shot him again, catching him dead in the chest. The mayor giggled and said, "You've got good reflexes. This old shell is unpleasantly sluggish."

So Gray shot the mayor in the face. He watched as the bullet bounced off, leaving a red dent beneath the mayor's eye.

The mayor leapt, reaching for Gray's throat. The second his hands touched Gray's skin, the world began to spin, as if Gray was going to faint, until the mayor jerked back, hissing.

"This won't do at all," he said, punching Gray in the gut with superhuman strength. Gray tumbled backward, dropping his gun. He couldn't breathe. The light in the cellar was a single bulb hanging from a wire. Gray found himself staring up into it, listening to the thumping of blood in his ears. He thought of Linda, lying in the hospital with all the tubes and wires trailing from her. Did she see a light? Did she follow it? Did it lead anywhere at all?

A shadow loomed over him. The mayor brought the broken neck of the wine bottle to Gray's throat. "Here's the problem," he said. With a twist of the jagged glass, he lifted the leather cord that bore the crucifix. He cut the cord with a single snap and flicked the wooden cross to the far side of the room.

He touched Gray again, his bony fingers hard against Gray's wine-wet throat.

In the weeks it took Linda to die, Gray had pondered whether or not people had souls. Was there some life force separate from the physical world, something that could endure even as the body failed? Or was man nothing more than muscle and nerves? Now Gray learned the answer. Because you truly, painfully know you have a soul when a demon sinks its claws into it and attempts to rip it from your bones.

Gray let loose a scream that echoed around the cellar. He tried to hold onto his own body, digging his spiritual fingers into his flesh, to no avail. Everything he was, every memory, every desire, every hope and fear and shame was being dragged out of the pores of his skin and there was nothing he could do to stop it.

"In the name of Christ, I command you to halt!"

Gray snapped back into his body with a force like the world's biggest rubber band. The mayor spun around, hissing.

"You can't stop me, Spare!" the mayor snarled. "Remember Atlantic City? Remember DC?"

Gray blinked, trying to recall where he was or even who he was. He saw a man in black robes standing on the staircase, holding a golden crucifix before him. Did he know this guy? The priest began to recite a prayer in Latin.

"Ooh, the old stuff," the mayor chuckled. "I'm trembling." Then he bent over and picked up Gray's fallen pistol and took aim at the priest. "Good-bye, Spare," he said.

A shot rang out. Gray looked at his own hand, which held the pistol it had found in the waistband of his belt. Smoke poured from the barrel in a neat white thread. He dimly remembered patting the priest down, then the whole evening flashed into his mind.

The mayor fell to his knees, crying like a slapped baby. He had his hands twisted behind his back, digging at the bullet hole. He raked wildly, ripping his clothes, revealing a bloody spine and torn flesh. His hands clawed faster, throwing gore around the room. Twisted black wings sprouted from the growing wound. The mayor's arms dropped, suddenly lifeless, as the wings grew and the shadow of a human torso emerged from the mayor's own torso. The mayor fell to the floor, limp as a week-old balloon, as the Eater stood up, now free of its human host. It was shaped, more or less, like a woman, with bony hips and a leathery hide stretched so tightly you could count her ribs. Her wings spread the length of the cellar, with gray vulture feathers falling with each spasm of her body. Her hair was a tangle of thick black worms. The atmosphere stank of rotten eggs.

"Now," said Spare.

Suddenly, there was a whisper. An arc of blood cut through the air beyond the Eater's throat. The Eater's wormy hair tilted at an impossible angle, then her head fell to the ground as her body toppled. Her head landed between her still twitching feet.

"Thank you, Hinako," said Spare. "Good work."

"Yeah," said Gray, now a true believer in invisible ninjas, "thanks."

The stairs shuddered as the sheriff's heavy cowboy boots stomped down them. He almost tripped as the made it to the bottom. He stopped, putting his hands on his knees, and started coughing so hard Gray was worried he'd vomit. He'd never heard anyone breathing so hard.

"Y'all… okay?" Bill asked between gasps.

"The mayor's dead," said Gray, looking at the pale, broken body before him. There was a stench to the mayor that hinted he'd been dead a lot longer than 45 seconds.

"It looks to me like suicide," the sheriff said, casting a glance toward Spare.

"No," Spare said. "That would cause undue burden on his family."

"We'll think of something," said Bill. "How are the kids?"

Gray crawled over to the boys. To his relief, they were breathing. He checked and found pulses in their wrists.

"Amber has an ambulance on the way," said Spare. "They'll be okay. The Eater probably drugged them, but he wouldn't have given them anything that would kill them. He needed them alive."

The grandfather clock up in the main ballroom began to chime.

Spare knelt over the body of the Eater. The whole of the corpse was writhing as if being eaten from within by maggots. With a wave, the body simply fell apart, collapsing into a vaguely human-shaped pile of steaming mulch, upon which pointy orange mushrooms instantly sprouted.

"It was female," Spare said. "A fallen angel. Jane was… ah."

"Jane was what?" the sheriff asked.

"Sheriff, can you take command of the situation here? Gray and I have unfinished business to attend to."

"We do?" asked Gray.

"Jane," said Spare. "I now know how to help her."

As Gray followed Spare back to the cruiser, he caught a brief snippet of the conversation Spare was having with Amber, but wasn't sure he understood it. Why would Spare be asking her to find a phone number for a hog farm?

Forty-five minutes later, they arrived back at the swamp. As they pulled up to the RV, the cruiser's headlights revealed Jane, still wearing only her trench coat, lifting the enormous engine with her bare hands and trying to shove it back into the RV's engine compartment. A skinny woman hefting a half-ton of steel seemed almost normal to Gray, a perfectly reasonable thing to be viewing after the rest of the evening.

"It doesn't really understand machinery," Spare said, sitting in the passenger seat next to Gray.

Spare got out as Gray shifted into park.

"Jane," said Spare. "You have to come out of there."

"Leave me alone!" Jane shouted, whipping around and throwing the engine. Fortunately, a steady diet of Everclear proved to have a deleterious effect on her aim. The engine splashed into the muck ten feet to the left of Spare.

"We can do this the hard way," said Spare.

"Then do it the hard way!" she screamed, charging at him, her hands clenched into fists.

Spare pulled the golden crucifix from his holster and she skidded to a halt in front of him. Spare's van, which had taken a different path to reach the swamp, appeared at the end of the road.

Gray got out of the car with his pistol drawn.

"I've got bullets filled with holy water," he said, as Jane eyed him.

"I should have known you'd not be grateful," Jane said.

"You're wrong," said Spare. "We couldn't have caught the Eater without your help. I know why you did it."

Jane looked at him as Spare's van cast a second set of shadows behind her. "You can't send me back," she said, sounding like a little girl.

"I could," said Spare. "But I won't. I was confused by the nephilim claim. It seemed so out of character. But, when I found the Eater was a female spirit, it suddenly made sense. A nephilim would claim the Eater was one of its own kind as sort of an ego boost, a little puffery to feel like they could be as powerful as a fallen angel if they wished to be."

"We could!" Jane screamed, her hands balled into fists.

"Even so, why would a nephilim betray a fallen angel? And then, I understood. We've killed your mother."

"Good riddance!" Jane snarled. "Filthy, filthy, filthy, filthy, filthy!"

There was a movement at Gray's feet. A small pink piglet trotted past, guided by the unseen hand of a seven-hundred-year-old ninja.

"I'm not the final judge of your fate," Spare said. "I'm not going to send you back to hell. But I can't let you ride this poor woman any longer. Get in the pig."

"Never!" Jane hissed.

"It's the pig," said Spare, "or hell."

Jane fell silent, and looked at the little pink beast that drew up beside her feet.

"A pig in a nearly endless muck," said Spare. "You'll grow fat and old out here. Wallowing in mud for a decade or two has to be preferable to spending a single day in hell."

"A single second," Jane said, sagging.

Jane shuddered violently, then fell limp to the dirt. The pig squealed loudly and blazed off into the night, a pink streak. Gray ran forward and stooped beside Jane, checking for a pulse. Her eyes fluttered open as his fingers touched her neck.

She looked at him, her expression dazed and distant.

"Where am I," she asked, in a bare whisper. "What am I doing outside?"

"It's okay," said Gray. "Everything's okay."

"We're here to help you," Spare said, drawing near. "Can you remember your name?"

"Carla," she said, her eyes darting around, trying to make sense of her surroundings. "Carla Reeves."

"Welcome back, Carla," said Spare. "Amber, can you check missing persons databases for… wow. That's fast."

Carla sat up, pulling the coat around her to hide her nakedness. "I feel sick," she said.

"You've had a lot to drink," Gray said, glancing at the empty bottle of Everclear.

"Oh God, this is so embarrassing," she said. "I've never drank until I blacked out." She looked at Gray's uniform, then at Spare's clerical robes. "Is this is some kind of costume party. Oh man. I don't even know what day of the week this is."

"Friday," said Spare. "There are some very worried people back in Kansas looking for you. Let's get you into town. You could probably use a shower, a hot meal, and a good night's sleep. I'll have Hinako secure you some new clothing."

"Friday? I sort of… I sort of remember it being Saturday. Just how much did I drink?"

"Don't worry about that," said Gray, helping her to her feet. She swayed, woozy, and leaned against him for support.

Yeah, he thought, Linda would definitely have wanted to hear about this night. He helped Carla toward his squad car, repeating, "It's okay," like it was his own personal mantra. And maybe things were okay. He'd stopped telling Linda about his nights while she'd been in the hospital. What had been the point of talking to somebody no longer there?

Tomorrow, he'd take some flowers out to Linda's grave. He hadn't been there in months. He'd sit a while and talk about his crazy night. And maybe—who knows?—she'd enjoy the story.

FOR TWENTY ODD years, Bigsby the Dwarf had run a little seafood shop near the docks of Commonground. The years had been odd indeed, given the cast of scoundrels that frequented his establishment. Commonground was a lawless city, haven of pirates, abode of goblins, home to thieves and thugs. Bigsby hadn't grown wealthy serving such a clientele. Still, he scraped by, and over the years had accumulated a treasure of interesting stories to share with friends over a pint of ale.

By reputation, Bigsby was a mirthful sort, good company in a bad city. Lately, Bigsby was rarely seen at his favorite bars. He spent his evenings in his shop, sullenly chopping at blocks of ice. His lantern burned late into the night. His face took on a pale tone, his eyes lined with red.

One evening, after he'd shuttered the windows and started to work on the ice, Bigsby heard a knock. He stopped chopping.

"It can't be him," he muttered.

The knock came again, more firmly.

"Go away," he shouted. "We're closed!"

He looked at the flat surface of the ice. With his ice-pick, he drew a line across the block. Even with good winds, it took three days to sail from the Silver City. If they left on the Feast's Eve, two days ago, they couldn't have arrived yet.

Again, the knocks came, swiftly followed by a thump, then a crash, as the door came off its hinges.

In the doorway was a giant of a man. The intruder was heavily muscled and horribly scarred, with a face that looked sewn together with bits from several different people.

Bigsby opened his mouth. A squeak issued forth.

He cleared his throat.

"F-Fish?" he said. "Are you here for…?"

"I'm here for you, traitor."

Someone else had answered. Bigsby glanced away from the monster. In the doorway stood another man, hardly any taller than himself. This stranger was hunched over beneath his tattered cloak, his body bent until his head was even with his waist. The hunched man leaned on a gnarled wooden staff. Rags tightly entwined his body, concealing every inch of skin. His eyes glowed like embers beneath his dingy hood.

Bigsby wiped away the sweat stinging his eyes.

"D-Did you say… t-trader?" he asked. "T-that I am. A humble trader in—."

The hooded stranger chuckled. "You have no secrets, dear Bigsby. I call you traitor with precision. You were a traitor twenty years ago when you cruelly poisoned Lord Brightmoon. Now you contemplate the betrayal of a friend. I know of the letter."

Bigsby hadn't heard the name Brightmoon in years. He'd all but forgotten the enormous price placed on his head. Countless souls in Commonground would betray him for the money, if they knew the truth.

Bigsby narrowed his eyes. He'd killed before. It was time to kill again. With desperate speed, he flung the icepick at the brute's throat as he dove from his chair. He swiftly pulled open the drawer that held his knives. It fell to the floor in a clatter. He grabbed his sharpest, longest blade and spun to face his attackers.

He was met with a bemused chuckle from the hooded hunchback. The icepick was buried to the hilt in the brute's throat, but the brute seemed unaware of this.

"You don't know who you face," the crooked man said.

"Then enlighten me, stranger," snarled Bigsby, holding his blade so that lantern light gleamed from its razor edge.

"Hmm." The hunchback nodded. "Stranger. That will do. My silent friend goes by Patch."

Bigsby stared at Patch and at the hilt of the icepick. The man wasn't even bleeding.

Stranger stepped forward. With a terrible groan he reached his spindly arm high and grabbed the icepick, freeing it with a grunt. He lay the pick on the block of ice.

"I'm not here for the reward," said Stranger.

"You'd be disappointed," Bigsby said. "I've never poisoned anyone."

"But you did receive a letter, yes? From a man named Jack Blade. You're meeting him as early as tomorrow. He's requested you lead him and his companions to the lair of the dragon, Greatshadow."

"Don't be absurd," Bigsby said. "I-I wouldn't know how to find Greatshadow. Why would anyone think that?"

"Because you drunkenly boasted of it one night. You said you'd stumbled upon the place and found it filled with riches. You wisely fled, of course."

"Ah," said Bigsby. "Perhaps I said such a thing, once, years ago, while drunk. It isn't true."

"Just another lie in a life of lies, then? But I see you speak the truth. You don't know how to find the dragon. But you won't admit this to Jack Blade. Instead, you plan to lead him on a wild goose chase into the Blackwater Swamp."

Bigsby felt limp hearing these words. When Stranger had spouted the truth about his distant past, Bigsby assumed the man had done some careful sleuthing. When Stranger had spoken about Jack's letter, he guessed the letter had been intercepted and read. But to know about his plans to lead the others into the swamp… he'd shared this with no one. Stranger was obviously a wizard. Bigsby swallowed hard.

"It's true," he said. "But this isn't betrayal. I've heard rumors that Greatshadow lives in the swamp. We might find him."

"You might meet your death by quicksand. But you'll never find Greatshadow in the swamp. Greatshadow lives in the mountain wastelands. The path to his abode is within my very blood. I shall lead you."

"Oh," said Bigsby, biting his nails. "Good."

"You'd as soon face the swamps," said Stranger.

"I saw Greatshadow once," whispered Bigsby. "Ten years ago, when the Armada of the Silver Kingdom sailed into this bay. I was watching from the window when night seemed to suddenly fall. My shop had fallen into the dragon's shadow. He passed over the water and breathed flames. It was horrible. The whole of the ocean was ablaze. Not a ship survived. Charred, bloated bodies washed ashore for days. I'm not eager to face the beast in his lair."

"My poor Bigsby," said Stranger. "What you are eager to do is unimportant. You'll do as I tell you, or I will reveal the price on your head to every soul in this accursed city."

Bigsby stared at his knife. He'd survived some terrible scraps over the years. But what chance did he have against a wizard? He let the knife fall from his grasp.

"Curse you," he mumbled. "I'll do as you tell me."

"It's not such a bad thing," said Stranger. "I promise you Bigsby, this is no journey of self-destruction. Greatshadow will meet his end. When he does, you may leave with all the treasure you can carry. Even with your small stature, that's immeasurable wealth. The dragon has more diamonds than the mer-king has pearls."

Bigsby rubbed his chin. Certainly, a trip to Greatshadow's lair was suicide. But, just in case, he would wear pants with really big pockets.

"Let us hasten," said Stranger. "You aren't the only ally I seek tonight."

Bigsby followed the wizard through the busted doorway. Patch picked up the door and leaned it into place. Bigsby shook his head with a sigh. The broken door was the least of his worries, but he dreaded the thought of haggling with Jardon the carpenter to get it repaired. The little goblin charged as if each nail was made of gold.

STRANGER LED BIGSBY to Blackstone's Barge. The squat ship glowed upon the dark water with the light of a hundred lanterns. The drunken men shouted and women squealed as they crossed the swaying plank. Stranger pushed open the door. Thick smoke rolled forth.

Inside, Bigsby hung close to Patch. Bigsby had been tripped over by more than a few drunken fools with foul tempers. But, drunk or sober, people got out of Patch's way. They moved through the crowd without brushing against a single body.

In the far corner of the room was a rough-hewn wooden booth. Sitting in this booth was a woman Bigsby knew by reputation. Everyone called her Infidel. She was a muscular woman, with dark eyes beneath a stern brow. Her red hair was cropped close to her scalp, and black tattoos ran the length of her arms. A scar ran down her left cheek, from eye to lip.

She sat alone, carving letters into the thick oak table with a dagger as she sipped a large flagon of mead. Bigsby was a good judge of body language. This woman wasn't in the mood for company.

"Infidel," Stranger said. "Well met this evening."

She glared at him.

"What the devil are you?" she asked.

"A humble traveler, in need of your assistance."

"Right. No, seriously, what are you beneath those rags? You sure as hell ain't human. You're not a goblin, neither."

"Madam, I suffer many deformities. How unkind of you to draw attention to them."

"Bullshit," Infidel said, reaching toward Stranger's hood.

Patch caught her wrist. It looked almost accidental, as if Patch had been moving his arm in her direction on a whim and happened to meet her hand. With his fingers clamped around her wrist, her arm was immobile. She strained to pull free, but Patch didn't budge.

"Let's forget about my face, Isadora," said Stranger.

Infidel responded by using her free hand to drive her dagger deep into Patch's elbow. With a twist of the blade, Patch's hand sprung open. In an instant, Infidel flew from the booth and tackled Stranger, the dagger pressed to his throat. His hood slipped back, revealing only rags that enshrouded his face.

"Where did you learn that name?" Infidel hissed.

Before Stranger could respond, Patch leaned over and grabbed the woman by her ears. She shrieked as Patch lifted her from the floor. If Patch felt any pain from the injury to his elbow, it failed to show on his impassive face.

"A bargain, Infidel," growled Stranger, struggling to his feet. "I don't speak that name again. You don't look beneath my hood."

Infidel responded by chopping down with the dagger, burying it deep into Patch's thigh. She pulled it free and struck again, and again. Patch didn't even flinch.

Stranger chuckled.

"There's another name you'll be interested in hearing," he ventured. "Tristram Castlebridge."

Infidel raised an eyebrow as she thrust the dagger toward Stranger, who stood just beyond its tip.

"You're one of his men?"

"Hardly," said Stranger. "We plot his demise."

"You certainly know the words a woman wants to hear," she said, a sudden smile upon her lips. "Drop me."

Patch let loose of her ears and she dropped to the floor, staggering to keep her feet.

"Goddammit," she grumbled, rubbing her ears. "Where'd you pick up the big guy?"

"Patch is an old friend," said Stranger. "Several, actually."

She pulled the bent remains of a gold ring from a particularly bloody spot on her upper ear.

"You owe me a new earring," she said.

"Treasures aplenty await you," said Stranger.

"Sure. Whatever. What's with the dwarf?"

Bigsby bowed politely. "Bigsby's the name. I'm—"

"You're that fish guy," she said.

Bigsby was surprised she had ever noticed him.

"If it makes you feel any better, I didn't fare any better against Patch than you did."

"That's freaking great. Wait until word gets out I'm no better than a dwarf fishmonger in a brawl."

"Killing Tristram Castlebridge will more than assure your reputation," said Stranger.

Infidel nodded. "Let's talk more about this killing thing."

She looked around the silent room. Everyone, man, woman, and goblin, stared at them.

"Hey!" she shouted. "Mind your business! Me and my buddies are plotting a murder!"

A few of the larger men laughed, while most of the goblins in the room turned a paler blue than usual. All turned away, and soon the room was awash in voices.

"Have a seat," she said.

Stranger twisted his bent body at awkward angles, grunting as he slipped along the bench. Bigsby climbed in beside him.

"You both look like you could use a little ear-hanging from the big guy," said Infidel. "Put a few inches on you, Shorty. Maybe take the kinks out of your back, Rag-face." She raised her arms above her head and stretched, her sinews popping. "Does wonders for the spine."

"Tomorrow, or in the days soon after, a ship will arrive," said Stranger.

"Ships arrive every day," said Infidel.

"This one carries a band of adventurers."

"Tristram's one of them?"

"He leads them," answered Stranger.

"He's the bossy sort."

"They've come to kill Greatshadow."

Infidel perked up. "And we tag along to watch them die? Could be fun."

"I think they will succeed," said Stranger.

"Shyeah. Right."

"Tristram carries Frostbite."

Infidel raised an eyebrow.

Bigsby thought "carries" was a strange verb to place before the noun. What was significant about some knight missing a few toes anyway?

"Frostbite's been missing for years," said Infidel. "How'd Tristram get it?"

"Unimportant. The sword will protect Tristram from Greatshadow's flames. The dragon's skin will have no resistance to its cold bite. A single cut will freeze the dragon's blood."

"So Tristram might actually beat Greatshadow."

"He'll claim this land in the name of the Silver Kingdom," said Stranger. "I would rather this island remain under… local control. So after Tristram and his friends exhaust themselves besting the dragon—"

"We take them out," said Infidel. "Gotcha."

"Excuse me," said Bigsby. "But if this Tristram fellow is tough enough to best Greatshadow, what makes you think we're tough enough to fight him?"

"We?" said Infidel. "Don't flatter yourself. Frostbite's a good sword, yeah, but it doesn't worry me. What do you bring to the party, fishmonger?"

"Bigsby has a friend among Tristram's party."

"Jack Blade," said Bigsby. "He was kind to me when I lived in the Silver City. He helped me escape."

"Escape what?"

Bigsby clenched his fists. Stupid! Twenty years of caution thrown to the wolves.

"Taxes," said Bigsby. He grinned sheepishly.

"Yeah," said Infidel. "Taxes are a bitch."

THE SHIP SAILED into the harbor the following evening, under a Northsea flag.

"That's not a Northsea ship," said Infidel, as she, Bigsby, Stranger and Patch watched from a hill above the harbor. "Who's he fooling?"

"The dragon, possibly," said Stranger. "Ships of the Silver Armada don't have a lucky history in this port."

"It has three lanterns hanging from starboard," said Bigsby. "That's the signal."

"We'd better get a move on, then," said Infidel. "Slow as you three move, they'll be old and gray before we get down there. That'll scare Greatshadow. A bunch of toothless old men limping into his lair, waving their canes."

Bigsby thought a bunch of toothless old men would probably fare as well as anyone. He chased after Infidel as she loped down the hill. Despite her cruel humor, Bigsby felt safer near her than he did alone in the presence of Patch and Stranger.

Bigsby was out of breath by the time they made it to the docks. He looked behind him. Stranger and Patch were nowhere to be seen.

"Infidel," he called out.

She stopped and looked toward him.

"Yeah?" she asked.

"Stranger," said Bigsby, between gasps. "You trust him?"

"This some joke?"

Bigsby shook his head. "I have a rowboat. We could escape in it before Stranger finds us."

"Sounds like a plan. Go for it. But I'm sticking around. There's killing to be done."

She headed toward the ship. Bigsby looked back. Stranger could now be seen at the far end of the docks. There was still time to run. But once he made it to the boat, where would he go? He'd lived in Commonground most of his adult life. Plus, there was still Jack to consider. Bigsby could care less if Stranger and Infidel murdered Tristram, but Jack had once been his friend. It seemed only fair to warn him. Of course, if he did warn him, Stranger would know it. The bastard could read minds.

"Don't forget that," Stranger called out, now a dozen yards away.

Bigsby shook his head. Could things get any worse?

"Oh look," said Stranger, drawing beside Bigsby, his eyes fixed on the deck of the ship. "They have a Truthspeaker among them."

"Great," said Bigsby, staring at the black-robed figure on the deck. "They're even worse than mind-readers."

"Don't forget that, either," said Stranger.

FORTUNATELY, THE TRUTHSPEAKER remained on the deck of the ship as Jack Blade bounded from the gangplank to the dock. He raced forward and grabbed Bigsby by the shoulders, lifting him in the air with his embrace.

"Old friend!" he said.

"Ixnay on the endfray," whispered Bigsby. "People don't know I used to live in the Silver City."

"Understood," said Jack, setting Bigsby back on his feet. "My, the years have been, uh, years since I've seen you. Put on a little weight, I see."

"The years have been kind to you," said Bigsby. And they had. Jack had aged in twenty years. He still had the same long flowing tresses, and sported the same fancy silk cloak over his immaculate black leather armor. Bigsby could see his face reflected in Jack's polished thigh-high boots.

"Wearing clothes like that around here's asking for trouble," said Bigsby.

"Let trouble come," said Jack. "It's important to look good in public."

"You look like you're on your way to a ball instead of a dragon hunt," said Infidel.

Jack smiled. "Bigsby. You've brought friends."

"Um. Yeah. This is, uh, In—"

"Ingred," said Infidel.

"Charmed," said Jack.

"Whatever," Infidel replied.

"And this," said Bigsby, "is Patch."

Jack looked at the hulking figure, and managed a smile. "A pleasure," he offered.

"Finally," said Bigsby, motioning toward the robed hunchback, "this is, uh, Stranger."

Jack's smile wavered a little as he studied Stranger's ragged form.

"I'm not a leper, if that's what you're thinking," said Stranger.

"Jack!" A voice thundered down from the deck. A silver-haired man clanked down the gangplank, his armor gleaming red in the fading sunlight. Without introduction, Bigsby knew this to be the famed knight Tristram Castlebridge. It was clear from the steely gleam in his eyes, the noble thrust of his chin, and the frost-encrusted scabbard that hung from his waist. Plus the name "Castlebridge" was stitched in gold thread around the hem of his flowing purple cloak.

"Is this the fellow you spoke of?" asked Tristram.

"May I introduce you to Bigsby, the Fish Baron of Commonground."

Infidel snickered.

Tristram cast his gaze upon her. She stared back. He looked down at Bigsby.

"Is she with you?"

"Yes," Bigsby said. "I thought an extra blade might come in handy."

"It confirms all I've heard about Commonground," said Tristram, "that the best man you could find for the job is a woman."

Bigsby dared a glance toward Infidel. She didn't have her hand upon her sword.

"I also brought Patch." He gestured toward the monster behind him.

"Beefy fellow, aren't you?" said Tristram.

Patch stared silently, as flies crawled about his face.

The hunchback stepped forward. "And I am Stranger."

"I see," said Tristram.

Stranger said, "Bigsby has told me of your desire to rid the land of Greatshadow. I share your desire. I know I am nothing but a withered old man, but I beg you to allow me to accompany you. I speak the language of every tribe upon this island, even the Dragontongue."

"Hmm," said Tristram. "That could be useful."

"Tristram!"

It was a deep, booming voice that called out the knight's name. It was like the voice of thunder, the voice of the heavens. Down the gangplank strode a man in a black cotton robe, a thick, gilt-edged book held in his right hand, a jagged, rust-spotted scythe carried in his left.

"Thomas," said Tristram. "Good of you to join us. This is Jack's friend Bigs—"

"Can you think of any reason for me to know the names of this lot?" interrupted Thomas.

Tristram seemed to flinch at the question.

"You there." Thomas the Truthspeaker extended a long, bony finger toward Bigsby.

The dwarf looked into the man's dark eyes, like pools of ink with little pearls gleaming in them. He felt faint.

"Yes, sir?" he asked.

"Why do you offer your services to us? Answer truthfully!"

Bigsby tried to lie. Because I humbly wish to be of service to your noble cause. His heart skipped a beat. Because I can think of no greater duty… he couldn't complete the thought. It felt as if the Truthspeaker's bony fingers had reached into his chest and gripped his heart.

"Because we seek to enrich ourselves with the dragon's treasure when you perish!" Bigsby blurted out.

"Hah!" laughed Tristram. "This quest will not end with our deaths, but with the dragon's! You have too little faith in us, dwarf."

The Truthspeaker smiled. The expression didn't suit him. "Let us have an understanding. We will tolerate your heathen presence, as well as this band of rabble you've gathered, because we need your knowledge. In return, we shall provide you a modest share of the dragon's wealth. There is no need for you to like us, and no need for us to like you."

"Wow," said Infidel. "It's like I think it and you say it."

"In our kingdom," said the Truthspeaker, "women speak only when spoken to."

"Not your kingdom," said Infidel.

"Since you choose to dress like a man, you can help unload the ship. You also," Thomas commanded, pointing toward Patch.

Stranger nodded. Patch lumbered forward. Infidel stood silent for a moment, her hand edging closer to her sword. Then, with a shrug, she headed up the gangplank.

THE CARAVAN OF ADVENTURERS left at dawn, while the cutthroats of Commonground were still sleeping off the previous night's revelries. This was Bigsby's favorite time of day. Usually by now he'd been working for a few hours, and would take a moment at daybreak to step outside his shop and watch the sun come up at the mouth of the bay. He would smoke his pipe and listen to the gulls and be filled with a tremendous sense that all was right with his world. He wondered if he would ever feel that way again.

Commonground was a long city, but a narrow one. It stretched for miles along the hilly shores of the bay, but once one ventured over those hills, even the half-hearted pretense of civilization was left behind. Commonground was located on the southeastern shore of a large island marked on most maps as the Isle of Fear. Bigsby had never much worried about what lay beyond the hills of Commonground. Now, he was being forced to think about it by another one of Jack's companions, a man named Magidance, who'd made his appearance only moments before they'd departed.

"...Wildcats, wolves, and wyverns," finished Magidance, who'd spent the last several minutes counting off the various threats that lay before them, starting with, "Ants: giant, man-eating."

The band of treasure seekers marched at a vigorous pace. Bigsby struggled to keep stride with Infidel, but kept slipping behind, to find himself once more within earshot of Magidance at the rear of the party.

"Seventy-three species capable of killing a man," said Magidance.

"If you're so worried, why are you here?" Bigsby asked.

Magidance shrugged. "I may have been drinking a little when Jack talked me into this."

Bigsby couldn't guess why Jack had recruited such a sickly looking fellow. Magidance was a pale, scrawny man, with bags under his eyes and thinning hair. He was armed only with a dagger, and Bigsby wondered if even the dagger was too much for him to handle.

The rest of the Jack's companions looked brawnier, consisting of a half dozen men-at-arms with well-kept weapons, and another ten burly men brought along to carry gear.

"Shame we can't have horses," sighed Magidance. "How long did you say this would take? Are we close?"

"We haven't traveled an hour!" said Bigsby.

"Horses are particularly favored by dragons," said Magidance. "Domestic animals are plump and slow compared with a dragon's normal fare. That's the real reason people haven't settled here. Dragon's don't give a damn about people as food, but civilization is built on livestock. I'll bet there are no cheese shops in Commonground."

"The goblins make a kind of cheese from the milk of cave goats," said Bigsby. "It's seasoned with the husks of firespiders."

"Sounds intriguing. I suppose I'd try it. I'll put anything in my mouth at least once. When I was up north, I had some fantastic cheese in a village of the snowmen. It was made from whale's milk of all things, and was half-transparent, like ice riddled with air. Master Solodon wouldn't touch the stuff. Said it smelled like rotten teeth. It did, I suppose. But it was salty on the tongue, like anchovies."

"Solo ... did you say Solodon?" asked Bigsby.

"As in 'the Great and Wondrous Master of Mysteries Solodon,'" said Magidance. "Formerly master of me, as well. I apprenticed with him."

"You? You're a wizard?"

"Not according to Thomas the Truthspeaker. He says I'm a thrice-damned liar who shouldn't be suffered to live. Fortunately, he gave Tristram his word he wouldn't kill me."

"Why does he think you're a liar? Aren't you a real wizard?"

"Magic is nothing but a lie you tell the universe," said Magidance. "The trick is to make the universe believe it. Truthspeakers and wizards are eternal enemies. But dragon hunts make for strange alliances."

"Thomas seems like a very mean man," said Bigsby. By now he and Magidance had fallen far enough behind that they could speak freely, though not so far back that they couldn't dash for the safety of the group should a strange growl come from the bushes.

"Thomas is a very righteous man," said Magidance. "As was Solodon. Only someone with weak morals could see them as mean."

Bigsby frowned. He had expected a sympathetic ear, not a scolding.

"Perhaps it's true," said Magidance, with a shrug. "There may be a Hell, and it may be my fate. Better than sharing Heaven with that bastard, eh?"

A scream came from the trail ahead.

Bigsby ran toward the safety of the larger party. He could see one of the carriers thrashing about on the ground, as Infidel dove into the tall grass.

"Snakebite!" someone shouted.

Magidance ran past Bigsby, trailing a stream of obscenities.

"Got it!" yelled Infidel. She stood. On the end of her dagger writhed a yard long white snake with black stripes.

"I didn't hear 'zebra snakes' in your list," Jack said to Magidance.

Magidance fell to his knees beside the snakebite victim. He produced a small sack from his cape. The bitten man thrashed about, screaming between gasps.

"Hold him!" Magidance shouted.

Jack and two other men grabbed the man's flailing limbs, pinning them.

Magidance pulled the tiny, toothful jawbone of a snake from his pouch. He pressed this into the man's flesh above the wound, then below, all the while humming rhythmically. He then blew a pinch of white powder into the man's eyes. The man cried in pain, then fell still and silent.

"Not even noon and we've lost a man," complained Tristram.

"He'll live," said Magidance. "I've cured worse."

"Will he be able to travel?" asked Thomas.

"Not soon. He'll sleep the rest of the day. Tomorrow, he'll be too weak to walk. But in a week, he should be good as new. If we take him back to the ship—"

"No," said Tristram. "We'll set up a tent here. Leave him food and water. We journey on."

"Leave him? Alone?"

"He won't stand a chance out here," said Bigsby. "There are monsters about. Man-eaters!"

"All the more reason for haste," said Tristram. "It would slow us to carry him."

"Sir," said Magidance. "Perhaps we could –"

"Enough!" said Thomas, in a tone that silenced even Tristram. He knelt beside the now peaceful form of the victim. "This isn't open to debate. I've known this man since he was a boy. His name is Pious, and he is a good and faithful servant. He deserves the best possible fate."

Thomas cradled Pious in his arms. Bigsby could see better now. Pious was a young man, barely old enough to shave. His face was angelic in slumber.

"Wake," said Thomas.

Pious stirred, his eyelids fluttering open.

"You have lived well," said Thomas, bending to place a kiss upon the young man's brow. "You are welcomed home."

As he said this, a breeze stirred the tall grass and wispy clouds dimmed the sun. A chill ran down Bigsby's spine. Pious closed his eyes. His chest fell still. Thomas looked up with a dreamy smile.

Magidance swayed as if about to faint.

"You …," whispered Magidance. "You killed him."

"I saved him," said Thomas.

Magidance started to speak, then stopped. He stood trembling, his hands in tight fists. He turned, his face red, and stomped away. As he passed by Bigsby he mumbled, in continuation of his list, "Zealots."

IN THE FOLLOWING DAYS, the pretense that Bigsby was guiding the party grew thin. Whenever directions were asked,

Stranger would be the one to jump in with an answer. Bigsby never even approached the front with Stranger, Tristram, and Thomas. Instead, he stayed as far away from them as possible, at the rear of the party, usually in the company of Magidance, and now Infidel, who seemed to enjoy Magidance's dry humor. If she did enjoy it, she was in luck, for Magidance seldom shut up.

Magidance carried a folded leather map that he made notes on as they traveled.

"Most maps in refer to this as the Isle of Fear, though some still call it the Isle of Fire. The coast is mapped reasonably well, but the interior is all guesswork. I did find a five-hundred-hundred-year old atlas that called this place Myhryrha, which is an oldtongue word for wine. It showed several fair-sized cities on this island. That's the real reason I agreed to come. The thought of finding the ruins of a lost civilization. That's the sort of stuff that gets your name remembered through the ages."

"I've heard goblins speak of hidden cities," said Bigsby.

"Hell, I've been to three of them," said Infidel. "Me and Boggy McBee used to do a little tomb scavenging. I gave it up, though. Too much digging, not enough gold."

The talk of lost cities caught Bigsby's imagination. Every shadow in the forest, every strangely shaped rock, hinted that they passed through ancient ruins.

The land gave his imagination plenty to work with. This was rocky ground, with huge stones the size of houses all around. Ahead, low mountains loomed, their round peaks gleaming domes of white stone.

On the evening of their ninth day of travel, as they journeyed around the base of a stony mountain, the air filled with an incredible stench. Stranger led them to the source of the smell. It was an enormous turd, the size of a small horse, black with flies.

"We're near," said Stranger.

Magidance stepped closer to the dragon dropping, carrying a small glass dish.

"My God," he said, brushing away flies and scooping some of the brown-green excrement into the dish. "On the mage markets dragon's dung sells for its weight in gold. It's useful for an invisibility spell. This alone covers the cost of our trip."

"We've not come this distance to content ourselves with dung," said Tristram.

"We should leave," said Stranger. "The goblins who live nearby will be drawn to the smell. They use the dung for—Aanh!"

Stranger fell forward, a small, rough-hewn arrow jutting from his back.

Suddenly, the air was filled with high-pitched trills and the whistling of hundreds of arrows. All around Bigsby, men began to fall. Fortunately, Tristram stood between him and the brunt of the attack. The arrows bounced harmlessly from Tristram's gleaming armor. Magidance, meanwhile, had taken shelter behind Patch, who stood stoically as arrows sank into his broad chest. Magidance shouted words in a language Bigsby had never heard. A strong wind swept up behind them, blowing the poorly made arrows back in the direction they had come. Tristram ran forward, sword drawn.

From behind rocks and shrubs, Bigsby could now see the dirty blue faces of dozens of goblins. Bows were thrown to the ground and jagged blades drawn as the goblins readied for hand-to-hand combat.

Tristram, Jack, and Infidel were upon them in seconds, their swords biting into goblin bone with each hack. Thomas joined in, swinging his scythe in a wide arc, liberating heads from their torsos.

In less than a minute the battle ended, with a score of goblins dead on the ground and the rest vanished into the sheltering brush.

Jack knelt over one of the bodies left behind.

"Look at this," he said, holding up a small shield.

"Dragon hide," said Magidance when he saw the finely scaled skin that covered the shield. "Where would—"

"The dragon keeps a harem of young female dragons," said Stranger, through teeth gritted with pain. Patch stood by him now, helping him back to his feet. The bloody arrow yanked from Stranger's back was still in Patch's hand. "Greatshadow kills them after they first give birth, before they grow old and powerful enough to challenge him. He tosses their bodies, and the helpless male chicks, into a deep gorge not far from here. Female chicks are allowed to live, for his future pleasure. The goblins must raid the gorge for the bodies."

"Then we're near," said Tristram.

"With a brisk march, we could be at his lair in less than an hour," said Stranger.

"Stay away from him!" shouted Infidel.

All eyes turned to see the female warrior with dagger drawn, standing between the Thomas the Truthspeaker and one of the carriers, who lay bleeding on the ground.

"I'll not stand by and witness another act of mercy on your part," Infidel said, her eyes narrow slits.

"You will not stand at all," Thomas said. He stretched his arm toward her and commanded in a rumbling voice, "On your knees!"

Infidel's body swayed drunkenly. Her knees bent, her legs trembled, but she did not kneel.

"Your resistance prolongs the inevitable," said Thomas.

Infidel staggered forward, her dagger rising toward the holy man's throat.

"Halt!" Thomas thundered.

Infidel jerked like a dog reaching the end of its leash. Sweat poured down her face.

"You cannot win this fight," Thomas said. "I see into your very soul."

Infidel growled, as she moved her limbs in spastic jerks. A trickle of blood flowed from her mouth.

"Your bravado masks the heart of a frightened girl," Thomas said, his voice calm. "I see a great shame within you. There have been times when you've contemplated taking a dagger to your own throat. No doubt, that would be for the best."

Infidel grunted as her dagger moved toward to her throat.

"No!" Bigsby cried out. He ran forward, his knife drawn, and plunged his blade into the Truthspeaker's thigh.

Thomas fell backwards, knocking Bigsby to the ground.

Infidel fell, limp as a puppet with its strings cut.

Bigsby struggled from beneath Thomas, only to find a hand on the back of his neck. He was lifted from the ground, dangling in the grip of Tristram.

"Traitorous wretch," Tristram snarled. "You cannot strike a holy man in my presence and live!"

Thomas struggled back to his feet with the help of one of the men-at-arms. He faced Bigsby. His eyes once more looked like inky pools of night.

"I can see into you now," said Thomas. "Your cowardly attack has revealed your true nature. There is a terrible sin in your past. Confess!"

"Ahhhn!" Bigsby bit his lip to silence himself, but it was to no avail. His mouth moved against his will.

"It's true! Ahhhhhhh! Oh, God. I poisoned Lord Brightmoon! Nnnnah!"

"Truly?" said Tristram. He tossed Bigsby roughly to the ground. "Then I won't break your neck after all. It would be rude to deprive Brightmoon's son of the pleasure."

Tristram looked toward one of the henchmen. "Tie him up. And the woman."

But when they looked to where Infidel had fallen, she was gone.

"How shocking to learn the truth about one's companions," said Stranger with a sigh.

Jack Blade turned his face away as Thomas looked in his direction.

"Three hours," said Tristram, looking toward the darkening sky. "Very well. We make camp here. The goblins should be too frightened to return, and the stench of his own dung should keep the dragon from catching our scent. We'll leave for our assault on the dragon come daylight, with every able-bodied man. And Thomas?"

"Yes?"

"Allow Magidance to tend to the wounded. Your wound as well."

"As you wish," said Thomas with a nod and a scowl.

THAT NIGHT, BIGSBY sweltered in the heat of his tent. The stench of the nearby dung stung his eyes until tears rolled down his cheeks. He couldn't wipe them away. His hands were bound behind his back with a stout rope, making it impossible to lay comfortably. He couldn't have slept anyway. After all these years, his secret was out. His future led to the gallows.

From outside the tent, there was a faint groan. The flap of the tent was lifted, allowing cool air to flow over Bigsby.

"Stay quiet," whispered Infidel. She crawled forward and cut the ropes that bound him.

He rolled onto his back, rubbing his wrists. Infidel was already slipping from the tent. Bigsby hurried after her.

Outside, he couldn't see her. At his feet lay one of Tristram's men, his throat slit.

Infidel's hand fell upon his shoulder. She dragged him into the bushes. They traveled for several minutes across the rocky ground, before Infidel motioned for him to stop.

"I won't lie to you," she said. "We're probably going to die."

"I'm a dead man anyway, if I fall into their hands."

"I have to go back," Infidel said. "Steal what I can. We won't make it far with only the clothes on our backs."

Bigsby nodded. Then he asked, "Why did you save me?"

"Did you really kill Lord Brightmoon?"

"Yes," said Bigsby quietly. "My father was his cook. Lord Brightmoon was a cruel man. He would have my father beaten for the smallest trifles. 'this soup scalded my tongue! Have the chef beaten.' 'this ham is too salty! Have the chef lashed.'"

Bigsby looked down at his hands. "My father was younger than I am now, but his hair was gray, and his face lined with wrinkles. Lord Brightmoon was killing him one day at a time. When I began my apprenticeship, I returned the favor, and poisoned the bastard."

Bigsby began to weep.

Infidel lowered her head.

"My father paid the price for my sin," said Bigsby. "When I fled, I left a note confessing… no, boasting of my crime. I later learned they executed my father anyway. I… maybe I do deserve to hang."

"No," said Infidel. "I witnessed Tristram's reaction to the news. He was gleeful, laughing. Lord Brightmoon's death brought Tristram closer to the throne. But the hypocrite was all tears and sobs at the funeral. God, even then he was a bastard."

Bigsby wiped his cheeks. "You knew Tristram?"

"Worse," Infidel said. "I loved him."

Bigsby sniffled, and stared at the muscular, tattooed woman before him. He didn't know what to say.

"I was born into wealth," Infidel said. "My father was an advisor in Tristram's court. I was a stupid little girl who imagined that when I grew up, I would win Tristram's heart."

Infidel sighed.

"When I was thirteen, Tristram returned from battle. After the death of Brightmoon, there had been a minor uprising in the southern provinces. Tristram had been gone for a year, helping to suppress the uprising.

"I was warned," said Infidel. "Some of the older girls told me that when Tristram returned from battle he carried a terrible temper, that he could fly into brutal rages.

"I was pleased by this. If the other women avoided Tristram, I would have a chance. I'd let him see that I was different, that I would love him even in his darkest moments."

Infidel rose from the rock she was sitting on. She stalked to a nearby tree, and sunk her dagger into it with an overhand thrust.

"I waited in his chambers, only to talk. And the bastard attacked me," she said, her face turned from Bigsby. "He beat me with his fists, kicked me when I fell, and laughed at my tears. The servants pulled me from the room more dead than alive. When my father learned of the attack, he was furious. Not at Tristram, but at me. He said I deserved it for startling Tristram in the privacy of his quarters. He banished me to a nunnery."

She looked at Bigsby, shrugging. "It didn't take. I fled the nunnery. I've spent the rest of my life on the road."

"I'm sorry," said Bigsby.

"Don't be," said Infidel. "I understand Tristram now. I understand the deep satisfaction of violence. That rush of power that comes when the sword leaves my scabbard. That electric thrill when I see my opponent's blood. It's better than sex. Tristram made me who I am. I can't wait to thank him properly."

Bigsby didn't know what to say to this.

"A touching tale," said a voice from the darkness.

Two shadows moved toward them, resolving into Stranger and Patch. Patch tossed two packs onto the ground.

"You'll never make it back to Commonground without supplies," said Stranger. "Not that reaching Commonground will do you much good. You'll both be fugitives, and where will you go when even Commonground can't hide you?"

"We'll survive," said Infidel.

"You can do much more than survive," said Stranger. "You can triumph. You can perform the duties you agreed to, and kill Tristram once he kills the dragon."

"I used to stay up nights dreaming about killing Tristram," said Infidel. "But now…? Now I'd really like to kill that damn Truthspeaker."

"I don't want to kill anybody," said Bigsby. "I just want my life back."

"If none of Tristram's party survives, your secret is safe," said Stranger.

"But Jack… and Magidance…"

"They stood by you earlier, eh?" said Stranger.

"I'm in," said Infidel.

"I guess I have no choice," said Bigsby.

"Follow me," said Stranger.

They marched through the darkness for an hour. Stranger led them to a small cave and told them to rest while they could.

"From here, you can watch the entrance to Greatshadow's lair. Once Tristram's party enters, you must follow swiftly. Have no fear of being seen. Tristram and his men will be too focused on what's before them to worry about what's behind them."

"Patch and I will be with Tristram. After the battle, his men should be no match for Patch. Tristram himself may be another matter. But I have faith in you, Infidel."

"What about Thomas and Magidance?" asked Infidel. "How do we counter their magic?"

"Should they survive Greatshadow, I will handle them," said Stranger.

"What about me?" asked Bigsby. "I'm no match for any of them."

"You did well enough striking Thomas from behind," said Stranger.

BIGSBY WAS WIDE-AWAKE when dawn came. Infidel had slept a little, but stirred as light seeped into the cave. Across a rocky valley they could see a huge gash in the mountain's face. Bones lay in great heaps at the entrance.

Before the mists of morning burned away, Tristram and his men appeared. Tristram led the way, followed by five men-at-arms bearing spears and shields. Thomas, Stranger, and Magidance followed with Patch shuffling behind.

Searching the shadows, Bigsby spotted Jack Blade, well in front of the others, creeping among the bone mounds at the lair's mouth.

Stranger cast a single glance their way, and nodded. Infidel slipped from the small cave and crouched behind a boulder. Bigsby followed.

A moment later, Infidel peeked around the rock.

"They're almost there," she whispered. "Can't see Jack. Must be inside. C'mon."

Infidel scrambled across the rocky ground, keeping low. Bigsby breathed deep to gather his courage and chased after her. Quicker than he would have liked, they reached the bone field. Up close, the jagged rock revealed itself to be covered with intricately carved demons. Stairs were cut into the rock, leading into darkness.

"I've seen carvings like this before, when we robbed the tomb of Kuranath," said Infidel. "This place was a temple."

Without waiting for Bigsby's reply, she raced up the steps, staying close to the wall. She motioned for him to follow.

As he reached the top step, Bigsby caught his breath. He could see himself reflected in the floor. For as far as he could see, the floor was made of seamless, gleaming silver. The room was enormous, hundreds of yards deep with a ceiling that vanished into shadows high overhead. From cracks in the rock, shafts of light pierced the darkness.

In the distance, the room held more stairs, rising into an immense, shadowy chamber. Tristram and his men gathered at the foot of the steps. Jack was near the top step, moving cautiously.

Infidel grabbed Bigsby and dragged him into a niche in the wall. She held a finger to her lips.

Jack crept forward into shadows.

Then a scream, abruptly halted, echoed through the chamber. Tristram and his men readied their weapons. Jack's head came bouncing down the stairs.

From the shadows emerged a strange creature, almost human, but taller than Patch. It had four arms, each carrying a sword of flame. It wore armor that glowed red as if fresh from the forge.

"Run!" shouted Magidance.

Tristram's men hurled their spears. One missed, clattering on the gleaming steps. The other four spears crumbled to ash as they touched the glowing armor.

"Halt!" cried Thomas, motioning toward Magidance. The wizard's legs stiffened and he tumbled, skidding across the polished floor.

"Fool!" screamed Magidance. "That's a godslayer! A soldier of the wars between Heaven and Hell! We cannot best it."

Tristram's men looked like they had doubts as well. They drew swords, but crept backwards as the godslayer stepped toward them.

Thomas alone held his ground.

"I fear thee not, Devil!"

The godslayer raised a sword overhead, preparing to strike the Truthspeaker who strode boldly forward.

"You are an abomination," cried Thomas, holding his holy book before him.

The godslayer staggered backwards, as if struck a powerful blow.

"An obscenity!" shouted Thomas.

Again, the Godslayer was thrust backwards. It spun about, and fell to one knee.

"Accursed soul!" Thomas raised his scythe over his head. His body glowed with brilliant blue light. He brought the scythe down with all his might, into the center to the godslayer's breastplate.

A crack of thunder shook the chamber. The godslayer's armor and weapons shattered, falling in jagged shards. Naked now, the godslayer was revealed as a bronzed-skinned, well-muscled youth, with golden hair and a serene smile. Bigsby couldn't help but notice the creature also had the longest penis he'd ever seen.

The tip of Thomas' scythe rested against the creature's chest, but had not scratched it. With a grunt, Thomas raised his scythe to strike again.

Still smiling serenely, the godslayer grabbed the fallen spear from the steps. With a single motion, he brought the tip of the spear up to the Truthspeaker's belly. Thomas cried out, his body rising from the floor, his scythe clattering to the ground.

"Now!" cried Tristram.

His five men charged, swords raised against the godslayer. The smiling devil kicked out at the first to reach him, catching him firmly in the chest. The man's sword flew from his grasp as he fell. With a graceful sweep of his lower left arm, the godslayer plucked the sword from the air and used it to sever the head of the second man-at-arms. As the man fell, his sword, too was captured. In a blur of motion, the four-armed youth waded forward, killing two more men before Bigsby could blink, and arming himself with their swords. The final man gave a panicked cry and fell forward, his sword thrust with both hands toward the godslayer's chest. The godslayer danced aside, slow by a second. The man's sword drew a thin red gash across the devil's ribs. The godslayer repaid the scratch with a dozen savage blows that tore the man to bits.

Bigsby limbs felt like lead. He watched helplessly as the godslayer descended the steps.

Only Tristram, Stranger, and Patch remained standing. Magidance tried desperately to regain his footing, slipping and sliding across the gleaming floor in his panic.

Tristram pulled Frostbite from its scabbard. Impossibly, a gentle snow began to fall inside the chamber. Bigsby's breath suddenly came out in clouds.

"I see you can bleed," said Tristram, addressing the godslayer while tightening his grip on his shield.

The four-armed devil leapt forward in a whirl of blades. Tristram grunted as two of the blades fell against his shield, while another slipped harmlessly across his breastplate. The godslayer's final sword was parried by Frostbite. The blade iced over. The godslayer struck again, and again Tristram blocked the blows. This time, the impact of the godslayer's attack caused the blade touched by Frostbite to shatter.

The godslayer's brow furrowed as he glanced at the now bladeless hilt held in his upper right arm.

Tristram attacked, driving Frostbite's tip into the creature's chest. The godslayer drew a sharp breath of pain and raised his lower right arm, bringing his blade up under Tristram's armpit, slipping it between the joints in his armor.

Tristram cried out and fell back, his sword-arm useless at his side. Frostbite hung for a second in the godslayer's chest, then slipped out and clattered noisily at his feet. A crust of red ice quickly sealed over the wound.

Stranger motioned toward Patch.

"Goddammit," grumbled Infidel, rushing from the shadows.

The godslayer struck at Tristram, more savagely than before. Tristram's shield splintered, and one of the beast's blades cut a deep gash into Tristram's neck. Tristram staggered backwards, his hand over the gash. He turned to flee, but the godslayer kicked out, tripping him.

The godslayer readied to deliver the killing blow. Before he could strike, Patch reached him, landing a solid punch to his nose.

The creature looked bewildered, as if he hadn't noticed the huge man. Patch struck him once more, causing a trickle of blood to run from his nose.

The godslayer struck with his remaining blades, piercing the patchwork man, then twisting the swords with a growl.

Patch's torso came free of his legs. He fell forward, locking his hands around the godslayer's neck as his legs stumbled away.

The godslayer began to spin around, hacking at Patch's arms. On his third rotation, Patch's torso and left arm flew free, leaving only his right hand around the godslayer's neck.

And then Infidel reached the godslayer.

She used her momentum to slide forward, between the godslayer's legs. As she passed, she grabbed his manhood with both hands. She stood suddenly, yanking with all her might, and the four-armed devil fell forward.

Infidel released her grip on the godslayer's member and drew a sword in one hand, a dagger in the other. As the godslayer hit the ground, she struck, drawing each blade across the creature's hamstrings. The godslayer rolled to his back, his legs useless as he raised himself on two arms. He still carried a sword in each of his free hands, and used these to strike at Infidel, the blades flashing in silvery arcs.

Infidel easily avoided the blades, then leapt forward, dropping her dagger, thrusting her sword with both hands into the godslayer's throat. She used her momentum to vault over the creature, as the tip of her blade dug ever deeper, nearly twisting his neck from his body.

The godslayer fell limp, a bubble of red blood rising from his lips. Infidel kicked at his head, then kicked again, and again. The head tore free, rolling across the floor to where Magidance had fallen. The mage was now nowhere to be seen.

"Heh," snickered Infidel, wiping her mouth. "Heh heh heh."

She walked to Tristram. He was alive, still conscious, but his life seeped between his fingers with each heartbeat.

Infidel knelt over him.

"Hey," she said, touching his cheek. "The name Isadora mean anything to you?"

Tristram stared at her, his eyes wide with confusion.

"No?" she said. "Hell, why should it?"

Then Tristum stiffened. His lips moved, forming the words, "My God."

"I've hated you for so long," she said, her voice trembling. "So do I kill you now? Or do I sit and watch the life drain from you? What will give me the most satisfaction?"

The decision was never made. A roar rumbled through the chamber. Infidel vanished in a rolling wall of flame. Bigsby felt himself pushed from his feet by an unseen hand. The weight of a man fell upon him, as flame roared above his head. Strangely, he felt no heat. Indeed, he felt as if he'd been plunged into ice water.

"Remain silent," whispered Magidance, unseen. The weight rolled from Bigsby's chest.

As the flames receded, Bigsby could see the smoldering remains of Infidel, still kneeling over the blackened corpse of Tristram. Stranger alone survived, standing calmly as his robes burned.

From the chamber beyond came Greatshadow.

Bigsby wet himself.

The dragon was impossibly large, having to crouch in order to slither into the enormous room. Greatshadow's skin was black with soot. The stench of sulfur filled the air. The dragon spoke, in a language Bigsby had never heard, yet understood instantly.

"Bold fool," Greatshadow growled, drawing his head near Stranger. "Do you know what you've cost me? Centuries. Three centuries of incantations are needed to enslave a godslayer. I'm pleased you survived. Your crime deserves a long, painful punishment."

Stranger pulled away the last of his charred rags and padding. He stood revealed, a dragon seven feet long from snout to tail, with a red scaly hide and a pair of wings upon his back, one twisted at an unnatural angle.

"You made my life a long, painful punishment," said Stranger. "From the day you plucked me from my mother's womb and threw me still wet into the gorge."

"Bigsby," whispered Magidance. Bigsby glanced over his shoulder to see the wizard, Frostbite in his grasp. "We can still snatch victory from the jaws of defeat. This land shall belong to the Silver Kingdom. Our fate rests in your hands."

Magidance held the enchanted blade toward him.

"Take this. While Stranger distracts Greatshadow, you must strike swiftly."

"But—"

"There is no time for debate," said Magidance. "I have transferred my invisibility and can hide you as you approach. You must do this, Bigsby."

"But—"

"Hurry. At this distance, dragons read thoughts. Shielding our minds weakens me with each second. Hurry!"

Bigsby took the sword. Instantly, he realized Magidance was right. The sword filled him with power, gave him strength and courage. A single blow, it whispered to him, and I will rob Greatshadow of his fire.

Bigsby stalked forward, the sword gripped in both hands.

"You amuse me, little Brokenwing," said Greatshadow. He pushed Stranger to the ground and pinned him with a single claw. Stranger kicked and bit, to no avail.

Bigsby reached Greatshadow. The dragon crouched in such a way that Bigsby could strike at the beast's throat just above the chest.

The sword whispered to him, filling him with cold resolve. He would kill Greatshadow, and liberate the land from his fiery rule.

With a gasp, Bigsby dropped the sword, and cried out, "Greatshadow!"

Across the room, Magidance toppled to the ground, unable to shield Bigsby further.

The enormous dragon snaked its head around. Now that he no longer held Frostbite, Bigsby could feel the furnace-like heat of Greatshadow's breath.

Greatshadow stared right through him.

"Hmmm," Greatshadow said. "Perhaps the blade would have killed me after all. You believed it could, at least."

"Take it," said Bigsby. "Destroy it. It's the only threat you face. All I ask is that you allow us to leave."

"You are in no position to ask anything of me," said the dragon.

"No," said Bigsby.

"But you don't have enough meat on you to be worth eating," said Greatshadow. "Go. Take this failure with you."

He rolled Stranger over on his belly, and twisted the disfigured wing, breaking the bones with a sickening snap. Stranger squealed. Greatshadow flicked his claw, sending the small dragon skidding.

"Little Brokenwing," Greatshadow growled. "A life of pain awaits you, if you flee this island. But should you choose to remain here beyond the dawn of the third day, I will find you, and grant you swift death."

Bigsby ran to help Stranger to his feet.

"Yes, Father," said Stranger, between gasps of pain as he rose.

Bigsby helped support Stranger as they limped from the ancient temple. On the steps, drenched in sweat, Magidance waited.

"Well, that was just great," he said. He spat in Bigsby's direction. "We were so close, and you chickened out."

"I found my courage," said Bigsby. "I won't ask you to understand my reasons. Now, will you help me? We have three days to get Stranger off this island."

"Not Stranger," the small dragon said. "He gave me my name. I am Brokenwing."

Magidance looked the dragon over.

"Hmm," he said, gently touching the damaged wing.

Brokenwing winced.

"I think I can set this to heal properly," said Magidance. "And I know places to hide you until you grow stronger."

"You would help me?" asked Brokenwing.

"How many chances will I get to study a live dragon up close? We'll never make it back to Commonground in three days, though."

"We can make it to the Red River by nightfall," said Brokenwing. "We can build a raft and let it carry us to the sea."

"What about the men we left in camp?"

"They're too far away to reach and still make it. They're on their own," said Brokenwing.

Magidance scratched his chin. "Ah, what the hell. It's not like any of them owe me money."

NIGHT FOUND THEM on the Red River, afloat on a crude raft. The moon turned the water to a silvery sheet as smooth and gleaming as the floor of Greatshadow's lair. Bigsby was skeptical that the raft would survive the night, given the haste with which they had assembled it. But, even with his concerns, he couldn't keep his eyes open. He stretched out beside Brokenwing, who was already sleeping, as Magidance stood over them, using a long stout pole to move the raft around obstacles.

"So, try me," said Magidance. "I'm dying to hear."

"What?" Bigsby asked, drowsily.

"Your reasons. Why didn't you kill him?"

"Greatshadow keeps this land wild," said Bigsby. "When he falls, this place will be overrun with farms and churches and men like Tristram."

Magidance nodded. "That was the plan."

"It wasn't my plan," said Bigsby. "I like this place as it is, untamed and untamable. I think the world still needs a place where the wicked can hide from the righteous."

Magidance raised an eyebrow.

"Damn," he said. "That's not a bad reason at all."

Tornado of Sparks

For, behold,
the Lord will come with fire,
and with his chariots like a whirlwind,
to render his anger with fury,
and his rebuke with flames of fire.

~ Isaiah 66:15 ~

VENDEVOREX STOOD BEFORE the trio of sun-dragons, juggling a white ball of flame between his foretalons.

"All fire is subservient to my will," he said, allowing the crackling orb to fade into a coal-black lump, which he crumbled to dust. Though he didn't mention it, light was also Vendevorex's plaything. The wizard bent light in a dozen subtle ways to enhance his appearance. The sky-blue scales of his hide glistened like wet gemstones. The diamonds that studded his wings cast rainbows with every movement. The silver skullcap that adorned his brow was wreathed in a shimmering halo. Vendevorex hoped to impress the king by looking more like a being from another world than a humble sky-dragon.

"Your so-called magic has an odor to it," said Zanzeroth, the sun-dragon who stood behind the king. "It reminds me of the scent of a storm. It smells like… trouble."

Zanzeroth was the king's most trusted advisor. Vendevorex knew it was vital to win him over. "Your senses are finely tuned, noble Zanzeroth," Vendevorex said, in a flattering tone. "Only a few dragons are refined enough to detect the aroma of true magic. Of course, magic is trouble… trouble that may be directed against the king's enemies."

Though he delivered his comment to Zanzeroth, Vendevorex carefully watched King Albekizan for a reaction. Albekizan was a giant bull of a sun-dragon, a creature who, even resting on the azure silk cushions of his throne pedestal, looked like the embodiment of raw power. Sun-dragons were the unquestioned pinnacle of the food chain, beasts with forty-foot wingspans and toothy jaws that could bite a horse in two. With symmetrical features and muscles sculpted beneath a hide of ruby scales, Albekizan looked down on Vendevorex with the assured poise of a creature confident he could kill everyone in the room.

Vendevorex was half the size of the king. It was the height of arrogance for him to seek admittance as a peer in the court. Sky-dragons earned places of respect in the kingdom as scholars and artists, but they were seldom found in positions of true authority. Vendevorex knew it would be a challenge to convince the king of his value. So far, he'd demonstrated abilities that he was certain the king would find useful in a personal wizard. He'd turned invisible, he'd populated the room with doppelgangers, and he'd conjured fire from thin air. Albekizan had greeted these feats with indifference, even boredom.

Vendevorex looked toward the king's companions. Zanzeroth, a dragon over twenty years the elder of the king, gazed at him with suspicion. To the left of Albekizan sat Kanst, the king's younger cousin, openly scowling. Vendevorex had studied all the residents of the palace invisibly before requesting an audience with the king. He knew that persuading either Zanzeroth or Kanst would lead to acceptance by Albekizan. Alas, the sun-dragons were proving more skeptical than he'd hoped.

"Other conjurers have come before us," Zanzeroth said. "They present us with mirrors and juggling and dare to call it magic. What makes your claims any different?"

"Better mirrors," Vendevorex said, as he willed his eyes to appear as dark pools full of stars. "I've journeyed to the abode of gods and stolen their secrets."

"Your talk of gods falls on deaf ears, little dragon," Kanst said. "What use has the mighty Albekizan for your illusions?"

"Illusions?" said Vendevorex. He spread his wings wide, to show that he had no hidden devices. In truth, most of his magic was mere illusion, but he possessed genuine power as well, the ability to manipulate matter with but a touch. "You misjudge me. The king is indeed mighty. I, however, am master of an unseen world. I hold power over fire and wind and stone. I'm no simple conjurer. Behold."

Vendevorex leaned down, allowing a wreath of white flame to envelop his foretalon. He touched it to the marble floor and melted his talon-print into the stone. He stood up, the outline of his claws in the marble still spitting jets of flame.

He looked the king once more in the eyes. "You sit there," he said, aware of the arrogance in addressing the king so brusquely, "the proudest dragon ever to have lived. Your pride is well earned. In far-away lands I've heard of you, Albekizan. I've heard of your hunger for power. What I've done to this marble tile I could do to a mountain. There is no fortress your enemies can hide within that I could not burn to ash. I am power, Albekizan. And for a price, I will be a power at your command."

To his relief, Albekizan looked more intrigued than angry at his bold display.

"What price?" the king asked, in rumbling voice. It was the first time Albekizan had spoken to him.

"An appointment to your court," said Vendevorex. "A home within the confines of your castle, and a position of authority as your chief consultant on all matters of magic."

Zanzeroth asked, "With your boasts of power, why would you desire these things?"

"Noble Zanzeroth," Vendevorex said, with a slight bow. "When I say I have been to the home of the gods, I do not speak metaphorically. I've traveled outside the ordinary world to gain my knowledge. The price I've paid is great; I can no longer return to the land of my birth. My choice is now to wander the world, an eternal stranger, or seek a new home. King Albekizan is the mightiest of earthly dragons. It's natural that I desire to serve him; he's the only dragon alive who can grant me the wealth and status that I feel are my rightful due."

"Why would you need wealth?" Zanzeroth scoffed. "Instead of defacing the king's floor, couldn't you have turned the marble to gold? Those diamonds in your wings… are they mere glass?"

"I measure wealth in more than gold and jewels," said Vendevorex. "True wealth comes from being valued in one's work and knowledge."

This answer seemed to please Albekizan. His eyes brightened as he said, "I can think of many uses for a dragon who may become invisible."

"Such as a spy?" Kanst asked. Kanst was a dragon nearly as big as Albekizan, even more heavily muscled, but with a certain blockiness to his features that made him look less intelligent than his companions. "How do we know you aren't one? Or an assassin in league with the Murder God?"

"If I were a spy, would I not simply linger in your midst invisibly to learn your secrets?" Vendevorex said, deciding that Kanst's question was too dangerous to leave unanswered. "And if I were an assassin—"

"If you were an assassin you could have killed us unseen," said Zanzeroth. "Or made the attempt, at least."

Vendevorex tried to judge from the older dragon's tone whether he was leaning in support of him, or simply annoyed by Kanst's poor reasoning.

"No," said Zanzeroth, narrowing his gaze. "You're no assassin. You are, however, a liar, to come here and speak to us of gods. I don't know the source of your 'magic,' but I know a falsehood when I hear one."

"Lie or not," the king said, glancing toward the imprint in the marble, "I'm intrigued by your abilities. You could burn a stone castle?"

"I call the flame I control the Vengeance of the Ancestors," said Vendevorex. (In truth, until that exact second, he'd only called it "flame," but he felt that his presentation needed more dramatic flare.) "There is nothing the Vengeance will not consume, and it responds to my will alone."

The king rose and moved toward the far end of the hall, which was open to a night sky full of stars. He spread his broad wings and said, "I'd like a larger demonstration. I'd also like no further damage to my floor. Follow me."

The king leapt into the air. Winds swept the hall, buffeting Vendevorex, as Zanzeroth and Kanst joined the king, beating their enormous wings. Vendevorex, unsure what the king had in mind, turned invisible. He found the large leather satchel he'd hidden behind a pillar. This bag contained all his worldly goods, including the true source of his powers. He opened the satchel and dipped his right foretalon into a jar of silver powder, coating it with a fresh dose of the miraculous stuff. The dust immediately vanished into his hide. Then, he closed the jar, slung the satchel over his back, and gave chase to the king.

The head-start the sun-dragons possessed proved little challenge for Vendevorex. Though sky-dragons lacked the sheer physical power of sun-dragons, they were much faster and more graceful in the air. Invisibly, Vendevorex drew to a glide behind the royal party. When the sun-dragons flapped their wings, it sounded like gusts from an enormous bellows. Vendevorex's own flight was utterly silent as his sensitive wings rode on the turbulence left in the trio's wake.

Kanst flew directly beside Albekizan, which came as no surprise to Vendevorex. The roles of the king's companions had become evident during his surveillance. Kanst possessed an arrogance that came from knowing he was related to the king by blood. Zanzeroth followed behind the king, perhaps slowed a bit by his age. But as the elder dragon looked over his shoulder, searching the sky, it soon became apparent that the true reason Zanzeroth lagged behind was to watch the king's back. From what Vendevorex had learned, Zanzeroth didn't boast any sort of royal lineage. He'd lived the earliest years of his life feral, a wild young dragon surviving purely on wits and instinct, before being discovered by Albekizan's father. The old king had treated the task of civilizing the savage young Zanzeroth as an obsessive hobby. The civilizing hadn't fully taken. To this day, Zanzeroth was respected as the most effective hunter in all the kingdom, the only dragon who dared to best the king during recreational hunts. Zanzeroth was, at heart, a creature ruled by instinct, and Vendevorex gathered that the elder dragon's instincts were not to trust him.

Albekizan led them to a nearby cornfield. It was late summer, and heat still rose from the dark earth. Corn stalks fluttered in great waves as the wind of the king's wings beat down upon them. He was coming down for a landing near a stone cottage. Vendevorex had spotted the place during his flights around the castle and knew something of its history, as the residence had been discussed by the king's tax collectors. Until recently, the cottage had sat empty. The king's soldiers had killed the former residents for reasons Vendevorex had yet to discover, and in the aftermath no humans claimed the abandoned property. That had changed in the spring, however, when a human family had moved in and begun repairs. Apparently they were migrants, with no claim to the place. Within the king's bureaucracy, there was a debate as to what was the wiser course—to allow the humans to return the farm to productivity, or to kill them for squatting.

The king tilted his wings to use the air as a brake and landed before the cottage, allowing his shadow to loom over the place. The moon was a dim sliver; the stars were cottoned by the humid air.

As the sun-dragons landed, Vendevorex swooped in front of them, coming to a gentle landing. He allowed his invisibility to fade away and gave a deep and dramatic bow. With his unseen and silent approach, it looked as if he'd known the destination and had been waiting here all along.

"This cottage is no castle," Zanzeroth said.

"But its walls are made of stone," said the king. "Since I've chosen it on a whim, our would-be wizard can't have prepared the structure with any trickery."

"Clever," said Kanst.

"You'd like me to burn this hovel?" Vendevorex asked. "It's hardly a challenge. I'd prefer to demonstrate on something more impressive." Vendevorex instantly regretted saying the words. He could see a look of skepticism flash through the king's eyes. "Still, if it is your will, it is done."

He turned toward the cottage. It wasn't much to look at. The walls were slightly off plumb, and the roof no doubt leaked in a dozen places. The whole structure was tiny by the standards of sun-dragons, and far too cramped for even a sky-dragon. Though he was no taller than most humans when he stood on his hind claws, if he stretched his wings they would reach from end to end of the dwelling. While the cottage was fashioned from thick slabs of river rock, the walls were so badly constructed that, from many yards away, Vendevorex could hear a man snoring within. He pondered if he should do something to alert the humans. Living in such poverty was bad enough; to die without warning on the whim of a king only added to the unfairness. Then, looking back at the Albekizan, Vendevorex steeled himself.

He turned to face the stone dwelling. He concentrated, forming giant orbs of glowing plasma around his foreclaws. With a thrust, he threw the flames against the stone. Instantly, the walls ignited in bright orange gouts of flame. Seconds later, a woman began to scream.

"Step back," Vendevorex said to the king as he walked away from the cottage. "The smoke is poisonous."

"Poison is the tool of the Murder God," said Kanst.

"The poison is a necessary result of the basic chemistry," said Vendevorex. He worried for a brief instant that he'd revealed too much, then decided that the word "chemistry" was probably as strange and open-ended to the sun-dragons as the word "magic."

Within the cottage a man's screams joined the woman's. There was the sound of frantic activity, until, after only a few brief seconds, both voices trailed off into hoarse coughs before falling silent. The smoke had already claimed them. At least they'd be dead before the flames ate their flesh.

"I thought you could control this," said Zanzeroth. "Yet your own magic creates poison fumes you fear?"

"I've no fear of poison," said Vendevorex. "The flames are completely under my control. It's only your safety I have in mind. Flames create their own wind. The smoke moves in ways that are difficult to predict."

"I'm pleased to see the flames eating the stone," said Albekizan. "Still, if the poisons would endanger my own armies...."

"My king, you will no longer need armies to lay siege to a castle. The heat and smoke are no hindrance for me. Watch."

Vendevorex walked back to the cottage. The flames were spreading aggressively across the roof. The wooden door was completely ablaze. With a wave of his wings, Vendevorex caused the flames eating the door to flicker out, leaving only glowing embers on the edges of the blackened wood. Before he could open the door he noticed a sudden movement in the field behind the castle. There was an old barn perhaps twenty yards away. Something moved near it. It was difficult to make out clearly through the haze of smoke, but it looked like a human running from the barn toward the field of corn. A man, if he wasn't mistaken, or at least an older boy.

Vendevorex looked back, wondering if the king had seen the human. Albekizan was focused solely on him. Only Zanzeroth seemed to be gazing beyond the house. Still, he'd been charged with the mission of burning the cottage, not killing every last human on the property. He decided it was best to carry on as if he'd seen nothing.

He pressed forward, reaching out to touch his foretalon to the charred wooden door, which disintegrated at his touch. He stepped into the burning room, the smoke pushed before him in a perfect arc by the bubble of fresh air he gathered. He moved further into the cottage, his heart sinking as he looked upon the ragged possessions of the family. It was the lot of humans in the kingdom of Albekizan to live modestly, but this family had been especially impoverished. He moved into the next room, at the rear of the cottage. The flames had yet to reach this far, though the heat made the air shimmer and the smoke from the other room rolled across the floor in a thick black cloud. Vendevorex's eye was caught by something rising above the smoke—a crib. He crept closer, afraid of what he would find. His worst fears proved true. There was a baby in the crib, a girl if he judged correctly, though human infants mostly looked the same to him. She lay still as death. Then, as he drew closer, she coughed. Though still alive, she was pale. He reached out and placed his claws on her chest. The silver powder he'd covered his foretalon with swirled from his skin, coating the infant, before vanishing into her flesh. He closed his eyes in concentration as he looked inside her body. She'd inhaled trace amounts of smoke, knocking her unconscious, but had suffered no permanent damage. Now that she was within the circle of clean air that followed him, her breathing grew more comfortable.

He decided that the only merciful thing to do was kill her.

He placed his foretalon over her mouth.

Her tiny fist moved reflexively in her sleep to grasp the claw that lay against her cheek.

He changed his mind. Killing this child would do nothing to bring him favor in the king's eyes. He scooped her up and placed her into his leather satchel. She was bundled tightly in a gray, fibrous blanket. She looked, atop the jars and pouches and notebooks he carried, more like a neatly packed provision than a passenger.

He willed the stones around him to burn even faster and headed toward the front door once more. He moved his wings to fill the doorway with smoke to make his exit more dramatic. He stepped into the doorway as the walls began to moan and crack. The whole structure collapsed behind him, filling the night sky with a tornado of sparks. Vendevorex strode forward confidently, emerging from the wall of smoke unscathed. Albekizan looked pleased with the drama of the moment. Even Kanst seemed impressed. Only Zanzeroth still wore a scowl.

"I trust this has answered any doubts about my powers?" Vendevorex said.

"Sire," said Zanzeroth, leaning in close to the king before he could answer. "We should consult further on this matter."

Albekizan glanced toward the older dragon, looking ready to argue, then nodded in agreement.

"Return to my court tomorrow at mid-day, wizard," said Albekizan. "You shall have my decision then."

Albekizan leapt into the air and headed toward the castle. Kanst stood for a moment, studying the mound of burning stone, before turning to give chase to the king.

Zanzeroth lingered, his red scales even redder in the flickering light. He drew close to Vendevorex and said, in a low hiss, "I don't know who you really are or what you really want. The only thing I know with certainty is that you don't smell right. To be blunt, I wouldn't enjoy the atmosphere of the castle with you in it. Do us both a favor… fly far from here tonight, little dragon."

Vendevorex kept his face expressionless as Zanzeroth turned away and launched himself with a mighty down thrust of his wings.

As the king and his entourage vanished into the night, Vendevorex opened his satchel and removed the baby. Laying his foretalons upon her once more, he used his abilities to mend the small damage that had been done to her lungs. The girl responded by drawing a deep breath, then unleashing a loud wail. She continued to scream for the next half hour as Vendevorex moved to the barn in search of any other survivors. He found no one. He waited a while longer, thinking that soon neighboring humans might turn up to investigate the blaze. Unfortunately, anyone who had seen the fire must also have seen the sun-dragons. No one came.

Vendevorex cradled the baby and stroked her tiny pink cheek, trying to comfort her. It didn't work. She cried all the louder. He thought for a moment about simply leaving her in the barn. Sooner or later, someone would come and discover her. Then, he sighed, and placed her into his satchel once more. He moved to investigate the cornfield and discovered footprints and a trampled stalk near the area where he'd spotted the human. He flapped his wings and lifted skyward. From above the cornfield, his sharp eyes could spot the bent and broken stalks that marked the path the human had taken. He swooped across the corn, arriving soon at the distant edge of the field, which was bordered by a large stream. As he circled the area, searching for any signs of movement, the baby's cries fell to a few half-hearted sobs. Seeing no one, Vendevorex landed gently on a well-worn pathway that ran along the stream. To his relief, the baby settled into silence.

He searched the site, at last finding the scrape of a footprint on the sandy pathway. The object of his pursuit had headed toward the forest that lay upstream. Vendevorex remained on the ground to follow the trail, keeping a keen eye for further clues. The path was apparently popular with humans and cattle. He wasn't certain he was following the right footsteps until he found a cow patty that had been deposited at some point the previous day. The whole of the patty was swarmed by beetles, save for a flattened section at the edge, where a foot had stepped quite recently. Beetles hadn't yet disturbed the newly exposed dung.

Soon, he found himself at the forest's edge. It was dark beneath the trees. Spotting footprints was no longer possible. He moved ahead, following the path, feeling certain that the human wouldn't be able to see any better than he could and was unlikely to stray far from the stream.

At last, in the distance, he heard the sound of someone crying. He turned invisible and crept forward. A teenage boy sat on the thick root of a tree by the stream, his arms limp at his side, his face twisted in grief. No doubt, this was the person he sought.

Remaining invisible, he asked, "What's your name, boy?"

The boy stopped crying and snapped to attention. He jumped up, brandishing a fist-sized rock. "Who's there?" he said, his voice trembling with fear, or rage, or both.

"I asked first," Vendevorex said.

"I'm Ragnar," the boy said, turning toward Vendevorex's voice, then twisting his head further, searching the shadows.

"Ragnar, I mean you no harm," Vendevorex said.

"Where are you?" Ragnar said. "Who are you?"

"A friend," said Vendevorex. "At least, not an enemy. I'm here to return something you value."

Ragnar spun around, raising his rock to throw, then spun around again, still seeking a target. "Are you one of them?" he demanded. "A dragon?"

"That isn't important," said Vendovorex. "Did you live in the cottage in the cornfield? Were you in the barn?"

"You are a dragon," Ragnar snarled, his face becoming a mask of rage. "You killed my family!"

"Did you have a sister? An infant?" Vendevorex said, keeping his voice calm, swaying his long neck to make his location harder to pinpoint.

"Jandra?" Ragnar said.

"She's alive," Vendevorex said. "I've brought her to you. Put down the rock. Turn around. I will place her at your feet. I'll also leave diamonds. They cannot replace what was taken from you tonight, but they will help you flee here and begin a new life."

"This is a trick!" Ragnar screamed, lunging toward Vendevorex's voice. With a violent grunt, he hurled the rock. Vendevorex easily leapt aside. The sudden jolt caused Jandra to start crying.

Ragnar picked up another rock from the stream bank and threw it toward the sound. Vendevorex jumped from its path, but it was followed instantly by another, then a third.

"Stop!" he cried out. "You'll injure your sister!"

"I don't care!" Ragnar cried, finding a large, dead branch near the path. He lifted it with both hands and wielded it like a club. He chased toward the sound of the crying baby. Vendevorex ducked and darted among the trees as Ragnar shouted, "I'll kill you! I'll kill every damn dragon in the world!"

Ragnar swung his makeshift club with such force it splintered against a tree. The end of the club spun through the air and caught Vendevorex on the cheek. He let out a hiss of pain and Ragnar charged toward the sound. He dodged away at the last second, then, with a flap of his wings, vaulted to the other side of the stream.

"Calm yourself!" he shouted. "Think of your sister!"

"I'm thinking of your blood!" Ragnar screamed, twisting and turning, searching both for the source of Jandra's cries and a new weapon. He spotted a sharp stone on the ground and lifted it, then eyed the far side of the stream. Vendevorex took a deep breath. Ragnar wasn't an adult, but he was still big and in good health, a farm boy with a body chiseled by labor. Judging from the force with which Ragnar had splintered his own club, he could no doubt injure Vendevorex with a lucky blow, or kill Jandra with an unlucky one.

To his relief, Ragnar made the mistake of stepping into the stream, wading into knee-deep water. Calmly, Vendevorex leaned forward and allowed the dust from his talon to fall over the stream. With a thought, the stream turned to ice, trapping Ragnar.

Ragnar gave a cry of alarm, beating the ice around his legs with the rock he carried.

"You'll injure yourself if you're not careful," Vendevorex said. Invisibly, he loosened his satchel and removed the screaming infant. She was still swaddled in the blanket, a neat, if noisy, bundle. He lay her on the ice, placed three diamonds on her chest, and shoved her toward her brother.

"Take care of her," Vendevorex said.

The bundled infant slid across the ice until she came to a halt against Ragnar's knee. Ragnar looked down, confused, seeming to calm a bit. Then, he raised the rock over his head.

"I'll take no gift that's been touched by a dragon!"

He plunged the sharp stone toward the infant's head.

It never connected. From nowhere, a thick red tail flickered out and knocked the stone from Ragnar's hand. In a flash, the tail whipped back, catching the boy full in the face. He fell backwards, still frozen at the knees, completely unconscious.

Vendevorex looked up. In the tree that towered over the stream, Zanzeroth crouched. Vendevorex had never seen a sun-dragon resting in a tree before. Their size and weight normally made them unsuitable for such perches. Zanzeroth moved gracefully as a cat as he leaned down and swooped up the infant with his foreclaw.

He brought the screaming infant to his face. The baby looked tiny against his giant jaws. He could devour her without bothering to chew. He sniffed her, the delicate white feathers around his snout fluttering like smoke. The baby instantly grew wide-eyed and silent.

"She's soiled herself," Zanzeroth said. "She'd probably be quieter if you kept her dry."

In the dark, his eyes seemed to glow with an emerald flame as he turned toward Vendevorex and offered the baby to him. Vendevorex took the infant and clutched her to his chest.

"I can't believe he would have killed his own sister," Vendevorex said.

"Human's aren't like us," Zanzeroth said. "They're beasts driven by primitive urges they cannot fully control. Fear, anger, hatred, lust… they have the same emotions as dragons, but lack our ability to keep them in check. They're all instinct and no reason."

"I've known humans who would prove you wrong," said Vendevorex.

Zanzeroth shook his head. “Think what you wish, but I've hunted humans for many decades. A good hunter understands his prey with a certain… intimacy.”

“Why did you save the baby?” Vendevorex asked.

“Why did you?”

Vendevorex sighed. “I’m not a creature who enjoys needless death. I killed her parents only as a consequence of proving myself to your king. But I don’t regard humans as prey. I saw no need for her to die when there was a possibility of reuniting her with a family member.”

“I knew you’d seen the boy flee the barn,” said Zanzeroth. “Your body language betrayed you. I was curious when you didn’t mention it. When you exited the house, I smelled the baby in your satchel. Again, you kept it secret. I've followed you to find out why.”

“I had no idea you were following me,” Vendevorex said.

“I’m the most experienced stalker in the kingdom,” said Zanzeroth. “Your invisibility doesn’t impress me.”

Vendevorex once more placed Jandra into his satchel. By now, the water of the stream had backed up over the dam of ice and was flowing over its surface, half submerging Ragnar, who was still out cold. Vendevorex waded forward carefully. The ice beneath the water was slick; he dug his sharp claws in for traction. He reached Ragnar and melted the ice around his legs, then dragged him to the riverbank.

“I’d rather not see him drown,” Vendevorex said.

“You're going to let him live?”

“Why not?” said Vendevorex. “He’s more a threat to himself than to me. Still, I’m not going to leave Jandra with him. I'll have to care for her a bit longer, I’m afraid, until I can find a suitable home.”

“The king wouldn’t look kindly upon this softness, wizard,” said Zanzeroth.

“I’ll kill for the king when I am his subject and obeying his orders,” said Vendevorex. “For now, I’m a free dragon. I will be as soft or as hard as my conscious commands.”

Zanzeroth slinked down from the tree, standing next to Vendevorex, drawing up to loom over him.

“Within the castle, the king keeps hundreds of humans as slaves. They do the menial labor of the place, the cleaning and cooking. You can find someone there who will care for the infant.”

“As long as I've saved her life,” said Vendevorex, “I’d as soon not deliver her into slavery. Besides, what does it matter how many humans live within the castle? You've told me to stay away.”

Zanzeroth stared at Vendevorex for a long moment. "Use your own judgment as to the baby's fate. It isn't my custom to hunt human females, so I don't care what her eventual destiny may be. And yet wizard… you should know I have something in common with this child, no matter how improbable that may seem."

"Oh?"

"I, too, was an orphan. I endured many years on my own, but I've no doubt I would never have survived to adulthood had I not been shown kindness by a dragon who had every right to kill me. Albekizan's father had compassion; Albekizan does not. It would be useful, perhaps, to have a voice in the king's court willing to stand for mercy."

"I can be that voice," said Vendevorex.

Zanzeroth nodded. "Perhaps." Then he said, "Kanst, doesn't trust you. I saw him back at the cottage after you left, poking through the ash."

"Do I need Kanst's trust?" Vendevorex said.

"No," said Zanzeroth. "The king enjoys his cousin's company but is wise enough not to listen to his counsel."

"The king listens to you, though," said Vendevorex.

"On occasion," said Zanzeroth. "Come to the castle at the appointed time. The king leans in your favor. I won't oppose you."

"Thank you, Zanzeroth," Vendevorex said.

"Save your thanks, wizard," Zanzeroth said, turning away. "I still don't like the way you smell. My instincts tell me that the day will come when I'll be the dragon that guts you."

Vendevorex wasn't certain what to say to that.

Zanzeroth stepped over the body of the unconscious boy and glanced back at Vendevorex. "Fortunately, unlike our sleeping friend here, I'm a being whose reason is in control of his instinct. As long as you don't give me an excuse to kill you, you may yet die in your sleep."

The giant dragon leapt toward the sky, his massive wings knocking aside branches as he rose into the night.

Vendevorex let out a long, slow breath. He looked down at the little girl in his wings, who stared up at him with big dark eyes. "Perhaps he's right," he said to her. "Perhaps, in this kingdom, there aren't any humans who've been raised to value reason over instinct."

Her mouth moved into what he interpreted as a smile. He stroked her pale cheek with the back of his scaly talon.

"At least," he said, gently, "not yet.

Girl's Night Out

AMELIA, I CAN'T BELIEVE YOU brought your stupid Bladerina costume," Sarah says, rolling her eyes.

"I brought both our costumes," I say, pulling her bright blue Sky-Girl tights out of my bag. We're on the observation deck of the Empire State Building; normally, it would be full of tourists at this time of day, but she's already told everyone to leave and I'm holding the doors shut with my mind. We can change in privacy.

"You're as crazy as Dad," she says, not taking the costume. "I'm not going to play superhero with you."

"Playing has nothing to do with this." Then I take another glance a down 5th Avenue and grimace. "Even if the thing does look like a doll."

Several blocks away, a giant is stomping through the Flatiron district. The thing is at least three hundred feet tall and, yes, it looks almost exactly like an enormous baby doll. Only, where its head should be, there's a huge revolver. Hopefully, the thing only has six shots; it's already fired three bullets. At least a dozen buildings have been flattened by the creature's rampage.

"Look," I say. "If you saw a man having a heart attack, are you telling me you wouldn't give him CPR? Even though you've had the training to do so since you were, like, eight?"

"You aren't going to change my mind by saying things that are really, really stupid." She waves my question away with her hand. "I don't see how this situation is even remotely parallel."

"We have the power to fight this thing, Sarah. We have a duty to help where we can."

"My powers aren't going to be useful here," she says. "That thing's got to be a robot. I can't change the mind of a machine."

"Can't you at least try? Even if you can't tell it to stop, you can help with the crowds. Keep them from panicking."

"When a giant doll is about to stomp you like a bug, how is keeping calm going to help, Amelia?"

I don't argue, not because I agree with her, but because I'm too busy fighting with my stupid tights. I'm trying to dress so fast I didn't notice that one of the legs is inside out.

She shakes her head as she watches me. "If you're going to fight it, I don't know why you need that stupid costume."

"If we're going to be superheroes, we should look the part."

"It's not like you have a secret identity to protect. Our costumes don't even have masks."

"It's about inspiring confidence. We need to project a professional image, something that will make the public more comfortable despite our differences. It's the same way the uniforms of police officers make people feel at ease despite the fact they all carry loaded guns."

"If cops showed up wearing bright red tights and a miniskirt I don't think anyone would be more comfortable," Sarah says, crossing her arms. "Admit it, Amelia: You've bought into Dad's little superhero fantasy. His brainwashing worked. You're totally into this."

"Can we debate this some other time?" I finally get the tights on and straighten out my pleated skirt. I pull on my jacket and close the steel zippers with my mind as I adjust the chinstrap on my hat. "I've got a giant to slay."

Feeling as if this sounds sufficiently brave, I turn my back to Sarah and vault over the safety rail. I used to need Sarah to ferry me around, since anything she touches is just as immune to gravity as she is. Now, I've mastered my own form of transportation. I've always had a sixth sense, the ability to feel all the iron atoms anywhere near me. With my eyes closed, I still 'see' people, since I have a picture in my mind of all the iron in their blood stream. It's like seeing ghosts, since the atoms appear as a translucent cloud.

But after years of training, my sixth sense has led me to a seventh one. I not only sense the iron atoms near me, I sense iron atoms that aren't yet there. Father says that all matter breaks down into finer and finer components, so that what we sense as solid objects are actually subtle vibrations of tiny loops of space-time. Just as I can grab a steel bar with my thoughts, I can "pluck" these tiny vibrating loops and cause them to manifest as pure iron.

Which is a long-winded way of saying that, instead of plummeting to my death after jumping off the skyscraper, I'm able to summon an iron rail from thin air as I clad my feet in heavy skates. The wheels of the skates lock perfectly onto the rail and I roll toward the Flatiron district with a metallic clatter, kicking to gain speed. I don't turn back to see if Sarah has chosen to follow. I hope she has. Certainly her grudge against our father won't lead her to turn her back on people in need.

Ahead of me, there's a thunderous boom. Above the rooflines, I see that the giant has unleashed another bullet, punching through the roof of a nearby building. Flames gutter from the hole; he's probably ignited a gas line. My first priority, obviously, is to disable that gun before he can fire his last two bullets.

I stretch my arms toward his gun-face… and nothing happens. I can't 'feel' the atoms of his weapon. I close my eyes, since sometimes my vision distracts me from my more subtle senses. Still nothing. He's invisible, like he has no iron at all inside him. This makes no sense; I'm certain this thing's a robot. There's no way a living creature could be this big without his bones snapping under their own weight, and, besides, if it had blood, I'd "see" it. Could anyone actually build a robot this large without using any iron for the supporting structure? Why would you even bother, unless you specifically planned on defending against me? Who even knows I exist?

So many questions. For answers, I'll try the direct approach. I pluck a two-handed sword from thin air as I swoop past his ribs. All my training pays off. I keep my balance as I sink the blade into his flesh. I use my momentum to slice him for at least thirty feet before I zoom away. I curve my rail around to survey the damage and find he's not slowed down at all. I'm not terribly surprised, since I didn't feel my blade hit anything all that hard. He's not bleeding though, more evidence that this is a robot.

As I swoop around for another strike, I glance back at the Empire State Building. I don't see Sarah. I really hope she's decided to help. I know this isn't what she wanted to do for her birthday. We're in New York because Sarah turned sixteen today and wanted to come here as her present. Mother accompanied us. She and Sarah have enjoyed themselves shopping, but I've been on edge all day, since

Sarah's choice of destinations is suspiciously close to Hoboken. I know she still exchanges emails with Vance.

Distracted by wondering about Sarah's location, I don't notice the gun-giant turning toward me. When I look back toward him, I find myself staring right down the barrel of his face. There's a sudden flash of fire and smoke and a huge black cylinder flies at me. I've trained to stop bullets by wrapping them in an iron jacket and holding them with my mind, but I've never tried anything at this scale. I manage to get a thin shell around it, but the momentum is more than I can handle. It slams into me, shattering both my concentration and my rail. I try to breathe and it feels like I've got a knife in my ribs. I'm tumbling toward the pavement, too dizzy to stop my fall.

On pure instinct, I wrap myself in a protective cocoon with crumble zones barely two yards above the sidewalk.

The world turns black.

SMELL OF RUST. Taste of blood in my mouth. I crack my eyelids then clamp them shut when metallic dust rains in. Every bone in my body feels broken.

On willpower alone, I roll to my side, since I don't want to throw up while I'm on my back. Choking on my own vomit would be a very ignoble way to die. I heave until I'm hollow.

The ground trembles and I remember why I'm sprawled out on this sidewalk. The rust around me is what's left of my iron cocoon. I swirl it back around me until I'm encased in armor, with only my face exposed. I stand by moving the armor with my mind. The giant has moved on, smashing through another half dozen buildings in the time I've been out.

I search the sky for any sign of Sarah. I don't see her, but I do see the giant bullet that took me out. It's bounced across the street and taken out a fire hydrant. There's something weird about it. I limp toward it and place my hand on the black surface. It's soft and rubbery, slightly translucent.

Unlike Sarah, I've paid attention to my father's chemistry lessons. Silicone. It's made of silicone.

I face the rampaging monster, looking at its pink flesh quivering with each toddling step. It's obviously covered with a silicone hide. But, it still has to have something solid inside, doesn't it?

I will a rail into existence and jump on. If Sarah were here, she'd tease me about relying on a rail. In theory, I should be able to fly by lifting my iron shell with my thoughts, the way I can hold the rail in midair. In practice, I freak out if I don't have something underneath my feet. Sarah makes flying look easy, but if I don't feel at least some connection to the earth, I get disoriented. It's not that I'm afraid of heights; I can ride my rails up a mile or more. I need something to ground me.

I crouch, leaning like a skier as I trigger an electromagnetic wave through the rail that grabs my boots and shoots me forward. I stretch my arms before me and clasp my hands together into an arrow shape, growing long razor blades several yards out to each side. I hit him from behind, coming in low, tearing through his ankle at what should be his Achilles tendon, digging deep to hit bone, or whatever's inside this thing.

It's like slicing a blob of Jell-O. The line I cut through the thing presses back together and closes. I look up to see if I've caught its attention. It's turning toward me again. The hammer on its revolver face pulls back and I watch the cylinder click into place with a fresh bullet.

So fast I'm not fully aware of what I'm doing, I grab an I-beam from the nearby rubble and thrust it heavenward, shaping it, compressing it into a perfect plug for the looming gun barrel.

The hammer flies down just as my plug jams the barrel. The gun barrel peels back like a banana as smoke and fire fly out from the back of the cylinder. The monster's limbs go limp and he collapses, landing in a jiggling heap. Almost instantly the gun barrel starts knitting itself back together. It looks like it can regenerate pretty fast.

I can hurt it faster.

There's several hundred tons of twisted metal within range of my extended senses. I grab it all and hurl it, not even bothering to reshape it, hammering the thing with cars, manhole covers, twisted I-beams, and about a thousand knives from what must once have been a restaurant. The creature takes the attack in eerie silence, showing no sign of pain as it tries to rise. As resilient as silicone may be, I quickly reduce it to shreds. It's increasingly looking less like a giant pink baby and more like a giant pink blob. Then, I blink, and it's gone.

"What the hell?" I mutter, staring at the rubble where it had been a second before. I spin around, searching for it. There's no way it could move that quickly. I ride my rail into the sky, searching for any clue as to where it went. The devastation goes on for a half mile in every direction. An earthquake couldn't have done more damage. Who made this thing? Why did it attack? What was the point of all this?

The questions will have to wait. There are survivors among the wreckage. As tempting as it is to dive in and start finding people one by one, I need to prioritize. New York has its own emergency personnel, firefighters and paramedics better trained than I am. They'll have a hard time getting to the core of the damage due to the complete gridlock of cars.

I'm wiped out and could probably use some medical attention myself. Breathing deeply, I push the pain and weariness from my mind. I grab a dozen cars with my powers and lift them skyward, keeping the doors sealed so that the panicked drivers can't make a jump. I guide the floating cars to Central Park, then grab another dozen, then do it again, clearing the roads for the rescue squads. As I lower the cars and release the doors, the drivers all run, looking confused and scared. Some injure themselves as they trip and fall. Sarah could calm them.

I don't bother searching the sky. I know where she's gone. My anger cuts me far sharper than my broken ribs. Does she really think she'll get away with this?

IT TAKES ME FIVE HOURS to finish clearing the streets. Mother is probably having a fit, either not knowing what's happened to Sarah and me in the midst of this chaos, or, worse, having found a television and seeing exactly what's happened. She hasn't exactly signed on to Father's vision of us being superheroes. To keep her from a complete nervous breakdown, Father agreed to defer his plan to introduce us as a "teen brigade" and wait until Sarah and I were adults. I'm 18 now, but had wanted to wait until Sarah was old enough to join me before making my debut. As much as I believe that my father is right, and that there's no more noble cause than to use our powers in the service of mankind, I confess that I've been terrified of the day I'd finally appear in public. How will the world react to discovering how different I am from other people? After my fight with the giant and the resulting clean up, I'm certain I've been filmed and photographed a dozen times over. As to how the world will react, I find myself utterly indifferent. I took the only course of action I could; there was no way I could stand by and do nothing.

I'm hoping that Mother is at the hotel. It's several miles uptown, far from the destruction. With any luck, Sarah has gone back to be with her. It's a faint hope, but I cling to it nonetheless.

I ride my rail to the roof and shed my iron shell. I'm completely drenched in sweat; I wish I'd thought to stop and grab my civilian clothes at the Empire State Building, assuming they're still there. I undo the lock to the roof door and go down the stairs slowly, my legs feeling like rubber. The stairs are pitch black; the power is out all through the city.

I unlock the door to our room with my mind and push the door open, slumping against the doorframe.

Mother gasps and runs to my side.

"Is Sarah here?" I whisper as she wraps her arms around me.

"I thought she was with you!"

I press my lips tightly together.

"What's happening?" she asks. "Why are you in your costume?"

"You honestly don't know?"

"The phone lines are all dead. Without electricity, I've had no television. I tried to go to the lobby, but the elevator is out of service. When I tried to use the stairs, an employee of the hotel told me it was probably safest to stay in my room."

"There was… an attack," I say. "Some kind of big monster. It… it killed a lot of people. I… think I stopped it."

"Interesting," says a voice behind me.

I turn around to find a man standing at the far end of the hall. He's all in shadows; I can't make out his face.

"Because, from where I stand, it looks to me like you started this, Amelia."

"What?" I ask, stepping toward him. I instinctively scan him for weapons, but find that I can't see him at all with my sixth sense. Like the giant, there's no iron in his body. "Who are you? How do you know my name?"

"You can call me Rex Monday. I've been watching you a while now. I know all about your little superhero fantasy, 'Bladerina.' If your father thinks he can unleash his own private army of superhuman goons to enforce his will upon the world… well, two can play that game. Baby Gun was only a sample of what's in store if you choose to escalate this war."

"War?" I ask, stepping toward him. "What are you talking about? Was… Baby Gun that giant? What did you have to do with him?"

"Your father's not the only one capable of breeding monsters," says Monday.

"If you're responsible for this," I say, "consider yourself under arrest!"

I summon iron bands around his arms, to no avail. It's like trying to grab smoke. I take another step toward him and realize I can faintly see the wall behind him. I look down and spot a small glass disk on the floor. I kneel to take a closer look.

"You're a bright girl. You've probably figured out I'm a hologram. I'm certain you've seen the technology in your father's lab; though I doubt you've seen a hologram projected with a lens built of a plastic explosive ten times more powerful than C4. Good-bye, Bladerina."

The lens explodes, but not before I've wrapped a shell of iron around it. All I hear is a faint *whumph*.

"Oh god," says Mother. "I told your father this was foolishness! I told him there would be consequences! But even the death of Alex—"

"Mother!" I snap. "Father and I aren't to blame for this."

"But…"

"Go back to the room," I say. "I'm going to reinforce the doors and walls and cover the windows with bars so that nothing can get inside."

"You're going to put me in a cell?"

"It's for your own safety while I'm gone."

"Gone?" she sounds confused. "You only just got here and now you're running off?"

"Sarah," I say.

She nods. With that one word, she requires no further explanation.

I FORM MY RAIL low over the Hudson, since the skies are now swarming with helicopters. I'm heading for Hoboken to retrieve my rebellious sister.

On her last birthday, she asked to attend a Nine Inch Nails concert by herself, without even me as chaperone. My parents agreed, assuming she couldn't get into too much trouble, given that, thanks to my father's telepathy, she had to know that he was keeping an eye on her. But, at the concert, an older boy named Vance had snuck in a bottle of booze and shared it with her. She apparently got buzzed enough to forget that Father was watching. He woke me up to tell me it was time to intervene. I was still in my pajamas when I found Vance's van. Sarah had her top off and her jeans bunched up around her knees when I peeled back the top of the vehicle and expressed to the lovebirds my extreme disapproval.

And was Sarah punished for her rebellion? On the contrary, she acted as if she was the victim, and extracted from Father a promise not to look into Vance's mind anymore, claiming that she was uncomfortable that Father might peek into his head at a moment when Vance was remembering their encounter. Father agreed that this would be something he, too, would wish to avoid, and said he would block Vance's mind from his awareness if Sarah agreed to behave more responsibly in the future.

Father, being an honorable man, has no doubt upheld his bargain; Sarah, being Sarah, has not.

In the intervening year, she's been sharing emails with Vance. I know because I peeked over her shoulder as she was reading her email. Before she closed the email, I saw she was corresponding with "HobokenBoy69." When I'd intervened at the van, I examined his driver's license and repeated his Hoboken address so I could say in a menacing growl, "I know where you live." When Sarah expressed an interest in visiting New York, I took note of the close proximity to Vance, but didn't argue against the trip since mother seemed excited about the opportunity to attend the ballet. My superhero moniker of Bladerina comes from my early years of dance practice. Now that I've heard it uttered by my very first supervillain, I'm having second thoughts. The name isn't really one to strike fear into the hearts of criminals.

I skate among the buildings unnoticed. The streets below are packed with cars and people even though it's almost two AM, no doubt refugees from the city. If Sarah's not with Vance, I might never find her in this chaos.

But, I do find her, easier than I hoped, plainly visible through a window on the fifth floor of a brownstone, where she's sprawled out on a ratty couch with an equally ratty guy bent over her, his hand between her legs.

I take out the window.

He jumps up and spins around.

Sarah yells, "Don't—"

I do, wrapping my fist in iron and landing a punch that's going to cost Vance a lot in dental work. He flops to the floor, blood streaming from his mouth. For half a second, I'm certain I've killed him, but then I feel the iron still ebbing and flowing through his veins. He'll survive.

"What the fuck are you doing?" Sarah asks, rising into the air, her fists clenched. "What fucking right do you have to barge in here and—"

"If you keep yelling at me I swear to God I will hurt you," I say.

"This is my life, Amelia! Stay out of it!"

"This is the life you want? Running from the scene of an emergency, running away from people who need your help so you can live out your selfish fantasies?"

"Don't talk to me about fantasies when you're dressed like Spiderman," she says, crossing her arms. "You're the one living in some fucked up dream world. I'm the one who wants a normal life."

"Normal?" I say, rolling my eyes. "You're feet aren't even touching the ground as you say this! And how can any relationship you have be normal when you control people's minds with your—"

Her eyes narrow. "I! Do not! Control! People's minds!"

"Fine," I say. "Whatever it is you do, people sure get excited about following your every command."

"I'm just persuasive. At least with everyone but you. So, let me ask you nicely… please go away. Please, pretty please. Seriously, I'm done. I'm done with all of Dad's crazy training. I'm never going back to the island. Vance and I are going to move in with a friend of his in Brooklyn and start a life together."

"Yeah, that'll work out swell," I say. "How are you going to support yourself?"

"Vance and I can get jobs."

"Maybe he can, but you're not even an American citizen. You can't legally work in the US."

She shrugs. "People will help me out."

"Sure. You can rob people blind with your voice."

"I'm not going to rob anyone. I want to pull my own weight, just like a normal person."

"Stop saying that word."

"What? Normal?"

I nod.

"Normal. Normal. Normal!" She stamps her feet for emphasis, though there's no sound, since she's not actually touching anything but air.

"Open your eyes, Sarah. The only way you'll ever feel normal is to accept who you really are." I wave my hand around the squalor of the apartment. "This isn't what you were born for. You're better than this."

"I don't want to be better," she says. "I want to fit in. I want to be accepted… to be loved."

"We love you, Sarah."

"Not the way Vance loves me."

"You've not even spent a full day in his company. You aren't in—"

"We've been emailing," she says. "We… we've got a real connection. He's the only one who's ever understood me."

"Does he understand you can fly?"

She doesn't say anything.

"How on earth did you explain what happened the first night you met? The way I peeled off the roof of his van?"

"Ah," she says. "Um, I didn't explain it. I asked him to forget what had totaled his van and blame his missing memory on some bad weed."

"Wow. That's a healthy start to your relationship, you wiping his memory."

She grimaces. "I know. It sounds bad. But, since then, we've only swapped emails. I haven't used my abilities on him at all. He really, really loves me."

"He's a teenage boy. He might tell you it's love, but he just wants to have sex with you."

"That is love," says Sarah. "It's right there in the name—making love. I know what I feel when he's kissing me. It's the best feeling in the world."

"That's just lust."

"What would you know?" she says bitterly. "You've never dated anyone. I don't even know if you like boys."

"I've got other priorities. You should to."

"You're the one with twisted priorities," she says. "So what if all I'm feeling is lust? What if all Vance wants from me is my body? Watch even an hour of television. Go to a newsstand and look at the covers of magazines. Sex is the axle that the rest of the world spins around. You think your abilities make you powerful? You can't know how powerful it is to feel wanted the way that Vance wants me."

I sigh. "You think dad is going to keep his agreement to stay out of Vance's head once he learns you've run away?"

She frowns.

"You've got to come back."

She sits down on the couch, shaking her head. "I'm never, ever going to lose my virginity, am I? I'm doomed."

"I wouldn't call that doomed. There are virgins in this world who have quite fulfilling lives."

"Name one."

"The Pope?"

"Oh, shut up." Her face is unreadable as the cogs inside her skull whir and click. I know she's hunting for a way to have what she wants, but isn't finding it.

I change the subject.

"We've got a supervillain."

"Huh?" She looks confused.

"You can't honestly have forgotten that when you last saw me I was charging off to fight a giant baby doll?"

"Right. How'd that work out?"

"I almost got killed. A lot of people got hurt. You would have been very useful if you'd stuck around."

"Don't guilt trip me. I never volunteered to be a superhero. Maybe you enjoy running toward danger. I want to retain my right to run the fuck away, like a… a…"

"Normal person?"

She nods. "I was going to say intelligent person, but that works."

"I didn't volunteer either," I say. "I was drafted. My number came up in a genetic lottery. Like it or not, I was born to be a soldier."

"Mom really hoped we were born to be ballerinas," she says.

"I'm changing my name," I say. "My superhero name."

"Yeah, it's lame. What are you going to be called now?"

"I don't know. I'm thinking it over. I want something more menacing. Like I said, we've got a supervillain now."

"You didn't destroy the doll?"

"I did. But some guy named Rex Monday is taking credit for making it. I've got to find him."

"Dad will track in down in ten minutes," says Sarah.

"Maybe. But Monday seemed to know a lot about us. Maybe he has some way of hiding himself? If so, I really need your help. Dad and I can turn up leads; if we find even one person who knows where Monday is, you can make them lead us to him."

She nods. "Yeah. I guess. It's… the least I can do. But, I'm not going to have a code name. And I'm not going to wear a fucking costume."

I think of something funny and try not to smile, since it's been a very unfunny day.

"What?" she says.

"I'm a little relieved you don't want a costume. Given your obsession with sex, you'd probably be one of those comic book women who fight crime wearing nothing but a thong and a push up bra, like you're more intent on giving bad guys a thrill than putting them in prison."

Sarah's eyes light up.

I've a sinking feeling that I've said something really, really stupid.

REMY HAD BEEN SITTING alone in the cell for twenty minutes when the guard-drone appeared at the bars, its laser scanner flickering over the vizcode above the lock. "Inmate 1313269, Jansen, Marcus Richard. Your mother has posted bail." The door to the cell slid open.

Remy had no clue who Jansen was. Neither, apparently, did the drone. Billy Big Lips had told him that every now and then you could glitch up the drones by smudging the vizcodes. Luckily, Remy had an abundant supply of drying blood to test the theory. He still couldn't believe it worked.

"'Bout time," Remy said, as the drone held out a baggie containing Jansen's wallet, watch, and keys.

Remy sauntered out of jail holding his head high, unafraid of the facial recognition in the cameras. He'd had the good fortune of being arrested by one of the few human cops left in Houston. He'd appealed to the cop's shared humanity to give him a pass. The cop had responded that he had nothing in common with a low life bean runner. Remy had kindly pointed out that the cop's mother had a different opinion, which she'd expressed the night before with extreme physical enthusiasm. The cop had then used his nightstick to knock out two of Remy's teeth, break his nose, and turn his left eye into a purple swollen mass the size of a baseball.

Remy walked three blocks before inspecting the wallet. According to his license, Jansen was 48 years old. The photo showed a bald Caucasian man with a drooping left eye, a bent nose, and several missing teeth. Other slots of the wallet held a condom, a fortune cookie fortune *(Time mends a broken heart),* and a three week old lottery ticket. No credit cards, just one lonely digibuck. Remy pressed the dollar sign. The balance blinked $9.63.

Remy, a 23-year-old Asian with thick, jet-black hair and, until today, far more symmetrical features, put on Jansen's watch. 6:30 p.m. He'd missed by half an hour the deadline to deliver the beans to Space Gorilla Max. 100 pounds of prime Columbian java were stuffed into the seat linings of his '27 Chevy, now unreachable in the police impound lot. Remy was dead. Space Gorilla Max didn't tolerate failure. The big ape barely tolerated success. The best Remy could hope for was that Space Gorilla Max would kill him by breaking his neck in one smooth, crisp snap, the way he'd finished Billy Big Lips. He definitely didn't want to be strangled with his own intestines like poor Vinnie.

Poor, poor Vinnie.

Remy's own intestines grumbled angrily. When the cop had pulled him over, he'd choked down the few dozen coffee beans stuffed in his jacket. The Thardexian's had negotiated an intergalactic ban on the beans after most of their population got wired on coffee and a bloody civil war had broken out. Coffee smugglers usually got the death penalty. Every muscle in his body felt tight and tense as caffeine leached into his bloodstream. His fingers wriggled with unspent energy. Crazy thoughts sparked like neon in dark corners of his mind.

Remy had one chance. He had to get off planet. Better still, out of the solar system. He needed a rocket ship. Nine bucks wasn't going to turn the nut on any legal option. It was time to break into the piggy bank.

As luck would have it, the central rail station was practically next door to the jail. He strolled in casually, ignoring the people casting glances at his mangled face. He found his locker. Fortunately, the retinal scan was tuned to his right eye.

He removed the backpack and slung it over his shoulder. With his caffeine-jazzed strength, he thought it felt a little light. He headed for the men's room and ducked into the first open stall. Unzipping the pack, he saw the bills. 30 grand in Canadian brown backs, one of the last paper currencies recognized by the Empire of Texas. With a little wheeling and dealing, 30 grand might score a ticket to Mars. He knew, however, that this would be a one way trip. Once he left earth, he wasn't coming back. Which meant he had something else he needed to do with the money.

He boarded the centerline, heading north toward the Galleria. Few people on the train gave him a second glance. Anyone with money traveled via the fleet of robotic taxis that ceaselessly roamed the streets. No one worth robbing or begging from would ever be caught dead on the centerline. From the number of drab uniforms, he suspected every other passenger was on their way to one of the government mandated jobs at least one member of each household was required to hold down. Since robots now filled all the essential low skilled niches in the labor market, most of the remaining jobs came with some element of symbolic humiliation. Though robots could do the job better, some wealthy people still liked to have people bow in front of them to shine their shoes, tote their bags, gather up dog poop, or wax their pubes.

Reaching the Galleria, he wound his way through the service tunnels that concealed the workers from the shoppers as they trudged to their jobs. He went down the dimly lit hall to the back of the Brazil Salon. He rapped lightly on the door.

Serena, the manager, opened the door and gasped. "Remy!"

"Shhh," he said, placing a finger to his lips. "Tell my mom I need to see her."

"Your face…"

Remy waved away her worries. "Fell down some stairs. Looks worse than it is."

Serena went back inside. A few seconds later, the door opened again. His mother's face turned pale when she saw him.

"Oh, Remy," she whispered.

"I'm okay," he said.

"I know a broken nose when I see it. And your cheek! You might have fractured your zygomatic bone."

Twenty years ago, Remy's mother had been a surgeon in the Independent Commonwealth of California. Now, the thought of human hands wielding steel knives on flesh was considered barbaric. AI surgeons guiding nanobots had rendered his once esteemed mother obsolete. She now maintained her government benefits by giving bikini waxes.

Remy handed her his backpack. "Don't open this until you get home," he said. "But… you don't need to work here anymore."

His mother's face sank. "This is jitter money, isn't it?"

"It's freedom," he said. "Just take it. I don't need it."

She shoved the bag back into his hands. "Did one of your hoodlum friends do this to your face?" she said. "Was it that gorilla?"

"If it was the gorilla, my head wouldn't be attached to my shoulders," he said.

"You act like you already don't have a good head on your shoulders. You're a bright kid, Remy. You had good grades. You could have gone to school."

"To study for a career that a robot's going to take from me inside a decade? The only real job security is the kind of work done in the shadows, Ma."

"How secure can your job be if you have to worry about some gorilla killing you?" asked his mother. "You've got better options. You know your uncle would let you work on his farm."

His uncle ran an organic pot farm back in California. There was a decent market for artisanal dope. Not coffee money, but at least it was legal. Alas, he could think of few things worse than for Space Gorilla Max to catch up to him at a place with a lot of picks and shovels.

"It's too late for that now," he said.

"It's not too late. California doesn't extradite to nations with death penalties."

Remy sighed. "Extradition is the least of my problems. I have to go. I... I might not see you again. Keep this to remember me." He dropped the backpack at her feet.

"Remy!" she said as he walked away. She began to sob. He didn't look back.

He headed down the tunnel toward the centerline, thinking through a dozen different plans on how he could get to Mars. He knew a lot of friendly baggage inspectors with the commercial rockets. Too bad Space Gorilla Max knew the same people. He couldn't trust anyone.

His best bet was to jack a private rocket. As luck would have it, the Galleria had a touchdown lot for bigwigs who dropped in from their mansions on the moon for a little shopping and dinner at Sal's. In fact, unless the big ape had changed his itinerary, Space Gorilla Max and his boys were dining at Sal's right now. Which meant his rocket would be waiting in the lot.

Remy grinned, though only briefly, since his face hurt too much to maintain the expression. Five minutes later, he was on the roof, staring at Space Gorilla Max's swanked-out, fire-colored, ten-story space phallus, with its mirror glass portals and gleaming chrome fins.

Yeah. This was exactly what the universe owed him.

Remy spotted Tyro and Wilson, two of Max's goons. They were vaping weed, shooting the breeze, their backs to the vehicles. Remy hugged the shadows, darting from rocket to rocket. Remy had noticed once before that Space Gorilla Max didn't lock his doors when he left his ride—why bother? Nobody could possibly mistake his rocket for someone else's, and anyone stupid enough to even brush against a tailfin would have his limbs ripped off. But Remy wasn't stupid. He was desperate and buzzed. He had to get to Mars, then to Saturn, then to Thardex One.

Remy climbed the ladder to the cockpit and slipped into the leather pilot's seat. The controls were in protected mode, but Remy had a way with machines. It took him a sweaty three minutes to hotwire the launch sequence. With white knuckles, he gripped the joystick. He punched the pedal to the floor and hit 9 g's inside a quarter minute. The haze of the city sky quickly cleared to reveal the stark black velvet of space.

Next stop: Mars.

Fortunately, Mars was closer than it used to be. The distance shrank when the Thardexians arrived, drawn by signs of industrial life visible in a spectroscopic analysis of our atmosphere. The Thardexians had been amused by mankind's quaint notions about gravity. They'd erupted in big, alien, belly laughs when they realized we'd explained the discrepancies between our theories and our observed movements of galaxies by postulating that 96% of the universe was made up of dark energy and dark matter.

"Really?" the Thardexian Chief Science Poohbah had asked. "96% off didn't seem suspicious?"

Thardexians modeled space-time as a kind of nine dimensional, spiky, knotted pretzel. It was possible to jump from spike to spike without passing through intervening space. When human physicists pointed out that the Thardexian model made no sense, the Thardexian's couldn't grasp the concept that reality should make sense. Honestly, it was all over Remy's head. All he knew was, using the Thardexian spike-space map, Mars lay six hours away via ultra-fast, swoopy-sleek rocket ship.

Remy steered the stolen spacecraft through the airlocks covering Valles Marineris. 30 million humans lived in the Valles, plus 15 million Thardexian refugees. He only needed one Thardexian if he wanted to live through this, and his best hope rested with his ex-girlfriend, Susanne. The ship touched down gently as a drifting rose petal in the fine red dust of her front yard.

His stomach had settled somewhat. The sparky, jittery rush of the caffeine was gone, leaving a more mellow, steady hum.

Susanne opened the door before Remy knocked. Oh, right, the precognition. Tall and curvy, with skin as blue and creamy as Earth's sky, and long curly hair whiter than milk, Susanne wore a clingy green hugger that left nothing to the imagination.

Remy strolled into her living room as if it were routine, as if he hadn't run out on her two years ago after emptying all the money out of their joint accounts.

"Hey babe," he said, flashing a pained grin. "What's up?"

"Remy," she said. "Some guy called here five minutes ago asking about you."

"Crap," said Remy. All Thardexians were dangerously honest by Remy's standards. Trying to explain lying to them was like explaining a rainbow to a dog. He hoped Susanne's precognition hadn't kicked in.

"I wish I could have helped, but my precognition didn't kick in until I hung up. I told him I had no idea where you were. I said I hadn't seen you in two years, that you'd walked out on me after you freaked when I told you I wanted to have your baby."

As it turned out, the Thardexians had also been puzzled by the very limited scope of human reproduction. Thardexians boasted they could mate with anything with a genetic code. They claimed to do so frequently, and with gusto, although the actual interspecies mating process remained a mystery to human biologists. Ordinary intercourse never seemed to get anyone knocked up. If any humans had participated in a successful mating, no one was talking, but all these pregnant Thardexians had to come from somewhere.

"Baby, I've changed my mind," said Remy. "I've grown a lot these past two years. I think you and I should get into my rocket ship and high tail it back to your home planet where we can breed lots of happy sprogs."

"You wouldn't like my home planet," she said. "It has oceans of ammonia and three times Earth's gravity. And of course, there's the war."

"As long as I'm with you it will be like Heaven."

"You're in bad trouble, aren't you?" she said.

"You wouldn't believe," he said.

"Gorilla trouble?"

Remy nodded.

Susanne sighed. "I suppose, as a Thardexian, I bear some of the responsibility."

"I really don't hold you at fault for gorillas being jerks," he said. When the Thardexian's had first arrived, they'd dispatched envoys to establish relations with the leaders of every government. Since they weren't initially certain of what, precisely, constituted a human being, they'd wound up sending an envoy to a troop of gorillas in the Congo. Exposure to the Thardexian's universal translation software had a profound effect upon gorilla intelligence. The apes had used their newly enhanced intellect to launch a gorilla guerrilla war against their human neighbors. They'd funded their fight by rapidly dominating the customary monetary streams relied on by human warlords, trading in slaves, weapons, diamonds, oil, drugs, and, most profitably, coffee.

Susanne clarified: "I mean that you wouldn't be involved in smuggling if my people hadn't made your governments outlaw coffee."

Remy shrugged. "I'd just be smuggling something else. I'm not cut out to make a so-called honest living by saying yes ma'am and yes sir a hundred times a day."

"True," said Susanne. "Which is one reason I was interested in mating with you."

"My bad boy charm, right?" he said, attempting a smile that turned into more of a grimace.

"Your inability to comply with authority," said Susanne. "With our planet in the midst of war, one hope for the Thardexians would be to introduce traits into our collective biological heritage that would reduce our tribalism. Your counter-authoritative instincts could be useful if they're genetic in origin, rather than environmentally acquired. This is why I invested so much time in analyzing you."

"My mother thinks I was born bad."

"Perhaps. But you were also born shortly after your world made first contact with a technologically superior spacefaring race. You've grown up amid economic, political, and religious upheaval. It's not easy untangling all these environmental influences from your genetic proclivities. Plus, your gut flora is seriously mutated by your caffeine addiction."

"What does my gut flora have to do with anything?"

Susan gave him a gentle smile. “I find it charming that humans think of themselves as distinct beings rather than walking ecosystems. When I study you for biological worthiness, I can’t just take your DNA into consideration. You’re also host to legions of viruses, bacteria, and multicellular parasites both benign and malignant that influence your behavior in subtle ways. Now that you’ve been gone for two years, my previous research with you is obsolete. Your biome has evolved in the interim.”

“All the more reason to take me back to Thardex One,” said Remy. “You can study me at your leisure. You said you still have connections there, right? That you could go back any time you wanted?”

Susanne crossed her arms as she fixed a hard stare at his mangled face. Then, her face softened. “You’re so damn lucky.”

“Why?”

“Since you've been gone, I've spent half my time hating you. The other half I've spent missing you. Life seems a little dull when I’m not getting swept up in your latest life-threatening scheme on a daily basis.”

“I hope you're in the second mood.”

“I said you were lucky.” Susanne wrapped her arms around him. He kissed her, ignoring the pain. Her lips were soft and sweet and slightly sticky, like she’d been eating honey. She smelled of lilacs.

For half a minute, Remy couldn’t recall why he’d been dumb enough to leave her. Then it hit him, deep in the pit of his stomach, the tiny black vortex of horror that he’d felt every time he’d touched Susanne. While Thardexians didn’t lie, they did deceive. They were shapeshifters. If their first encounter was with a human male, they took the form of sultry vixens. If they first met women, they appeared as tall, hard studs, muscles carved with the perfection of Greek statues. No one knew what they really looked like before they stepped out of their ships, aside from the fact that all Thardexians sported blue skin and white hair. Some tiny, distant voice in Remy’s head screamed every time he put his mouth on her. The thought of going to Thardex One and discovering he’d been kissing some tentacled, gelatinous, blue-white blob was too awful to contemplate. Only the last remnants of the caffeine and the looming possibility of gorilla decapitation made her touch endurable.

Susanne broke off the kiss and went to the bedroom, returning seconds later carrying two suitcases. “Let’s go,” she said.

"Thardexian women certainly pack faster than human women," said Remy.

A minute later they were on the ship, punching up through the ephemeral Martian atmosphere, following the Thardexian spike map to Saturn, nine hours away. From there, they'd jump from spike to spike until they reached Thardex One. In twenty-four hours, Remy would be in a place so unpleasant that even Space Gorilla Max wouldn't bother to hunt him down.

This plan seemed better back on Earth. His head throbbed with each heartbeat and tiny sparks floated before him. The caffeine was going, going, gone.

"I need coffee," he whispered.

"I knew you would," Susanne said, pulling a thermos out of her purse. She twisted the dispensing valve and the cabin filled with the nostril-stabbing aroma of Thardexian brew, thick and black as spent motor oil.

Once, her quirky and unreliable precognition had unnerved him. Now, as he lifted the thermos to his lips and sucked down a steaming gulp of bean juice, he recognized that her gifts had certain advantages. He emptied the thermos in under a minute and she produced a second one.

"I love you," he said.

"I've always known you would."

They spent the rest of the voyage in Space Gorilla Max's heart-shaped, satin-sheeted, banana-scented bed, taking full advantage of Thardexians' extraordinary flexibility. Remy felt like his life was turning out pretty well. Maybe it was Thardexian pheromone manipulation, maybe it was caffeine psychosis, or maybe it was love, after all.

In the afterglow, he confessed the biggest mystery of his relationship with Susanne. "I don't deserve you."

"I know," she said.

"Why do you put up with me?"

"I told you. Your potentially useful genetic traits."

"Yeah, but disobedience to authority? I mean, that can't be rare, can it? There are a thousand punks like me in the bean trade."

"True," she said. "But there's also your hair."

"My what?"

"Your hair," she said. "You're still young, but I can smell in your genes that your hair is going to turn this gorgeous, thick silver. Mmmmm-rrrroww!"

"My hair?"

"Look, I don't ask you to justify your sexual selection preferences," she said, sounding a little defensive. "I mean, if I were to design a human female, I certainly wouldn't waste resources on these ridiculously globular breasts," she said, arching her back to better display her generous cleavage.

"Um, I think big breasts help me choose a mate capable of feeding my offspring," said Remy.

"Other mammals choose mates perfectly well without prominent breasts," said Susanne. "But, don't worry about it. It's fine. You like boobs. I have boobs. Just accept that I like your hair. I mean, really, really like it. You're going to be amazing in another two decades." Her voice dropped an octave as she ran her fingers through his locks. Her eyes grew dewy as she brought her face close to his. Rather than kissing him, she licked the dried blood on the left side of his face. Her saliva numbed his pain. Her faint purring as she analyzed his genetic information unsettled him, but her breasts mashing against his chest quickly overrode any uneasiness.

Remy was recovering to the point he was ready to give her another sample of his DNA when the computer chirped their arrival at the Saturnian gravity knot. He went to the leather seat, took the joystick and started steering toward the next spike. Susanne came into the cockpit and massaged his shoulders. His fingers flew across the instrument panel and the ship turned, bringing the rings of Saturn into view.

This was why he'd been born. This was the payoff, the single moment of his life where everything was correct, sitting at the controls of a cherry red rocket ship, a blue-skinned babe wrapped around his neck, the rings of Saturn glowing before him. Maybe Thardex One would be a lousy place to live, but what did that matter? He loved Susanne, Susanne loved him. All was right with the universe.

This bliss lasted upwards of thirty seconds.

The rings of Saturn vanished, hidden behind a steel shark the size of a small moon that swooped down from above. The shark opened its iron maw and swallowed their vessel. The door of the rocket ship exploded from its hinges and a dozen goons stormed the cockpit.

They grabbed Remy and Susanne, dragging them screaming and kicking from the ship.

In the center of the vast, chilly hanger, Space Gorilla Max waited. The bloodied, beaten heads of Tyro and Wilson hung from his belt.

Space Gorilla Max wasn't happy. He was a big silverback, easily half a ton. His eyes were red as tomato sauce. When he spoke, his long canine teeth flashed ivory.

"Remy!" he shouted, his rank spittle fouling the air. "You sack of excrement! You dare touch my ship? Do you know what I'm going to do to you?"

Remy kept quiet, fearing his worst guesses might be taken as suggestions.

"The average human intestine is twenty-three foot long," said Space Gorilla Max. "Boys, bring me my tape measure."

"Look," Remy said. "Do what you want to me. But leave Susanne out of this. She had no clue this was your ship. She's innocent. Just ask her. You know she can't lie."

"I can't imagine why her innocence is important. I wonder what the average length of Thardexian intestine is?"

"Why not find out?" Susanne asked.

Susanne lurched, her body swelling from sleek supermodel to sumo in a span of seconds. Her legs thickened to tree trunk size, her torso leaned forward as a long tail sprouted to balance growing weight. Her head expanded to the size of a small car, taking on the form of a t-rex, only toothier. She opened her long, knife-filled jaw and gulped down Space Gorilla Max in a single bite. For several long seconds, his agonized, muffled shrieks could be heard from her belly.

All the gorilla's men fled the room, sobbing like children.

Susanne belched. Her outline slinked and undulated as she slipped from dinosaur back to dream woman. Only, now she was a very pregnant dream woman, her belly bulging like a beach ball. She wiped her glistening lips with a slender, dainty hand as Remy stared.

"I'm so sorry," she said, rubbing her belly. "I really think I would have decided to mate with you, given time. But it seemed more urgent to mate with Space Gorilla Max. I don't know if he has any other useful traits, but oh my god his fur! That silver mane—-oh, oh, oh. It makes my toes curl. Our babies will be fabulous!"

Remy nodded. "I'm, um, happy for you."

"Do you still want to go to Thardex One?"

"With Max gone, I guess it's safe to go home. I've got family in California. Maybe it's time for a fresh start."

"You aren't as upset as I thought you'd be," she said.

Remy shrugged. He truly wasn't upset. Perhaps his brush with death had given him needed perspective. Perhaps watching his girlfriend digest a gorilla had mutated his gut flora even further. Whatever the cause, he felt as if he was a little wiser, as if he saw the world a little plainer now. Shoveling manure beneath the California sun might make for a worthwhile life after all.

Time mends a broken heart.

And he'd damn well keep the rocket ship.

IN THE DIMLY LIT BEDROOM, Nyx tossed my pants onto a giraffe's head standing in the corner. Under different circumstances the big-game trophy might have made a good conversation starter, but Nyx wasn't in a talking mood. She leapt onto me, digging her nails into my back. She silenced my yelp of pain by pushing her licorice-flavored tongue deep into my mouth. We collapsed onto her bed, sending startled cats flying.

"Easy!" I cried out, as she bit my ear.

She responded by digging her nails in harder.

"If you didn't want to play with the panther," she growled, "you shouldn't have opened the cage."

NYX'S PARTY had broken up at midnight when the rain started. I'd been nursing a beer at the edge of the bonfire for over an hour. Coming out here had been Jerry's idea, but he never turned up. The only person I recognized other than the hostess was Conspiracy Dave and I wasn't drunk enough to talk to him. I barely knew Nyx, having only run into her a few times since she moved here from California.

I was contemplating making my exit when some sparks landed in the leaves of the nearby woods. The next thing I knew there was a wall of fire roaring northward. Everyone reached for their phones but no one had service out in the ass end of Chatham County. I sprinted to my car to grab a camera, not wanting a potential disaster to go to waste.

When I got back to the fire, Nyx had cranked her boom box to full blast. Distorted drumbeats thudded like rhythmic thunder. Inexplicably, she'd stripped off her clothes. She danced naked at the edge of the wildfire, stomping and kicking embers, waving her hands in the air. Hell yes I started snapping shots, managing to take a few dozen before the surroundings turned stark white and KABOOM, actual thunder deafened me.

Rain came down in torrents. The other guests ran for their cars, knowing better than to seek shelter in Nyx's house. Nyx owns, like, fifty cats, and the atmosphere inside is noteworthy. Alas, no one had warned me, so I sprinted toward her kitchen door. Nyx darted past with gazelle-like bounds, laughing wildly. For half a second, I wondered just how crazy she was and thought about bolting for my car. On the other hand, I had a track record of following unclothed women into dangerous places.

Nyx was well-maintained for a woman in her late thirties, certainly in better shape than I was, five years younger. Her skinny torso glistened white as milk beneath the florescent lights of her kitchen, with beads of rain upon her small breasts glinting like jewels. Only the lines of her face showed her age.

The smoke of the bonfire still filled my sinuses enough that the cat odor hadn't set off warning bells. She looked out her screen door at the dying fire and the taillights of the other guests heading down the driveway.

"I guess the party's over," she said, as another burst of thunder rattled the kitchen.

"I thought things were just getting interesting." I set my camera on the table and grabbed a roll of paper towels from her counter to dry it.

She eyed the camera. "Get any good pictures of me?"

A "yes" or a "no" was going to get me in trouble, so I hid behind a technicality. "I was really taking pictures of the fire. If it burned down half the county, I could have sold the photos to local papers."

"They pay for that stuff?"

"Not much," I said. "But every dollar helps."

"You make your living as a photographer?"

I shrugged. "More or less. Mostly less, according to my ex-wife. She wasn't thrilled when I quit my day job."

"What did you used to do?"

"Nothing remotely interesting. The world I saw from inside a cubicle was mundane and gray. The world I see in my camera is… better somehow. Perfectly ordinary things turn magical."

"You're fortunate you can reach that heightened state with only a camera," she said. "My ex-husband chased after the same feeling, but used copious amounts of drugs to get there."

"That's why he's your ex?"

"Among other reasons," she said. "I was completely honest about who I was when we met, but he somehow fell in love with the person he wanted me to be. Apparently, the real me is somewhat… difficult." She crossed her arms, covering her breasts, shaking her head. "I don't like to dwell on the past. I moved out here to get a fresh start."

"To new beginnings," I said. "I'd offer a toast, but I left my beer out by the fire."

Nyx smiled as she opened a cabinet door revealing shelves of booze. She took down a bottle of absinthe.

"I saved this for the true friends who'd still be here when the party wound down," she said. "I may not have as many true friends as I thought if a little rain sends them running."

"In fairness, it's a lot of rain," I said as she poured the green liquid, letting it soak through a sugar cube on a spoon. "We're lucky that storm rolled through."

"Luck had nothing to do with it," she said. "I asked it to come."

"Well then, good job."

"Since we're about to share a drink, I suppose I should ask your name," she said. "I feel like we've met, but can't place you."

"I'm Buddy. Jerry's friend. We met at the Haw River Ballroom. The Old Ceremony concert?"

"Right," she said. "So, Buddy. Didn't Jerry tell you I was a witch?"

"He told me you were Wiccan."

"Please," she said, rolling her eyes. "I'm part of something a lot older than that. Witchcraft predates civilization. The only part the Wiccans get right is the bit about being sky-clad."

"Sky-clad?"

"Naked. The energies I manipulate are the faintest tingles on the skin. You miss the signals entirely with clothes on."

"I see." She still hadn't gotten dressed and didn't seem to mind that I was getting an eyeful. "Are you casting a spell now?"

"Of course. After manipulating so much energy, I'm going to be up all night. I'm giving you this love potion so you'll keep me company. To new beginnings?"

She raised her glass. I clinked mine against hers, then sipped the absinthe. My lips puckered from the intense licorice burn. She took advantage of my puckered lips to kiss me, then pulled away, her dark brown eyes locked onto mine.

"That's a strong potion," I mumbled.

"Absinthe makes the heart grow fonder."

This time, I initiated the kiss. Anyone who can deliver a line like that with a straight face is all right by me.

THE NEXT MORNING, I stumbled through her house in the fog of a hangover. I took shallow breaths, the ammoniated atmosphere stinging my eyes. I found my shirt on the kitchen floor, still damp. What I didn't find was Nyx, despite looking through every room. The warning bells that hadn't gone off the night before started clanging. Nyx was something of a hoarder, with an unnerving collection of taxidermy, ranging in size from the giraffe head in the bedroom to chipmunks dressed in Victorian suits congregated on top of her refrigerator. Finding a dozen stuffed cats among all the living ones felt wrong. I stepped into the bathroom to relieve myself and glanced into her shower. Wax-penciled numbers and symbols covered the walls.

Thoroughly spooked, I retrieved my camera and made it to my car. I sped down the rutty road. I reached the paved road and put miles between us, feeling lucky to have escaped. By the time I reached Hillsborough, I started laughing, tickled by the over-the-top weirdness of the night. Most of all, I laughed at how freaked out I'd gotten by a lonely woman's poor housekeeping.

NYX DIDN'T CALL ME and I didn't call her. She didn't use computers, so I didn't have to worry about her stalking me online. For once in my life, I'd successfully pulled off a one-night stand. I usually wind up more entangled with my bed partners.

A month passed. Someone knocked on my kitchen door. Moving toward it, I spotted Nyx through the window. Worse, she spotted me; I really need to invest in some curtains. My approach to home furnishing since my divorce is somewhat Spartan. When my old life fell apart, I never quite found the energy to build a new one, at least not a new one with such niceties as drapery and furniture.

I opened the door. “Fancy seeing you.”

“Hi Buddy. Forget our date?”

“Date?”

She frowned. “You said we’d open a gate together. That you’d photograph me.”

“Um,” I said.

She sighed. “I should have written it down for you.”

“Details are hazy,” I admitted.

“You said you photograph magic?”

“I believe I was speaking metaphorically. The closest thing I have to a steady income is doing covers for indy-published fantasy novels. A few years back I did the photo for Stephanie Burant’s first book. There are enough Burant wannabees that most months I can pay my mortgage. I’m always on the lookout for things that look supernatural. I don’t actually believe in magic.”

“You shouldn’t,” she said. “Magic’s all crap.”

“This from a witch?”

“Being a witch is more science than magic.”

“Rain dances and love potions are science?”

“Alcohol’s ability to promote feelings of goodwill are well documented.”

“Sure, but the rain—”

“There’s nothing mysterious about rain.”

“I’m not saying there is. It’s just that, when you claimed to have summoned it you came off sounding…”

“Crazy?”

I managed to maintain a neutral expression.

She put her hands on her hips. “I’m sick of people doubting my sanity. I understand how the universe truly operates. It’s everyone else who’s crazy.”

“Okay,” I said, slowly.

“Let me explain everything to you,” she said. “I’ve gotten better at breaking it down into simple terms since the days of my doctoral program.”

“You have a PHD?”

“No. Dancing naked in moonlight isn’t, quote, an approved research methodology, unquote.”

"The narrow-minded fools," I said. "But, maybe you can explain the workings of the universe some other time. I'm not sure I've got the mental stamina at the moment to take it all in."

"Didn't you take a nap?" she asked.

"Why?"

"Since we'll be up late."

"Why?"

"To photograph me," she said. "You repeated the promise three times. How can you not remember?"

"Absinthe-mindedness?"

She stared at me blankly.

"Look, just tell me what you want."

"I need you to take pictures as I open a gate."

"That sounds… mundane."

"These aren't ordinary gates. They're portals to an intertwined reality."

"Go on."

"What do you know about the multiverse?"

"Like, from comic books?"

She plowed ahead with an answer that didn't have a lot to do with comic books, so I tuned out most of it. Something about splinter realities branching away from our own, sharing the same physical space, but separated by vibrational frequencies.

I interrupted her when she got to that part. "That's exactly how it worked in *Flash of Two Worlds*."

Now it was her turn to look confused.

"Not the TV version," I said. "The original comic book, *Flash 123*. I'd show it to you, but all my comics are currently stored at my mom's house."

"How old are you again?" she asked.

"Old enough to get a sense when someone I'm talking to hasn't been taking their… um…" My voice trailed off. It was a sentence I really shouldn't have started.

She raised her hand and waved away my words. "I've worked out the harmonics of the splinter reality most in tune with our own. At certain moments, in certain places, I can sync the vibrations and capture energy from this entangled world."

"By dancing naked."

"I've explained why that's important."

"And moonlight's required?"

"Not the light itself. The tidal forces help align the realities."

"If I went with you, and I'm not saying I will, what, exactly, would I see?"

She shrugged. "I don't know."

"You don't know?"

She shook her head. "I'm in a trance when the energy starts flowing. My memories of opening the gates are as fuzzy as your memories of promises."

"You're certainly making a convincing case."

She crossed her arms, frowning, looking like she might be about to give up. Then, she managed to smile, and said, "Worst case scenario: I'll get a good workout dancing while you take pictures of a naked woman."

"That's the argument you should have opened with."

SHE FAILED TO MENTION she'd be dancing in public. Hillsborough is one of the oldest towns in North Carolina. In fact, it's a lot older than North Carolina, having been a major hub of the Occanneechee Indians. I've never met an actual Occanneechee, but behind the courthouse there's a reconstruction of some of their grass huts. The ragged condition of the huts is a sad testament to the fate of the natives.

Did I mention the huts were right behind the courthouse? Under the full moon, Nyx's body practically glowed. If any trucks came over the bridge on Churton Street, they'd get an eyeful.

Increasing the odds we'd be discovered, she cranked her boom box to tooth-rattling. I gave serious thought to running, but figured what the hell. She was the one who was naked. I didn't even have to admit to knowing her. I snapped shots as she danced in front of the hut. It was pitch black inside. She waved her arms toward the darkness with seductive, come-hither gestures, as if trying to draw out someone. I kept taking pictures.

And then… I still didn't see anything but her dancing. I couldn't hear anything but the music. But glancing at the black doorway, the hair rose on the back of my neck. I felt like something was staring at me from the darkness.

A mangy cat yowled and ran from the hut, racing between Nyx's legs. She almost tripped trying not to step on the thing. I burst out laughing. Nyx frowned, running her fingers through her tussled hair as she watched the cat vanish in some nearby bushes. Then she grinned and gave a soft chuckle, which grew into an actual laugh. We laughed until we fell to the grass, completely breathless, tears in our eyes.

Which is why we didn't see the deputy until he focused his flashlight on us. Then we laughed even harder.

WITHOUT BOTHERING TO ASK if I was interested in trying again, Nyx said she'd be back in twenty-nine days. On the day of the next full moon, I tried to take a nap but couldn't sleep.

She rapped on my door as the sun was setting.

"Tell me about the Ice House," she said as I let her in.

"The what now?"

"When I told my sister about our experience at the huts, she asked if I'd thought of trying the Cameron Ice House."

"Oh, right," I said. "Behind St. Matthew's Church."

"She said it's really spooky in moonlight."

"It's spooky in daylight," I assured her. "It looks like a house that's been buried in the ground so that only the roof is showing. I've got a ton of close-ups of the wooden shingles. I use them for textures in Photoshop."

"And there's a door?"

"Sure."

"What's it like inside?"

"Who knows? It's locked."

"Could we break in?"

"The deputy might not be as forgiving if he catches us vandalizing a town landmark."

"Locks are the greater vandalism," she said. "If the place is set in the earth, it will have accumulated a great deal of energy. It will yearn to be free."

"How can energy yearn for anything?"

"Didn't I mention that all universes are sentient?"

I went back to the difficulty of getting inside. "The Ice House looks pretty solid. I doubt I could kick the door open."

"I've a crowbar in my trunk."

"If you need to dance in front of an open door, can't we just use my kitchen?"

She shook her head. "This place is too new. It takes a long time for the energy to build in a gate."

"I don't know that the Ice House is all that old. The foundation, sure, but I think it was rebuilt at some point. And, you know, the Indian huts are younger than my house. They were put up in the seventies."

"Ah," she said. "The huts might not be old, but the land has been lived on a long time. I could feel the flow. So could you. I saw it in your eyes."

I crossed my arms, not wanting to admit that, until the cat had jumped out, I had sensed something odd.

"You're still skeptical," she said.

"I'm a little old for fairy tales."

She nodded. "It does sound like a fairy tale. Have you never wondered why every culture has such stories? Haven't you pondered the universality of belief that there's a world just beyond our own, a world entered via holes in the ground?"

"I assume these stories exist because our ancestors weren't that bright."

"No! They were deeply in tune with the land. To have enough food to eat, they had to listen carefully to natural rhythms. Modern man has grown deaf to nature. Our ancestors heard the truth. There are worlds next to our own, worlds of elemental intelligence."

"The idea of intelligent worlds is hard to swallow."

"Most people can't accept it. We don't want to think that, as we assault the earth with our machines and pollution, we're hurting sentient spirits."

"If we're hurting them, aren't they angry? Isn't it dangerous to open gates and let them out?"

"Anger is an animal emotion. There are no angry trees. The intelligences I commune with are far older than animals."

"Whatever. I'm in. I'm looking forward to doing it with you again."

She put her hands on her hips. "Was that a double entendre?"

I grinned.

"Getting into the Ice House would leave me in a very pleasant mood," she cooed.

"I live to please," I said.

"Then please break into the Ice House with me."

"Leave it to a witch to know the magic word."

THE NIGHT WAS PITCH BLACK, the moon hidden behind clouds. Nyx disrobed, her body pale in the gloom. Fortunately, the Ice House isn't visible from the road.

I made short work of the lock. The Ice House was originally built by a rich family as a place to store ice during the summer. From the size of it, they must have really liked cold drinks. The open door revealed stairs descending farther than I could see via the light from my cell phone.

"Do you feel that?" Nyx asked.

I gave the question honest consideration and sensed a faint quiver in my guts, similar to what I felt at the huts, but purer somehow, humming down beneath the bass range.

"Get your camera ready," she said, turning on the boom box.

I stepped back as she started to dance. I'd been able to get clear photos in the previous month's moonlight, but in this darkness I was either going to have to use a flash or take such long exposures her dancing would be a blur. Worried that the deputy might investigate the source of the music, I decided in favor of the blur and kept the camera steady with a tripod.

She danced for half an hour, until the song faded to silence. She fell to her knees, panting. I moved closer. From a yard away, her skin gave off heat like a stove.

"Did… did it work?" I asked.

She rose, giving me a sultry stare. She threw her arms around my neck as I bent my face toward her. Just before our lips touched a static spark arced between our noses. I stumbled backward, cursing. She laughed. I tripped over the boom box and landed hard on my back, laughing despite the pain.

Then the deputy showed up.

He didn't find us funny at all.

THERE WAS SOMETHING FUNNY in the pictures, however. As expected, Nyx was a white blur in the long exposure. What I didn't expect was that she would have a dancing partner. I hadn't seen anything, but the camera caught something, a vaguely human shape in the open door, a fog with limbs, all blurred.

What if she's not crazy?

Or maybe crazy is contagious. Lord knows, I'd exposed myself. On our first absinthe-fueled romp we didn't bother with protection, so there wasn't much point in being cautious now that we were… well, it's not quite accurate to say that we were a couple. But she showed up at my house most nights at sunset, always slipping away shortly after dawn, leaving only her scent on my pillows. We never spent much time talking.

I tried to read up on her theories, but the Orange County Library didn't have much useful information. The math she assigned me to study was way over my head, and the mythology seemed pointless. From the *Encyclopedia of Fairies* I learned the difference between a faun and a pixie and an elf, but nothing that helped me make sense of what I'd seen.

Of course, I didn't spend that much time reading. Breaking into the Ice House had opened a door inside me I hadn't even known was closed. Long ago, I'd dreamed of being a photojournalist, travelling to exotic landscapes. My actual budget, alas, kept me mostly within the boundaries of my home town. But Hillsborough has its share of old, abandoned houses, closed up shops, and shuttered factories. I started exploring them all, crawling through windows, forcing open doors, usually in broad daylight. There's a house on Highway 70 that hasn't been lived in for decades, and the backdoor wasn't even locked. Inside, I found a life frozen in cobwebs. There were shoes next to an unmade bed, and dirty dishes still in the sink, like whoever had lived there had been planning to come back. I took hundreds of photos, feeling like I was finally capturing something that mattered, something truthful, even if the truth was that nothing mattered. At any moment anyone of us could simply vanish, leaving nothing behind but framed photos blotted out by dust.

And yet… whoever had lived here had, in fact, lived here. Every clue indicated that, until the moment things fell apart, this place had been someone's home, where they protected everything precious to them. If someone broke into my house, with its single plate and glass, and mattress directly on the floor, they'd probably think someone was squatting there rather than actually renting the place.

A WEEK BEFORE the next full moon, we were stretched out on my mattress when she said, "I want to try the cellar of the Colonial Inn."

The Colonial Inn is old enough that George Washington might have slept there, though as far as I know, he didn't. The building has been in limbo for years, too historic to be torn down, too big and rickety for anyone to afford to restore it. It's a majestic eyesore.

"That's a good target, if your main criteria is that the gates are creepy in moonlight."

She nodded. "Being creepy is a good guide. Have you ever wondered why some places make the hairs on the back of your neck rise? People can sense when another world intersects our own."

"Maybe. But people live right next door to the Colonial Inn. Can we do this quietly?"

She shook her head. "The beat has to be loud. The vibrations are key to opening the gates."

"Then we need to be away from people."

"Getting away from people is something I'm all too happy to do," she said.

She rose and went to the kitchen. She came back a moment later with a glass of water. "I think it's weird that you only have one glass and one plate."

"I moved in here with literally nothing but my camera gear and a bag of dirty laundry."

"Your ex got everything else?"

"I let her have it all. Well, except my comic books."

"Why?"

"I really like comics."

"No, I mean why didn't you try to keep more stuff?"

I shrugged. "I needed a clean break."

"Did it work?"

"Not in the least. But… my past doesn't provide a lot of fuel for nostalgia. As for my future, I don't know. I feel like I've had my life on hold. I'd really like to move forward, but can't seem to figure out what direction to move." Then, I smiled. "But you've inspired me. First thing tomorrow, I'll head to the Dollar Tree and buy another plate."

She laughed, but then her face grew serious. "I know how you feel. That longing for a new life, a new world." She ran her fingers through her hair. "And now, a longing for a new gate, since the Colonial Inn isn't going to work out. Any ideas?"

"If creepy is the criteria, I can hook us up."

THE NEXT FULL MOON found us hiking through the Cabe Lands. Long ago, the Cabe family owned a huge farm next to the Eno and now it's a state park. You can still find family tombstones among the trees. The Cabe Lands aren't far from the interstate. Even down by the river, you hear tractor-trailers. Still, it's a safe distance from anyone's house.

The Cabe's ran a gristmill on the Eno. All that's left is the stone foundation, looking like a miniature castle.

"Good call," Nyx said, as our flashlights played over the stone wall. "This is creepy."

It's not the wall itself that's spooky. It's the part of the wall that's missing. There's a big gaping hole in the rocks, like a giant punched his way out from inside the foundation. What's left is an arch of broken rock, like fangs on a sideways mouth.

Nyx whistled. "I feel the flow already. This is going to be amazing."

As she undressed, I set up tripods. I'd brought five cameras. I put a video camera inside the foundation itself, aiming it out through the gate. If another apparition did appear, I was ready for it.

Finally, I grabbed my handheld camera and climbed the bank opposite the gate.

"Ready?" Nyx asked.

"As I'll ever be."

She pressed play. Drumbeats pulsed into the night. She danced. I snapped photos.

Minutes passed. I squinted, trying to tell if what I saw in the gate was a trick of the light. A faint luminous fog swirled in the doorway. Nyx drew her arms back and forth, trying to draw it out. Whatever was on the other side of the gate responded by stretching out a long arm of glowing mist, the ephemeral fingers straining toward Nyx.

I blinked. The fog solidified into a furry hand. It snatched her from her feet and jerked her through the gate before she could even scream.

"Nyx!" I yelled, dropping my camera, scrambling down the hill. I paused before the hole in the wall, unable to see her. Nor could I see the video camera inside, even though it should have been only a few yards in front of me. With trembling hands, I found my flashlight and aimed it through the jagged gate.

The beam formed a bright cone in the haze, illuminating trees instead of the back wall of the mill.

"Nyx?" I whispered.

No answer, at least none I could hear over the pounding drum beat.

I carefully crept through the gate, swinging the beam from side to side. I straightened up, looking around. Enormous trees towered over me. I whispered, "Nyx?"

A loud snort answered. A figure leaped in front of my beam, crouched on all fours. At first I thought it was the biggest deer I'd ever seen, since it had antlers. My jaw dropped as I realized that the antlers jutted from the brow of an almost-but-not-quite human face. The nose and mouth were definitely those of a man, albeit covered in short tan fur. The eyes, however, were cat-like, glowing golden in the flashlight beam.

I turned and ran, making it through the gate, back into my own world. I was bowled over by a glancing blow from the creature's rear hooves as it sprang over me. By chance, my hand fell on the master remote I'd clipped to my vest and triggered all the cameras at once, filling the night with flashes and clicks. The creature didn't like the commotion. He let loose a growl then jumped from camera to camera, stomping the hell out of them. Finally, it focused on the blaring boom box, crushing it to splinters beneath its cloven hooves.

It paused, breathing hard as it tilted its antlered head toward the sky, sniffing the air. On its hind legs, the thing was twice as tall as me, not counting the antlers, which added another five or six feet. The time I'd spent in the library hadn't been a complete waste. This thing was the spitting image of a faun, though nothing I'd read had prepared me for it being so huge. Its eyes narrowed into angry slits as it sniffed the air and turned its head toward the rumble of trucks on the interstate. It drew back its powerful shoulders and unleashed a long howl. Then, it bounded up the brushy hill in eerie silence, barely disturbing the leaves covering the forest floor.

I sat for a moment, frozen, unsure if it was gone. My paralysis lifted when I heard the distant sound of a truck's air horn screaming through the night. The thing must have reached the interstate.

I rose on unsteady legs and staggered toward the gate. On the other side, the moon through the leaves was the brightest I'd ever seen. Ordinarily, a full moon obliterates stars, but I could see hundreds of them, maybe thousands, twinkling against a sky of perfect black. Was this what the heavens looked like before light pollution? This was an atmosphere that had never known a factory or car. The air was so pure I felt light-headed.

I heard a groan off to my left. I saw a pale form slumped across the roots of a giant oak.

"Nyx!" I yelled, running toward her.

Her eyes fluttered open. She had a knot on her left brow as big as an egg.

"What happened?" she whispered.

"A big-ass faun tried to kill you," I said, grabbing her by the hand. "We're on the wrong side of the gate! We've got to get back to our world before it closes!"

She rubbed her temple as I pulled her to her feet. "I don't think it wanted to hurt me. It wanted to dance. I was just too fragile a partner."

"It seemed pretty violent to me. It smashed up my cameras. Also, you'll be needing a new boom box."

"It's probably terrified," she said. "It's never seen any kind of technology. It's lashing out because it's afraid."

"Then I'd hate to be on I-85 right now. The thing made a bee-line in that direction. I can only imagine what it will think about cars."

"Oh no," she whispered. "We have to help it find its way back!"

"Finding it isn't my first priority. Getting you to an emergency room is."

"I've survived worse," she said. "My first husband once beat me so bad it dislodged my cornea."

I didn't know what to say to that.

I helped steady her as we moved back toward the gate. From this side, there was no stone wall. Instead, there was an enormous tree with a huge cleft in the trunk, like it had once been split by lightning. On the other side, I could see one of my mutilated cameras, the lens glinting in moonlight.

"I'm sorry," I said, as I helped her through.

"About what?"

"About… about what your husband did. No one should suffer that kind of bullshit."

"It's nothing you need to be sorry about. I don't hold all men responsible for the actions of one asshole."

"Then I'm sorry I didn't know. I mean, we've been sleeping together for a month and I haven't… I can't believe I know so little about you. It makes me feel like… like I've been using you."

"So what? I'm using you. We aren't children."

"You're an interesting woman, Nyx. I want to get to know you better."

"I'd like that."

With our arms around each other, we stumbled out of the gate into our own world. The change in the air was instantly noticeable. Unlike the comparative silence of the other forest, our own woods echoed with distant thumps and screams.

"At least we made it back before the gate closed," I said.

Nyx shook her head, holding her hand toward the gate, her finger's spread. "The flow's too strong. This gate won't shut before dawn. The photons from sunlight will provide the pressure to push back the tide."

"So… more of those things might come through?"

She shook her head again as she bent over her backpack. "There's no music to draw them toward the gate."

She pulled out a water bottle and drained it in one long gulp, then wiped her lips. "We have to lead it back. It can't survive in our world. It's only a matter of time before some cop puts a bullet into it."

I started to ask why that would be a bad thing, but checked myself. Deep down, I knew she was right. This wasn't an evil spirit. It was a wild spirit.

"Come on," she said, sprinting up the trail.

I chased after her. I'm not in bad shape, but I'm no runner. I strained to keep up with Nyx, even though she was injured, not to mention barefoot on a rough and rocky trail.

We'd taken twenty minutes to hike down to the old mill, weighed down with camera gear. We made it back to the parking lot in half that time, then ran through the ratty trailer park across the way. A dozen people stood around the trailers, staring toward the interstate barely thirty yards distant. Something was on fire, though I couldn't quite make out what through the trees. Heads turned as Nyx ran past, stark naked.

We scrambled up the bank to the interstate. A tractor-trailer had jackknifed from the northbound lane across the median to block the southbound lane. A Civic had swerved over the median to avoid the truck, only to T-bone an SUV. Now they were tangled together, burning, and traffic had backed up in both directions. The flames had jumped to the trees on the far side of the interstate, providing a fiery backdrop for the faun as it ran from car to car, screeching and yowling, kicking in windshields and pounding on roofs with its fists. Drivers ran from the scene, probably thinking the devil himself had come for them, as the flames painted the creature hellish red.

"We need a drum!" Nyx yelled. "We have to get it dancing!"

"I left my bongos in my other pants!"

"Improvise!" she shouted, running toward the faun.

I scanned the area, spotting an abandoned pickup. I found a large plastic bucket in the bed. I tucked it under my arm and whacked it with my palm, producing a vaguely musical note.

I'd spent enough time listening to Nyx's midnight drum CD to have the underlying beat burned into my memory. It's a DUM dum dum dum DUM dum dum dum that a B-grade western might use for Indians on the warpath. I just had to count to four, with the one being loudest. So, that's what I did, cautiously heading in the direction of the faun.

Amazingly, the beat caught its attention. Or maybe it was Nyx, now only a few yards from him. She froze as he cast his gaze upon her, then gracefully lifted her arms and began to sway her hips to the bucket beat.

The faun snorted as he watched. I approached as closely as I dared while Nyx danced vigorously, jumping into the air on each DUM and bouncing from foot to foot on the dum dum dum.

I nearly lost the beat when I saw the faun mimic her movements. She danced backward, little by little, heading toward the trailer park. The faun followed, entranced by her white body shimmering in the firelight. She seemed to float down the steep embankment; I've no idea how she didn't break her neck. I struggled to make it down without taking my hands off the drum. For a moment I lost the rhythm, and my beat and her dance were no longer in synch. The faun looked over its shoulder toward me, its brow furrowed.

"ONE two three four," I whispered, getting my act together.

We inched our way down the trail. I was vaguely aware of a crowd at my back. People from the trailer park filmed the faun with phones. I prayed he didn't notice and go on another rampage. He seemed mesmerized by Nyx's movements, and didn't even react when sirens wailed through the night behind us.

It took us forever to move down the path. Nxy's dance had a lot of stepping forward as well as stepping back, so our progress was decidedly incremental. I kept expecting a gunshot from some highway patrolman to bring a rapid end to our journey, but none came. No doubt they were too busy with the chaos up on the road to spend time combing through the woods in search of a late night drumbeat.

My arms felt like lead by the time the river came into sight. My fingertips had gone numb. Nyx was drenched in sweat, her wild hair clinging to her cheeks. I could see the strain on her face, thought about the knot on her head, and wondered how long it would be before she passed out.

Instead, she made it all the way back to the gate, dancing through the gap in the stone, drawing the faun toward her with beckoning gestures. The faun looked around nervously at the crowd of gawkers. Then, breaking stride from the dance, it dove through the gate. Nyx crouched, clasping her hands over her head as the thing leaped over her, before it bounded off into the primeval forest.

She straightened up, looking toward the faun as it vanished in the darkness. She turned back to me and said, "Toss me my pack."

I dropped the bucket. "What?"

"Toss me my pack," she said. "Hurry. It's almost dawn!"

"You'll be trapped in there!"

"It's not a trap. It's a choice," she said.

"There's no way I'm letting you go alone," I said, grabbing her pack and running toward her.

"You might never get home again," she said.

"I'd rather lose my home than lose you," I said.

She leaned close, standing on her tip-toes to kiss me. Then she ripped the pack out of my hands and pushed me hard in the chest, forcing me to stumble back to the other side of the gate.

"I love you too," she said. "But you're my only ticket back. I need you to open the gate again next month."

"You're crazy. I don't know how…"

"You've got pictures and recordings to study the moves. I trust you. And, I need you to feed my cats while I'm gone. In one month, you can—"

The first rays of sunlight dappled the leaves around me as the fog cleared. On the other side of the gate, I could see the single red LED of the video camera I'd placed inside.

THE EYEWITNESSES to what happened that night all sounded so crazy the cops didn't know what to believe. No one was seriously hurt in the traffic pileup. Airbags did their job and the drivers got out before the fire started. I watched the videos posted to YouTube. Nyx's dance with the faun is so shadowed and shaky, you can't be sure what you're looking at. As for my own video, from the one camera that didn't get smashed, it recorded nothing but fog. Staring at the fog on my monitor, I've a hard time convincing myself it all really happened.

Though, not such a hard time that I haven't ordered a copy of the drumming CD that Nyx played when she danced.

THE NEXT FULL MOON, I'm standing in front of the jagged gate. I'm not a good dancer. But then, I didn't think I was a good drummer, either.

I've packed a bag in case this works. Nyx will probably appreciate a change of clothes by now, assuming she's waiting on the other side.

If she isn't... I guess I'll have a new home. Because I'm going through to find her whether we can come back or not.

It's midnight. I strip off my clothes and stuff them into my bag. I balance the new boom box on a large rock and press play.

I dance.

About the Author

James Maxey's mother warned him if he read too many comic books, they would warp his mind. She was right. Now an adult who can't stop daydreaming, James is unsuited for decent work and ekes out a pittance writing down demented fantasies.

Readers interested in sampling Maxey's odd ramblings might enjoy his science-fantasy *Bitterwood* series, the secondary world fantasy of his *Dragon Apocalypse* novels, his two superhero series *Lawless* and *Whoosh! Bam! Pow! (*aka the *Nobody Gets the Girl* series) or the steam-punk visions of *Bad Wizard*. His short fiction has appeared in *IGMS*, *Asimov's*, and over a dozen anthologies, with the best of his work appearing in the collections *There is No Wheel*, *The Jagged Gate,* and *Life in a Moment*.

He also occasionally delves into non-fiction, with books like *Write! Daydream, Type, Profit, Repeat!* and *Cryptids: How We Know They are Real.*

James lives in Hillsborough, North Carolina with his lovely and patient wife Cheryl and too many cats. Cheryl joins James as co-editor and publisher of Word Balloon Books anthologies for kids, including *Beware the Bugs! Rockets & Robots,* and *Paradoxical Pets.*

To sign up for his newsletter, visit jamesmaxey.net, or use this QR code. He can also be found on Facebook by searching for the group Dragonsgate: The Worlds of James Maxey. Or, follow him on Twitter @JamesAllenMaxey.